"*A Letter for Hoot* is a well-paced murder mystery set against the backdrop of a summertime junior-level golf championship. The tale is full of fascinating characters and moves at a quick pace with new clues revealed in almost every chapter. A fun read for adults and middle-school-aged children alike."

"I loved *A Letter for Hoot*! The detail in describing scenes and action adds greatly to the effectiveness of the story. The character descriptions clearly define each person's unique personality. Clues along the way lead the reader to solving the mystery, but everything falls neatly into place at the end."

"*A Letter for Hoot* grabs the reader's attention in the first few pages. This book invites you into the storyline with relatable characters and a hometown feel. The character descriptions are so realistic, you might even see yourself or someone you know in them. The book is fun, suspenseful, and detailed. Preteens to seniors will enjoy this book."

W9-BIP-992

A LETTER FOR HOOT

November 2019

A LETTER FOR HOOT

Dear Rebello Family,
Please enjoy my
debut novel!
Holly Spofford

HOLLY SPOFFORD

A LETTER FOR HOOT

Published in the United States of America.
Hojo Publishing Company
Contact: hojo.spofford@gmail.com

ISBN-13: 978-0-9994143-0-9

Edited by Stephanie J. Beavers Communications
www.StephanieJBeavers.com / 610-247-9494

Cover design by Shezaad Sudar

DEDICATION

For my mom, my angel above

For my dad, my hero

ACKNOWLEDGEMENTS

John L. Spofford: I am forever grateful for your love and support both in life and in the writing of this book. Your deep sense of creativity helped to shape this book, as did our fireside readings and brainstorming walks. You are the best thing about me. I love you.

Holly Curry and Cheryl Flail: I am beyond thankful for your ongoing support, enthusiasm, and patience as you read through several drafts of my book. I am truly blessed to have you both in my life. I can never express what your friendship means to me.

Sheila and Jeffrey Lessin: Wonderful neighbors, dear friends. Sheila: My deep gratitude to you for reading more than one draft and cheering me on. Thank you for asking questions, making suggestions and being there during this process. You are a treasure.

Jeff: I am grateful for your frank honesty regarding your trepidation about reading a draft of the book. You will never know the impact on me of one single, sincere comment you shared after reading it. Thank you.

Lynn S. Surgner, Lauren McKinney, Aunt L, Uncle Biggie, Cuz Tucker, Lucy Carroll, I deeply appreciate your feedback and support.

To my friends and family members who consistently asked, "How's the book?" You kept me encouraged and writing.

Editor: Stephanie J. Beavers: Editor Extraordinaire. You helped me to fulfill a childhood dream. Among other things, you sanded down the rough edges of my first book and taught me invaluable lessons about the world of writing. My heartfelt thanks for everything.

Lastly, thank you to my readers who chose this book. I hope you enjoy it.

1

July 23, 1981

Tick, tick, tick. Round and round went the blades. Clay opened his brown eyes and focused on the white ceiling fan. Tick, tick, tick. He liked the rhythmic sound and comforting breeze. He lay still and absorbed the calming energy of the fan. The long day ahead would require his full focus. He filled his lungs with clean morning air that wafted in from the open window and closed his eyes again. He took a moment to envision each shot, feel each swing, and see each putt fall into the cup. Visualization was a critical part of a routine that helped him win his club championship the past five years. But something inside him felt off—something small, but annoying enough to concern him. Maybe a cup of rocket-fuel coffee would knock that feeling right out of him.

He sat up, swung his long legs over the side of the bed, stood, and shuffled to the open window. The sky was robin's egg blue and not a single cloud was in sight. He looked down and saw his neighbor Mrs. Day walking Caesar, her well-fed yellow Lab.

"Mornin', neighbor," he called from above.

"Mornin' to you, Mr. Clay. Another beautiful day's upon us," she responded and waved.

Clay waved back and watched her stop and wait while Caesar relieved himself on a tree. She always called him "Mr. Clay" even though his last name was Tyson.

He dressed quickly in the outfit he had laid out the night before—navy golf shorts, a white golf shirt, and a red leather belt, the same color scheme he wore in every club championship. Was it coincidence he had won five years in a row wearing the colors of a country he loved? He wasn't about to change course, especially now, with this weird feeling nibbling at the edges of his mind.

Outside, the newspaper landed on the ground with a loud slap. Daily, the paperboy lobbed the paper through the air like a grenade. If it landed anywhere near the middle of the driveway, Clay considered that a miracle. He retrieved the paper and sat down to breakfast, anxious to see how his beloved Phillies had done at the previous night's game. He turned to the sports page and saw they had suffered another loss. *At least I didn't stay up late to watch it. Well, they're young and have time to develop*, he thought.

Clay read the rest of the paper, crunched on his wheat flakes with sliced banana and strawberries, and washed it all down with a glass of juice followed by a cup of coffee. Glancing at the clock, he saw he had a little over an hour till his nine o'clock tee time. Time to get a move on. He went to the front hall table and grabbed his keys, wallet, a small blue notebook, and his good luck charm—a piece of blue sea glass. He then headed out to the garage.

Clay's golf bag fit perfectly into the back seat of his green Jaguar convertible XKE. He slid comfortably into the driver's seat and started the engine. *God, I love how she purrs to life.* He practically worshipped the car and cared for it like it was a baby. Three years earlier, he had spotted the car rusting away in the driveway of its heartless owner, and bought it from the man. Within six months Clay had lovingly restored the car to its current prime condition.

Maybe an open-air drive to the club would erase the nagging he continued to feel inside. The beauty of the day pushed the negative sentiment to the back of his mind as he drove down Quarry Lane. He felt the warm sun on his face and enjoyed the rich green foliage of the trees as he whizzed past them. "Highway to Hell" blared out of the radio speakers and, even though AC/DC wasn't his favorite band, the song pumped his adrenaline.

A quick check of his rearview mirror revealed to Clay that another car was tailing him. The music had been playing so loudly, he never heard the car approach from behind. They must be in a rush. He slowed down and waved at the driver to pass. The driver held steady behind, so Clay pulled his Jag to the side of the road to make it easier for the other driver to pass. Instead of passing, the driver of the other car followed suit and parked some thirty yards behind Clay. The reflection of the sun bouncing off the hood of the car made it impossible for Clay to see who was inside, but he saw two silhouettes.

Curiosity got the best of him. He stepped out of his car and squinted as the two people got out of their car and crunched their way over the gravel in his direction.

"Thought that was you," said one to Clay.

It took Clay just a second to recognize the voice. "Hey! What's up? Y'all okay?" he replied.

"Nah, we're fine. We just thought we saw something fall out of your car," said the second person.

"Oh, really? I hope not one of my clubs. Can't lose those. I'm headed to play for the club championship. You too?"

"Maybe in a little while. You sure don't want to lose those clubs."

"You're right about that."

"Hey, man, looks like your taillight is busted," said the second person as he pointed at the taillight.

"No way. I just had my car serviced," Clay replied.

"More importantly, double check to make sure you haven't lost a club," the first person said.

"Right, yes. Right now." Clay turned to check his clubs in the back seat of his car.

He never saw it coming.

Pain. Excruciating pain. He didn't know pain like that existed. Clay's six-foot-four-inch frame crumpled to the ground. His head spun like a tea cup on a children's amusement ride. He felt the warm slickness of blood ooze from the right side of his head. His instincts screamed, "Save yourself! Get away!" and he slowly rocked to his hands and knees, trying to focus. A scarlet ribbon snaked down his right cheek and plopped to the gravel. He raised his head slightly and saw shadows. People? Suddenly, one shadow raised its arms to the side and swung. The second blow was delivered with more ferocity than the first. The back of Clay's head cracked like a walnut. He lay crumpled on the ground and his white golf shirt turned deep crimson. Clay felt himself being dragged across the gravel road, his head bobbing like a doll's. He fought to stay awake. His efforts were futile. Pain took over.

* * *

Clay opened his eyes. His vision was blurry at first. He had no idea how long he had been passed out, but the tranquil air held the feel of early morning. He blinked and realized he felt different. He shook his head—the pain was gone. He put his hand to his head, expecting to feel blood. Nothing. No blood. Inside his chest, his heart shifted into high gear. His shirt was bright white. Why was there no blood? Where was the blood? Panic struck and questioning thoughts raced through his mind.

Clay stood, scanned his surroundings, and noticed everything—the trees, the grass, the flowers—looked more vibrant. He suddenly felt centered, weightless, calm. The panic he felt was immediately extinguished. His Jaguar XKE and golf bag in the back seat came into distant view, as did the driver's side door still hanging open. He closed his eyes and shook his head again. *Why is my car so far away? I was just standing beside it.* His head injuries must have been making him see things. A check of his trusty Timex told him the time was 7:58 a.m. He did a quick calculation in his head. *That can't be right.* Clay had left his house at 7:45, and more than a quarter of an hour had passed. Or had it? Voices emanated from somewhere nearby. He looked around and didn't see a soul—just a pale blue, almost white, sky. And the light. The light was clear and warm, and Clay found himself floating in it. Then, with stone-cold horror, he watched as two men lifted his lifeless body and carried it toward Serenity Lake.

He screamed, but no one paid attention because no one heard him. The sound resided in his head alone as he watched his body hit the water and sink to its dark bottom.

2

August 7, 1981

How could the night have gone so wrong? It was one of those rare summer nights that convinced the town folk of Cab Station, Virginia, that all was right with the world. No sticky humidity, no hungry mosquitoes, and the moon was a brilliant meringue pie set deep against the darkness.

The night was just dark enough for the children to blend in as they navigated their way along the well-worn trail to Serenity Lake. The light of the moon and the older kids' knowledge of the path eliminated the need for a flashlight, but the younger ones, skittish in the dark, held tight to each other's hands. The group thought they were being secretive, skulking out to the lake at ten o'clock at night for a swim. Little did they know that every generation before them had also enjoyed this childhood pastime during the sweltering summer months.

Serenity Lake was beloved as much for its solitude and beauty as for the fun and adventure it afforded. Families regularly used the park on the lake for picnics, parties, and weddings. Occasionally, an elderly person's last wishes included holding their funeral at the lake.

"Did y'all remember your bathin' suits?" Charlie asked his twin cousins Luke and Gabrielle.

"Sure did, cuz! We wearin' 'em," they responded together in happy voices. Like most young twins, Luke and Gabrielle often spoke in unison.

"I hope there ain't no eels swimmin' 'round tonight," squeaked little Larry, the youngest of the bunch at eight.

"Aw, Larry, they hide down in the dirt in the nighttime!" barked his older cousin Franklin. "If you're such a scaredy-cat, go on home to your momma!"

"Shut up!" Larry said. He didn't like that the others considered him a baby.

At fourteen, Carrie was the senior member of the group. She put an end to the bickering. "Can y'all keep it down? Your hollerin' is gonna wake the dead!"

Carrie's best friend Sheila added, "Yes! Hush up!"

Twigs snapped under the children's feet as they marched through the woods to the last row of towering pines where the path opened to the lake. The water was as still as the night. Moonlight bounced off the surface with enough intensity to make reading a book at that very time and place possible.

"Last one in's a rotten egg!" shrieked Carrie, and she dashed out of the woods toward the lake. The others all followed, tossing their clothes in haphazard heaps on the bank. They plunged in, and the liquid velvet cooled their warm skin. The soft silt under their feet squished between their toes. The water was not so deep that it was over their heads, but swimmers had enough depth to plunge beneath the surface to explore the lake's dark, secret world.

Larry and Charlie took turns dunking beneath the surface, each trying to hold his breath longer than the other. "I'll beat ya this time!" Charlie sucked in one long breath, hoping he'd win.

Larry watched him disappear. He closed his eyes and began, "One… two… three… four… five…" After a minute, Larry realized he had drifted farther out into the lake than usual and suddenly became afraid, though he did not panic.

He knew he'd be able to dog-paddle his way back to shore.
In the meantime, he saw that Charlie had popped back up
and was floating near the shoreline. "All right, Charlie,"
Larry panted. "You won this time," and he paddled in the
direction of his friend. Except that, when Larry reached him,
it wasn't Charlie. Charlie was shouting from the shore. Larry
looked again. "Ah!" he screamed. "Help! Help me! He's dead!
Help me, please!" Larry swam back to shore as fast as his
skinny body would go, swallowing water, gasping for air,
and screaming all at the same time.

Sheila dragged Larry out of the lake. "What is *wrong*
with you?" she asked.

"That!" He pointed with a shaking finger.

She squinted and looked out into the lake. "What the…
It's a log, you dummy!" Sheila then focused her eyes more
directly on what the sharp moonlight was illuminating. That
night, she, along with the rest of the gang, saw what no child
should ever see. Bobbing a few feet from shore, staring with
milky dead eyes, was the body of a man.

The children's screams ripped through the woods. They
ran wildly and blindly. Tears of fear and panic blurred their
vision. Branches scraped and scratched them. Sticks and
pebbles stabbed their feet. Their legs couldn't distance them
from the horror fast enough.

Larry was the first to reach home. He tore through the
back door into the small, tidy kitchen, his heart pounding
out of his bony chest. "Momma! Pop! Momma! Pop!" he
howled. "Where are you?" He had forgotten the late hour
and that they had gone to bed.

A deep voice thundered down the stair case. "Hey!
What's all the hollerin' about? Why aren't you in bed?"

"Pop! Pop!" Larry could not contain himself.

"Hold on a sec." Larry heard the squeak of his parents' bedroom door and the shuffling of their slippers on the stairs.

Blinking in the harsh kitchen light, his father said, "Spit it out, son. You as white as a ghost! What in the devil is goin' on?"

"I... I..." he stammered.

"Calm down, baby. Take a breath," Momma said in her soothing voice. She rubbed Larry gently on his back.

Larry inhaled deeply to clear his stunned brain. Finally, he told his mother and father about the horrible thing he and the others had seen at the lake.

Pop glanced at Momma and asked, "Are you sure that's what you saw? It ain't one of your silly friends playin' a trick?"

"Yes! It was a dead guy! I swam into it! Its face looked all waxy and puffy, like it was fake. Its eyes wouldn't stop starin' and it wasn't movin' or nothin! I screamed and Sheila pulled me out and then the others saw it and we all ran away!" Sobs shook Larry's body.

"We need to call the police," Momma commanded. She tightened her pink robe, shuffled into the hall, and made the call.

Larry was unable to hear exactly what was said, but when his mother returned, she said the police were sending an officer to their house and two squad cars to the lake.

Fifteen minutes later, there was a knock on the door. Pop opened the screen door and welcomed in two police officers. They were young, and each wore the fresh face of a civil servant all too eager to help the citizenry. Larry had never seen such tall men, except for the players on his favorite basketball team on TV.

"Evenin', ma'am, sir. I'm Officer Jackson Taylor and this is my partner, Officer Royce Lee Darman," said the taller of the two men. He removed his black hat. Officer Darman did the same.

Pop extended his massive hand, "Evenin', Officers. My name is Percy Alexander and this is my wife Janie and son Larry. We appreciate you comin' out at this late hour."

They stood in the hall and Officer Taylor addressed them. "I understand somethin' a little scary happened tonight at Serenity Lake."

Larry, who had never met a police officer, was fascinated by the gun saddled to the man's hip. "Is that a real gun?"

"Yes, it is, son."

"Do you shoot bad guys with it?"

Office Taylor smiled and squatted to be eye level with Larry. "Tell ya what. How about all of us head into the living room and you can tell me all about what happened tonight."

Larry shifted his brown eyes to his parents.

"It's okay, son," Momma said. "He's doing his job. I'll put on some coffee."

3

June 2011

The school year, as insane as it was, with three lock-down drills, six snow days, and science class with a totally wacko teacher who thought it was funny to keep gross eyeballs of dissected sheep in jars on his desk, was finally near. The end of school meant final exams. NT—officially Nicholas Tucker—Tyson hated studying for them, especially history. Too many names, events, and places to keep straight. History was the last exam he would suffer through, and then he would be done. Thank God.

At five feet six, NT was shorter than most of his classmates, many of whom had hit their growth spurts earlier in the year. NT was still waiting. He knew he could do nothing to rush that process, but his patience was running out. He wore his thick brown hair closely cropped, unlike his friends who preferred longer hairstyles. "It's easier to comb," he'd tell them. His hazel eyes, lively and intelligent, sat underneath slightly arched eyebrows that gave him a permanent questioning look. He was proud of the inch-long scar along the right side of his jaw that he had acquired when he was eight. A bad leap off his bed landed him face-first on the corner of his nightstand and earned him seven stitches.

NT was about to finish eighth grade at Wayne Middle School. He had figured out "the system" early on, and realized that by getting mostly *B*'s with an occasional *C*, he could stay under the radar. He was fine with that. He wasn't like a lot of his grade-driven, uptight classmates who freaked out if they got an *A* minus instead of an *A*. Grades weren't worth the stress. He preferred spending time playing sports, especially soccer and golf. On the soccer field, NT had a powerful foot and the speed to dodge defenders easily. And his middle school golf team had ranked him as their number one player. He had high hopes of securing a top spot on the varsity team the following year.

Sitting in a blazing hot room for study hall was beyond agonizing. What's with *study hall* anyway? The name was totally bogus because it wasn't a hall and no one studied. Rather, he and his classmates spent the better part of forty-five minutes watching the clock on the wall take its good old time to get from two o'clock to two forty-five—that magical dismissal time when NT and his peers were sprung for the day. At last, the bell shrieked and NT was free. Middle schoolers flooded the hallways, bumping off each other, laughing, opening and closing their lockers. NT stood in front of his, yanked out his ten-pound history book and tattered notebook, and shoved them into his backpack. He flung the backpack over his shoulder, slammed the locker shut, and headed toward the bus lines.

On the bus, NT made his way down the aisle. The aromas of bubble gum, body odor, and nail polish hung heavy in the air. Luckily, enough kids chomped on gum to somewhat hide the smell of his peers who hadn't yet discovered deodorant. NT slumped into a seat and prepared himself for the ride home. He lived the farthest away from school and sometimes fell asleep. On those days, Marge, the bus driver, would wake him when she reached his stop. Not today though. NT was wide awake when the bus screeched up in front of his house. He stood and stretched his arms, then grabbed his backpack and walked toward Marge.

"All right, hon, one more day. See you tomorrow," Marge cackled. She was digging through her enormous purse for her signature pack of Marlboro cigarettes.

NT stared at her and she winked back at him, ready for his warning. "Those things are going to kill you, Marge," he told her for the umpteenth time. Sort of their running joke.

"They ain't killed me yet, kid. Heck, if I can raise six kids by myself in a house with one bathroom, these ain't nothin'!" she replied with a chuckle that had the raspy quality of a life-time smoker. NT just nodded and said goodbye.

He walked down the stone path toward the yellow front door. His mother had said, "This cheery yellow will brighten things up." NT's parents were going through a divorce. He didn't understand why, but he thought brightening things up was a tough proposition. How a yellow door would help him feel any better was a total mystery to him.

NT made his way into the kitchen, grabbed a handful of cookies, and greeted his mother. She was leafing through cookbooks for new recipes for her catering business which, in the short time she had owned it, had become top-notch and popular with the locals. NT and his mom made chit chat about school and the summer, then NT told her he had to study for his history exam. "I'm going to shoot some baskets first," he said, and went outside to blow off steam. Thirty minutes later, he headed upstairs to study.

At his desk, NT smoothed the wrinkled study guide his teacher had given out. He sighed. So boring. He glanced over the section entitled *What You Need to Know* and checked off a handful of items he had already completed. The others were indicators of just how much work he had to do. He toyed with the pencil sharpener and glanced out the window where he saw the neighbor kids in their yard, running around playing tag. "Lucky dogs. They don't have to study for stupid exams."

NT's thoughts turned to the next day. School would be done and he'd be packing his suitcase. He so looked forward to getting to Virginia to spend the summer with his grandparents—his routine since grade school. This year was different. Since his parents' split at the start of the school year, he'd been going back and forth between his mom and dad's houses, and the thought of staying in one house instead of two would be a welcome change. He was still trying to wrap his head around his parents' situation. Their divorce made him sad and angry to his core, but he worked hard to maintain a happy face.

NT's grandparents, Mimi and BB, were on the young side of seventy. They lived in an old stone house—Shady Acres—that was wrapped protectively by a vast porch loaded with wicker furniture topped with comfy pillows. They weren't like other grandparents who wore sweaters when it was a hundred degrees, told the same stories over and over, or ate dinner at four thirty. They volunteered in the Cab Station community where they lived, took painting classes, and played golf at least four times a week.

They loved to take care of their house and its grounds. Every Saturday afternoon—following his early golf game— BB rode his ancient tractor and cut the acre-sized field that lay behind the house. NT was amazed the Jacobsen still ran. Even with its hood missing, the blue smoke it coughed out, and a ratty tennis ball covering the dagger-like point of the broken gearshift, the tractor ran. Somehow.

Mimi worked tirelessly in her vegetable garden. She took great pride in her tomato, pepper, and lettuce plants, and treated them with finesse. By late June, the plants always offered an early bounty.

Behind the field, Martin's Creek snaked its way through the woods and the golf courses at Cascades Golf Club where NT would spend a whole lot of time this summer. He couldn't wait.

"Are you studying up there?" His mother's chipper voice floated up the stairs and ripped him from his daydreaming.

"Yep," he yelled down, and added "unfortunately" under his breath.

"Okay, good. I have to run to the store. I forgot an ingredient for dinner. You stay put and I'll be right back."

"Okay."

The front door slammed and a minute later NT's mother backed out of the gravel driveway. Where food preparation was concerned, she was a true perfectionist. She spent days rifling through cookbooks and evenings preparing and testing new recipes. Since NT was the only other person in the house, he was the sole taste-tester of her new creations. Most times, he really liked what she made, except if the dish had fish. Never fish. Fish was gross.

Fifteen minutes later, NT's mother returned, and NT remained in his room studying for another forty-five minutes, until he had had enough. He couldn't deal with any more dates, events, or names of dead people. His mother was still working on dinner, so he wandered down the steps and into the kitchen where a small TV blared the news. Nine months earlier, his dad would have been in the kitchen, too. Now it was just NT and his mom at dinner time. NT missed seeing his father on a daily basis. Luckily, they texted a lot. But it wasn't the same as seeing him in the flesh. NT had friends whose parents had split, but he just didn't have it in him to talk to them about his own situation.

"What are you making?" he asked.

"Boneless short ribs over mashed potatoes and a salad," she said. Her eyes were glued to the TV. Rarely did any news item catch her attention enough to make her look away from her cooking, but a story about one of her favorite chefs had grabbed her.

"I'll set the table."

"Okay. Thanks, honey."

They finished dinner and talked about NT's trip to Virginia and when his father would pick him up on Saturday.

"Need help studying? I remember some things from history, you know," she offered.

"No, but thanks. I took a lot of notes earlier. I'm going to review them again now."

"If you change your mind, let me know."

* * *

Saturday had finally arrived. As promised, NT's father was at the house a little before eight. NT was up and ready to go. After the grueling and annoying week of exams, he was more than ready to leave it all behind. He heard the car door slam and the creak of the porch steps as his father walked up to the front door. NT opened the yellow door wide to let his father in.

"Hey, bud. Got all your stuff?" his father asked.

"Yup."

NT's mother walked into the front hall, wiping her hands on a dish towel. "Hi, Chris," she said. "Thanks for taking him."

"Hello, Georgia," he responded curtly.

An uncomfortable feeling permeated the atmosphere as the two just looked at each other. NT broke the tension. "Can we go? I'm ready."

"Sure. Have everything?" his father asked.

NT nodded.

"Including your summer reading book?" his mother asked.

NT rolled his eyes and responded, "Yes. *The Old Man and the Sea*. Ernest Hemingway. Right here." He hugged his mother goodbye and told her he'd call later that night.

4

After the five-hour drive down Interstate 95 from Philadelphia, NT and his father arrived at BB and Mimi's house in Cab Station. The town was home to some twenty thousand residents and had prospered in its early days thanks to its production of tobacco, corn, and peanuts. In time, Cab Station also became a popular location for several of Virginia's aerospace firms.

As they drove through town, NT observed that not much had changed since his visit one year earlier. The main drag, Tubman Avenue, was alive and well. Diners at Wellie's were seated at tables along the sidewalk enjoying an early afternoon cappuccino. People gathered outside the library to discuss the latest best-seller or were buried in their phones. Al's, the combination convenience store and gas station, was bustling. The white marquee above the Lessin Movie Theater caught NT's attention. "Dad, look!" He pointed at the titles. "They're showing movies from the eighties! That's awesome! One is *The Terminator*. NT loved "old" movies—the 1980s was his favorite era. "Me and Daisy'll have to see Arnold blowing stuff up!" He next noticed that the bench outside Sweetwoods Ice Cream Parlor had received a fresh coat of purple paint. He and Daisy probably ate ten gallons of Sweetwoods ice cream every summer.

Daisy. Daisy Kathryn Taylor, that is. She was unlike anyone NT knew—kind of like the sister he never had. He loved hanging out with her because he never knew what to expect. Her wild imagination led the way on all kinds of adventures. One day they'd be skipping stones on Martin's

Creek or gorging on ice cream at Sweetwoods. The next, they'd be involved in a séance taking place at the town graveyard.

The mass of curls in Daisy's long, red hair reflected her sometimes unruly, always adventurous, nature and flair for trouble. Her eyes were like clear emeralds. A smattering of freckles across her small nose reminded NT of cinnamon. Smart, inquisitive, and sassy, she sometimes teetered on the edge of disrespect. But NT knew when to stop her.

Daisy was born and raised a Cabbie, as those born in Cab Station were fondly called. She was number four out of four kids, the only girl. Her father worked long hours in town as sheriff and her mother was a teacher at Cab Station Middle School. As the only girl on the middle school golf team, Daisy proved her worth by continually thumping her male opponents. And her teammates in softball knew Daisy to be a deadly accurate pitcher, a description that was not an exaggeration—the summer before, when NT and Daisy were horsing around, she picked up an apple, hurled it in the direction of a tree twenty feet off, and squarely nailed a bird that had been perched on a branch. The bird fell to earth like a stone through water. The poor critter never knew what hit it. Daisy was horrified at what she had done, and ran away in inconsolable tears. But that was Daisy—sassy tomboy one minute, girlie-girl the next.

NT's father pulled into the circular driveway at Shady Acres. NT's grandparents were sitting on the porch, waiting for their arrival. BB was in his rocker and Mimi sat on the two-seater sofa.

"Hey, Mimi, BB!" yelled NT from the car window.

Mimi greeted NT and his father in the driveway, giving each a kiss hello and a hug. BB shook his son's hand and ruffled NT's hair.

"Was I-95 a parking lot?" BB asked.

"Not really," Chris responded. "Things slowed down near Manassas because of construction, but it wasn't too bad."

"They should be done that project soon," BB responded.

"How about we enjoy some lunch? I know I'm starving," Mimi said.

BB concurred. "Me too. Then maybe after lunch we can head over to the club for a quick nine holes?"

"Yes, please!" NT responded.

* * *

They returned home from golf in the early evening and enjoyed a steak dinner out on the porch. Over dinner, Mimi told NT that she had run into Daisy's mother in the grocery store. "I told her I'd have you give Daisy a call when you got into town."

"Oh. Okay." NT was secretly pleased but tried not to show it.

The next day, NT's father was up and out early. "Be good, son," he said to NT. "I'll be in touch when I can."

"Bye, Dad."

BB followed Chris out the door, as he had an early golf game with the Grumps, his men's group. He took NT's clubs along with him to store at the club so that NT wouldn't have to ride his bike back and forth with the bag strapped to his back.

NT would leave a while later, as he first called Daisy to make plans. One of her brothers answered and yelled as loudly as possible, "Daisy, your little boyfriend is on the phone!" NT felt his face flush.

"Give me the phone, Brett!" she yelled. NT imagined Brett, all six feet of him, holding the phone in the air over Daisy's head, making her jump for it.

"God, you are such a pain! Give me the phone!"

"Ouch! You didn't have to kick me!" Brett yelled.

"Obviously I did. Give me the phone or I'll kick you where it'll really hurt!"

NT knew she meant what she said.

"Fine. Have fun with your *boyfriend*." NT pulled the handset away from his ear when he heard what sounded like Daisy's phone clattering to the floor.

"NT? You there?"

NT reasoned it was safe to put the phone back to his ear. "Yeah. Hey, Daisy."

"Are you in town?"

"Yeah. I got in yesterday. Your brother's being a jerk again, huh?"

"Well, some things don't *ever* change."

"I'm going to the club. Want to come so we can hang?"

Daisy sighed. "I can't. I have to babysit this morning and all day tomorrow. But, hey, Sweetwoods has new flavors. Let's go soon."

"Sounds good. When are you finished babysitting?"

"Um, probably not 'til dinner."

"Oh." NT was bummed. He'd been looking forward to seeing her and telling her about his crazy year.

"You sound sad. Don't be. We have, like, the whole summer to hang out, right?" Daisy asked.

"Yeah. I'll talk to you tomorrow," he said.

"Cool. See you later," Daisy said, and hung up.

5

NT took his time riding to Cascades Golf Club. He went the long way, which took him past Daisy's house. He knew she wouldn't be home, but then again, maybe her plans had changed and she didn't have to babysit after all. However, when he rode past her house he saw no cars or bikes.

He turned into the driveway of CGC and absorbed the green beauty of the grounds. It was a beautiful and welcoming place with members of all walks of life. The red brick clubhouse with its wide white columns stood elegantly and proudly atop a hill. Two fun, but difficult, golf courses challenged players of all skill levels—Mill Course and Creek Course. Diners on the stone terrace enjoyed sweeping views of the first and eighteenth holes on the Mill course. The club also had a great practice area and the Grille Room served the best burgers NT had ever eaten.

After locating his golf bag, NT headed to the pro shop to grab some tees. He wondered if Jeff Gambone was still the head pro. Jeff was a really nice guy and always had a joke for NT. NT entered the shop and didn't have to wonder any more. Behind the desk was a man NT had never seen. *I guess Jeff's gone.* NT introduced himself to the new guy.

"Michael Gates. Nice to meet you, NT." They shook hands. "Your grandparents told me you were coming down for the summer."

"Yes, sir. I hope to play a lot while I'm here."

"That's great. But you'll first need to review the new rules pertaining to junior golfers. I established these rules, along with certain times for junior golfers to follow. If you don't, your play will be limited, understand?"

"Oh, I didn't know."

"Well, now you do. Right?"

NT nodded a quick "see ya." He couldn't get out of there fast enough. That guy was mean.

He followed the path down to the practice range. Hitting balls on the range took his mind off the sadness he felt about his parents' divorce. The hole he felt in his heart would not heal, but he was hesitant to talk to anyone about his feelings for fear he'd cry. He felt liberated from the anger at his parents when he hit balls.

NT kicked a small stone as he walked and heard a clink sound when it landed. Curious, he walked to where the stone had stopped and saw the metal shaft of a golf club nestled in the grass. He knew right away it was a putter. *That's weird. Who would throw a putter here? Maybe someone lost it.* He picked it up and let his imagination go to work. "Here we are on hole number eighteen. NT lines up the winning putt—"

A croaky old voice broke through the air. "Where'd you get that club, sonny?"

NT looked around and saw no one.

The voice croaked again, this time louder than the first. "Where'd you get that club?"

NT caught a whiff of cigar smoke on the light breeze coming from the same direction as the voice. He glanced thirty yards to his left where a run-down cottage sat nearly hidden under a large willow tree. For years, he had wondered about this shack. The washed-out gray exterior was the result of years of storms battering against the structure, and the moss-covered roof indicated neglect by its owner. A red door added a splash of sorely needed color.

For a brief second, he was reminded of the cheery yellow front door at home.

A thin old man leaned in the doorway. His face was shadowed by the tree and clouds of cigar smoke, but NT observed he was wearing khaki pants and a white collared shirt. The man shuffled into the sunlight and NT froze. The man just stared at NT, who did not know what to say. He stared hard. His dark eyes were prominent in his lean, wizened face. NT felt wholly uncomfortable until a large, friendly smile cracked the man's face. He waved NT over and removed the cigar from between his lips. "I'm James. Who are you?" he said, and extended a calloused hand.

"Nicholas Tucker. NT for short, sir." He shook the man's hand.

"Ha! *Sir!* The boy called me sir!" Guffaws echoed from deep inside the man's belly. NT felt his face go red. "Oh, Lordy, son. Just call me James."

"Okay," NT replied. He handed James the putter. "I found it in the grass, just off the path."

"Is that old man Gunderman's putter?" a male voice from inside the cottage asked.

"Yep," James responded.

"Man, I was catchin' heat from the boss man about that darned club. He was gonna make me pay for it out of my caddie money." The man's tone reflected relief.

NT was now fully curious about the shack and what went on there. He peered over James's shoulder and squinted to see inside.

Again the voice spoke from inside, "Y'all want to look inside here, Nicholas?"

"Um, yeah, if it's okay," NT said.

James nodded toward the door. In they went, and NT stopped and looked around in wonder. One wall was covered top to bottom with covers from *Sports Illustrated* magazine. They featured Jack Nicklaus, Arnold Palmer, Tom Watson, and other famous golfers. Against another wall, a half-dozen lockers bulged open with golf bags full of old or lost clubs. Rickety bookshelves above the lockers held books of all genres. The floor emitted painful groans with each step. Smells of mustiness and dampness blended with that of Old Spice aftershave to create an almost pleasant aroma. In the center of the room was a round wooden table with six beat-up chairs around it. Three other men, all dressed exactly like James, were seated at the table engaged in a card game. Cigarette smoke curled toward the ceiling. Considering the age of the building, it was in tidy condition.

One of the men looked up from the card game and asked, "James, you recruiting a new one? Man, he ain't even old enough to shave." The men all laughed. This gave NT the shivers and made him feel completely out of place. The man eyeballed NT and directed his next comment to him. "Boy, this is the caddie shack. You a newbie? You gonna be wearing that little yellow bib saying you a new caddie? You ready to carry two big ole bags? Only caddies are allowed in here. So, you a new caddie or what?"

"Uh, no. My grandparents are members here." Even to NT, his voice sounded hollow. "I was just outside and, I... well... I should go. I don't want to get in trouble." He turned toward the door, hoping no one noticed the redness that had crept into his cheeks. Just as he was about to step outside, the men broke out in laughter. NT stopped. He didn't know what to make of these men—the caddies—and felt foolish for having gone into the shack in the first place.

"Oh, son, you should've seen your face! Ole Sir got you good, didn't he? He's just yankin' your chain." James chuckled and threw an arm around NT's shoulder.

A deep voice floated from the back of the shack. "Y'all let him be." NT was surprised by this new voice. He had not seen anyone beyond the men around the table. "Come on back here and sit awhile."

James nodded his approval. NT walked to the back. Another man, this one seated in a rocking chair, came into view. On the table next to the chair was a small silver bowl that brimmed with golf tees. The man was broad shouldered, slender, and had close-cropped graying hair. Clear blue eyes—intelligent, kind, honest eyes— accentuated his deeply lined face that was darkened by many summer suns. The man smiled and NT caught a glimpse of a gold tooth.

"You never been in here, have you?" The man's voice was firm, yet gentle, like his demeanor.

NT stuttered a reply, "I've seen the shack... the... building... on the way to the range, but I've never been in here before."

"I figured. My name is Hoot." He stuck out a massive, leathery hand and shook NT's with confidence. The sense of calm and safety the man exuded helped NT relax. "You're Nicholas Tucker, right?"

NT stared at him, now wary. "How'd you know that?"

"Well, I know your grandparents, Miss Marian and Mr. Willy. They told me you were comin' down for the summer and just by looking at you, I knew you must be their flesh and blood."

"Oh." That made sense. NT asked, "Do you work here too?"

"Yep. I train the caddies and keep 'em in line. I just moved back here a few months ago. I left the area for a few years for work, but I missed it here. Glad to be back."

"Do you caddie too? My grandad tells me it's great money, especially if you carry two bags."

"My caddying days are mostly over. I only carry one bag now. Can't do two—not with this old shoulder of mine."

"Oh, what happened? Did you hurt it?"

"Y'all are curious, aren't you? I got shot up with some shrapnel in Nam—Vietnam. They operated, but some pieces were buried too deep, so they just left 'em in." Hoot answered as if he were talking about the weather.

"You were in Vietnam? We studied that in history."

"Yep. Spent time there, 'til this happened." He rubbed his shoulder. "Can't put weight on it anymore. Plus, the scar tissue is so thick it kind of froze it up."

"How long were you there?"

"Oh, about a year. We got in a firefight on Hill 425 and me and my boys…" His voice tapered off and he shook his head.

"Sorry." NT looked at the floor. One thing he did learn in history class was that most vets did not like to talk about their war-time experiences.

"Anyway, I'm glad I can still caddie. In fact, I've got a standing game every Saturday with your grandpappy. He can still smack the ball for his age!" Hoot laughed. "I also caddied for his big brother, your great uncle."

NT scowled. He'd never heard anyone in his family mention a great uncle. "My great uncle? Who's that?"

The question hung in the air like an unseen weight. Silence had swallowed up the caddie shack's previously happy atmosphere. All heads turned to Hoot. The only sound in the shack was the creaking of Hoot's chair. Hoot cleared his throat, looked at the frozen faces at the table, and responded to the boy's innocent question. "Nicholas Tucker, ain't no one ever told you about your great uncle Clay Tyson?"

"Nope. Never. Who is he?"

Hoot exhaled heavily. "Well, your Uncle Clay was a real gem of a man and a heck of a golfer. Everyone at this club knew him. He was bigger than life itself—kind to everyone—and we all loved him. He was considerate, and I loved caddying for him and Mr. Willy. He was also one of the smartest men I ever did know."

Hoot fell silent then rocked back in his chair and gazed out beyond the red door that still hung open. He was transported back in time, many years ago, to the day he earned the name Hoot.

* * *

"You're a hunnert and thirty to the green," Percy informed Clay.

Clay accepted his trusted nine iron club from his caddie and took aim for the white flag flapping gently in the distance, teasing him, beckoning him "I dare you."

Whoosh! Smooth as ever, Clay swung. The rectangular divot spun upward from the ground—another perfect shot.

"Woohoo! You hit that one on the screws!" Percy exclaimed. The ball was in perfect flight. It sailed over the greenish-blue creek. It landed on the green with a soft thump. Percy was amazed by Clay's accuracy. "Man, you hit every green."

"I couldn't do it without you, Percy," was the humble reply.

They crossed over Martin's creek feeling peaceful and relaxed. The sounds of their shoes squishing on the damp grass was the only noise they heard. Today was no different from any other—Clay and Percy out together, getting ready for another club championship.

The ball had landed about twelve feet from the cup. Another birdie opportunity awaited Clay. He squatted down to look at the line his ball would follow. He asked Percy, who read greens like no one else, if he thought the line broke much to the left.

"No. Maybe just a ball's width."

Clay took his stance, found his line and, like a knife through butter, made a smooth stroke. They watched as the ball rolled over and over toward the cup, creating little sprays of water from the dew. Seconds later, the ball disappeared into the cup with a satisfactory clunk.

"Woohoo!" Percy's enthusiastic outburst was so loud, the red-tailed hawks screeched in protest.

"Percy, you're going wake the dead with those loud hoots! Matter of fact, from now on, I'm going to call you Hoot," said Clay. He wore a broad smile and nodded in affirmation of the moniker.

Percy—now Hoot—laughed out loud, then shook Clay's hand in silent agreement.

* * *

Hoot snapped out of his daze and leaned forward in his chair to signal the conversation was over. NT wanted to know more about this mysterious relative. He looked to James and the other caddies, but they all shrugged their shoulders. Lawrence, a younger caddie, broke the heavy silence. "There's a picture of him up there." NT looked up and saw a lifetime of pictures taped and glued across an entire rafter in Hall of Fame fashion. Lawrence removed one of the photos and let out a low whistle. "Your uncle Clay was some kind of player."

"You knew him too?"

Lawrence said nothing.

NT leaned in close to get a good look. In the black and white photo stood a tall, handsome man with an easy grin. Positioned at Clay's feet was a trophy that reached his knees. To Clay's right stood a broad-shouldered man with clear eyes that had not dimmed with the age of the photo. Hoot's arm was draped around Clay's shoulder and he wore an enormous smile.

NT looked at Hoot who, in a hushed tone of reverence, said, "Five-time club champ and five-time state champ. With that swing, he was good enough to go out on tour, but he never had the chance. Not with what happened and all."

"What? What does that mean? What happened?" NT was beyond curious.

Hoot lifted those startling eyes to NT and shook his head in solemn response. "Ain't my place to tell you, son. Best to ask your grandparents."

6

Hoot's words echoed in NT's head. "Ain't my place to tell you, son." NT could only conclude that something bad must have happened to his great uncle Clay. But what? Did he cheat in a tournament and get kicked out of the club? That wouldn't make sense because Hoot had said everyone loved Clay. What could have happened that NT's grandparents should be the ones to tell NT about it? The mystery grabbed NT's imagination and held on tight. He couldn't do a thing about the matter at that moment, so he continued with his practice session and formulated a plan to ask Mimi and BB when he got home.

It felt great to swing a club again. The quiet calm of the range allowed NT to focus solely on his swing. He warmed up with his wedge clubs, then the irons, and lastly, his driver. As happened with many golfers, NT's own love-hate relationship with his driver was the bane of his existence. He never knew if he'd slice the ball off to the right or if he'd hit a nice draw where the ball started right and gently turned left mid-air. He was tired of his lack of consistency, and decided this would be the summer he would tame his driver once and for all. He hit balls for another half hour and decided he'd had enough for one day. A slight shift in his stance helped straighten out the ball flight, but his drive still needed work. He'd fix it.

NT pedaled home, hoping BB would be there when he arrived. He left his bike at the side of the driveway and noticed the garage doors were wide open and the garage was empty. In the kitchen, he found a note on the counter. "We are both out, but one of us will be home by 4:00." The clock had just struck three. A whole hour. *What a pain*, he thought.

Upstairs, NT changed his clothes. From his bedside table, *The Old Man and the Sea* stared up at him. He picked it up and read the summary on the back. *What's so great about some old man who catches a fish?* Exhaling loudly, he took the book and went out to the porch to read. After all, he did have an hour to kill.

The sound of Mimi's car in the driveway woke NT with a start. His book thudded to the floor when he sat up in the chair. He had no idea how long he had slept, but at least he had started his summer reading assignment.

"Hi, Mimi!"

"Hello, sweetheart. Would you please help me with these bags?"

"Yup."

"Thank you. They're heavy, so be careful."

Together they unloaded the groceries from the car and put everything away. When they were finished, NT asked, "Mimi, can I ask you a question?"

"Sure, but let me get changed first. Meet me out in the vegetable garden. I need to do battle with those weeds."

Ten minutes later, NT stood and watched as his grandmother yanked out the weeds that had sprouted among her Romaine lettuce. Every pull was followed up with a gingerly pat-down of the dirt around each lettuce plant.

"What did you want to talk about?" she asked.

"Well, I met that guy Hoot in the caddie shack at Cascades. He told me that he used to caddie for BB and BB's brother, a guy named Clay? One of the other caddies showed me a picture of him. Who is he?"

Mimi looked up, wiped her brow, and sat back on her heels. "Let's get one thing straight. You do not belong in the caddie shack. Ever. I'm happy you met Hoot—he's a lovely man. But the caddie shack is off limits to children. It's a place of work for adults, okay?" Her dark eyes signaled that she wasn't kidding.

"Fine," NT said. That was not the reaction he was expecting. "But, what about Clay?"

"Well, his name was Clayton. Clay for short. He was a few years older than BB, and a very kind and gentle man. He traveled a lot because he worked for the SEC as a compliance examiner."

NT asked, "What's the SEC?"

"You've heard of the stock market and brokers who handle other people's money?"

NT nodded.

"Well, Clay made sure that all those people followed the rules of legal trading and their bookkeeping was in order."

"So, like, he made sure no one was stealing money or cheating other people?"

"Exactly. Anyway, everyone loved him. When BB and Clay were young, they were inseparable and always played golf together. Clay won a bunch of club championships. I don't remember the exact number." Mimi paused, then looked up at NT with squinty eyes. "What exactly did Hoot tell you?"

"Kinda the same thing. But then he said something happened to him. What?"

Mimi sighed. "Nicholas, he's no longer with us. He died a long time ago."

"Oh. How'd he die?"

"It's a long story, but I'll tell you. I'm done here, so why don't we go to the porch and sit? I need some lemonade. You?"

NT and his grandmother settled on the porch, each sipping from a tall glass of homemade lemonade. Mimi smacked her lips as the drink refreshed and cooled her down.

"Well, are you going to tell me?" NT was ready to burst.

"Patience is not in your vocabulary, is it?" she joked. "Okay, here's the story. The year was 1981—long before you were born. Your great uncle Clay was scheduled to play in the annual club championship. Everyone was waiting at the club, anxious to walk with him and his opponent, Calvin Sweeney. Clay had quite the fan base. It was a beautiful day, not too hot. His trusted caddie and friend Hoot was waiting on the first tee. Clay's start time was 9:08 but, as his time got closer, there was no sign of him. He wasn't on the range, the putting green, or in the locker room. This was rather alarming. He was never late for a tee time, especially where the club championship was concerned."

"Where was he?"

"We didn't know. We could only assume he had overslept, so your grandfather and I called his house. There was no answer, so we drove to his house to look for him. Meanwhile, Hoot had the brilliant idea of checking the hospital to see if he was sick—or worse."

"And?"

35

"We got to his house, and his car was gone. BB unlocked the front door and yelled out for him. Again, no answer, but we knew he had been there earlier because of the breakfast dishes in the sink and box of cereal on the counter. We walked all through his house, calling his name in every room, yet, nothing. His neighbor told us she saw him leave at around seven thirty that morning." Mimi took a sip from her glass.

"So, he *did* leave to go play, right? I mean, if his car wasn't there, and his neighbor said she saw him leave, he had to have left for the club, right?"

"That's what we assumed. We decided to go back to the club to see if anyone had heard from him. To save time, BB took a shortcut down Quarry Lane. Then… we saw it at a distance." Another sip of lemonade and shake of her head.

"What? What did you see?"

"Clay's Jaguar. I can still see BB's white knuckles, squeezing the life out of the steering wheel. He sped to the car, which was pulled off to the side of the road, not far from Serenity Lake. Clay's golf clubs were in the back, but there was no sign of Clay. The rear taillight was broken, which was odd, because Clay cared for that car like it was a baby. BB opened the glove box and saw Clay's wallet, some papers, and a couple of scorecards. We walked into the woods toward the lake, calling his name over and over as we went along. I remember the panic rising in my throat. I fought to keep my voice level every time I called his name."

Mimi emptied her glass.

"After ten minutes of looking around the area, we decided we needed to get the police. BB stayed with the car in case Clay showed up. We both knew that wasn't going to happen, but we were too afraid to say it out loud. I drove to the police station, explained what was happening, and a patrol car followed me back to where BB was waiting. BB just shook his head as we approached—still no sign. We walked all the way around Serenity Lake and found nothing out of the ordinary. The police made notes of everything they saw and said they would collect anything that might be considered evidence. They asked us to go to the police station to make a statement."

"But, where was he? Did you find him?"

"Not that day, no. It was about two weeks later when he was finally found."

"What do you mean, 'when he was found?' Who found him?" NT thought his heart would burst, it was beating so hard.

"A group of kids went for a late-night swim in the lake, and one of the younger boys swam right into Clay's body. It was floating just offshore, and the poor child thought it was one of his cousins. The shock nearly killed him."

NT processed what his grandmother was explaining. "So, wait. Why was Clay near the lake if he was supposed to be at the club?"

"His car was near there, so we reasoned that he had taken Quarry Lane for the same reason your grandfather had—as a shortcut."

"He drowned, right?"

Mimi sighed. "That was our initial assumption. But the autopsy made it abundantly clear that the cause of Clay's death was not due to drowning."

"Then, what?"

"We did not see his body when it was pulled from the lake. Had we been there, we would have seen the real cause of his death." Mimi spoke her next words slowly and carefully. "The Medical Examiner, Doctor Nettleton, determined that your great uncle Clay died due to *blunt force trauma*."

NT had heard those words before on TV and was pretty sure he knew what they meant. But he asked anyway.

"It means, Nicholas, that someone hit Clay in the head so hard, it killed him."

NT sat paralyzed. His brain struggled to digest what he had just heard. "You mean someone murdered him?"

"Yes, Nicholas. Doctor Nettleton determined that Clay was hit on the side and back of his head with some type of heavy object, and it killed him."

7

NT struggled for the next two days to comprehend what Mimi had told him about his great uncle Clay. He was having a tough time figuring out where to put his feelings of anger, sadness, and confusion. If Clay was such a great guy, why did someone kill him? This thought consumed NT as he waited for Daisy on the bench outside Sweetwoods. He snapped back to reality when he felt sticky butterscotch and vanilla dribble run down his fingers. In his distraction, his ice cream cone had turned soupy and runny. He threw the mess into a nearby trash can and returned to the bench.

"Hey! What's up?" Daisy pulled up and parked her bike next to the bench. She plopped down next to NT.

"Nothing. You?"

"Why do you sound so blah? You should be happy. School is finally over and we can hang out. God, I am so glad school is done. I had some really weirdo teachers."

"Yeah, same here. I hope high school is better than middle school."

"Well, my brothers say you have a ton more freedom."

"Good."

What do you want to do?" she asked.

NT hung his head low and responded, "I dunno."

"What is wrong with you? You look like someone hurt your puppy," she said.

He was wrestling with what to tell her first—about his parents' divorce or Clay's murder. He picked the latter, and gave her a sullen response. "I just found out that my great uncle was murdered."

Daisy did a double take and stared at NT. "What? Murdered? Here, in this little nothing of a town? Wow!"

"I know, right?"

"I don't remember hearing anything about that!" Daisy's face lit up like a lantern. "How do you know? Who did it? How? Why didn't you tell me before?" Her questions were relentless and NT saw her brain working in overdrive. "So, that means... BB had a brother? Or Mimi?"

NT rattled off his responses. "Clay was BB's older brother. Mimi told me about it. You didn't hear about it because it happened, like, thirty years ago. We weren't even born."

"Oh," she whispered. "Sorry. I thought you meant it happened, I don't know, recently. Wanna talk about it? We could go to the lake?"

NT hesitated, but realized there was no point in saying no. Plus, he did want to talk about it. Even though Daisy acted a bit nutty at times, he knew she would listen.

They got on their bikes and rode down Quarry Lane to the lake—the same road where Clay's car had been found. NT replayed his grandmother's story in his head. He couldn't help but wonder what happened to Clay, who murdered him, and why. Those questions and others scrambled his brain. At the lake, they dropped their bikes and made themselves comfortable along the edge. The sun warmed their faces and Serenity Lake was calm and beautiful.

NT told Daisy the entire story, from discovering the caddie shack and meeting Hoot, to learning about the existence of his great uncle Clay, to hearing the horrific details his grandmother had told him of Clay's last day.

Daisy sat up quickly. "Why don't we try to find out more about him? We have, like, three whole months to investigate him. We can talk to your grandparents. And my dad. Maybe he knows about it. And I read tons of Nancy Drew books. We can do what she does! We can also read the report the police wrote about it!"

As enthusiastic as Daisy was, NT was not. He stared at her and thought everything she was saying sounded completely insane. "Really? Do *what* like Nancy Drew? Hide in the bushes and spy on people? Besides, Mimi said it was investigated." He sighed and rolled his eyes. "The only thing I could see going along with is checking with your dad. Since he's sheriff, he'd know something."

Daisy glared at NT. "Well, at least you agree on *one* thing." She just as quickly regained her enthusiasm and babbled on about how they could learn more about NT's mysterious relative. NT had almost had his fill when her chatter was interrupted by the sounds of splashing and laughing coming from the lake. Two women wearing floppy sun hats and yellow life jackets were happily paddling around in a red canoe. NT and Daisy waved to them. They waved back and simultaneously yodeled a "hello" that bounced over the lake.

"Is that you, Daisy Taylor?" asked one of the canoers. The woman tipped her gigantic sun glasses down for a better look, then rowed toward the shore.

"Hi, Miss Hardy!" Daisy called back.

"Well, what an unexpected pleasure to run into y'all," the woman said. "I was going to call you this evening, but this is better. Minnie and I are traveling to Myrtle Beach for

41

a few days next week. Would you be able to take care of our baby while we're gone?"

Daisy nodded. "Sure."

"Lovely. Stop by the house on Thursday to get the key. My sister and I will be home all day."

"Yes, ma'am. See you then." NT and Daisy waved goodbye as Miss Hardy turned the canoe back toward the center of the lake.

Just then, a furry pink head popped into view over the edge of the canoe.

"What the—?" NT asked. He blinked to make sure his eyes were not fooling him. "A pig?"

"Yup. That's Succotash, their baby. They take him everywhere." Like his owners, Succotash was wearing a yellow life jacket—only his was pig sized.

"Seriously? How do you know them?"

"They're the Hardy sisters. You'll love their names— Minnie and Cordie. They're sort of crazy, but really nice. They live near the edge of the fairway on the sixteenth hole. You know that big white house with the blue and green striped awning? They moved back here, I think in the spring? When they go away, I feed and walk Succotash. You can come with me!"

As if on cue, Minnie yelled to Daisy, "All right, dear, we'll see you Thursday. And bring your friend!"

Daisy and NT watched as the ladies paddled off with their pig in tow.

"Wow. That was totally random," said NT.

"I suppose," said Daisy. "You'll see them around town, I'm sure." Undeterred by the interruption, Daisy immediately returned to the topic of investigating Clay's murder. "What do you say? We have the whole summer."

NT thought about it. She was right. Three months was a long time. Plus, spending time with Daisy was always an adventure in itself. "I guess we won't be playing golf or going to Sweetwoods every day, so we might as well."

They headed back to Shady Acres, ready to start finding out as much as they could about Clay Tyson. In the sitting room, they eyed a stately oak desk that stood in a corner. NT had never paid much attention to the desk, as it had always been there, but the possibility that it contained paperwork of interest intrigued him. He slid the bottom left drawer open and saw it was filled with papers. Just then, he sensed another presence in the room. He stood and turned to see Mimi, who had entered carrying a silver tray with three glasses of lemonade.

"I thought you two would like something to drink. Come on out to the porch where we can sit and chat," Mimi said.

NT stuttered, "Daisy and I were looking for some paper."

Mimi smiled. "Of course you were. You and Daisy look as though you're on a mission. Maybe I can help."

NT and Daisy found the lemonade to be cold, deliciously sweet, and refreshing. They emptied their glasses greedily.

"So, why do you need paper?" Mimi asked, looking at them over her glasses.

"Well, I know that next year in school I have to write a report about a family member. And since I don't know a lot about Great Uncle Clay, I thought I would talk to people who knew him. And take notes," he answered.

"That certainly sounds interesting," said Mimi. "You may want to talk more with Hoot, or Mrs. Cavanaugh at the library. She and Clay were in school together. That'd be a good place to start. Oh, and two other people who knew Clay well are Minnie and Cordie Hardy. They recently moved back to the area and I know they spent lots of time with Clay."

"Wait. The pig ladies? We saw them today," NT said.

"I would refrain from calling them that," said Mimi. "But, yes, you might find them helpful in the course of your research."

"I have to go to their house on Thursday, so maybe we can talk to them then," Daisy suggested. "For now, let's start at the library."

"Awesome. Let's go there first," NT said.

"Hey, before the library, we should go to the police station and see if my dad knows anything about Clay's case," Daisy said.

"Uh, okay. But do you think he'll want to talk to us? He's probably busy."

Daisy shrugged. "There's only one way to find out, right?"

8

Miss Brenda was usually the first person people saw when they entered the Cab Station police station. Today, though, she was not at her usual front desk position. NT and Daisy heard a light clicking sound in the next office. They peeked in and saw Deputy Darman. He was hunched over a crowded desk, busily working away on his computer. From the hallway, they smirked as Deputy Darman's enormous sausage fingers hunted and pecked at the large keyboard, one letter at a time. Considering the mess of papers and folders on his desk, they were surprised he had room for a computer at all.

Deputy Royce Lee Darman was born in Tuscaloosa, Alabama, to parents who had graduated from the University of Alabama. The family moved to Cab Station when Royce was in fourth grade. Royce played youth football and went on to be the star player at his high school. The coaches loved his ability to crush the quarterbacks of opposing teams. At well over six feet tall, his hulking, muscular frame struck fear in the hearts of his opponents. For a big guy, he was quick-footed. He was also smart, and used his intelligence to his benefit. He, his parents, and his coaches never doubted he'd one day play for Alabama's Crimson Tide.

Royce loved his high school glory days playing under the lights on Friday nights—the cheers of the crowd, the smell of the grass on his battle field, the sweat dribbling down between his thick eye brows. But one night, the unthinkable happened. In one quick move, he felt a sickening snap of his leg. The opposing team's quarterback was in his crosshairs for a sack when Royce was blindsided with the force of an eighteen-wheeler. And, just like that, his football career was over. No more playing under the lights, no cheering crowd and, worst of all, no Crimson Tide. He made the best of his situation by graduating from high school and completing the necessary two years of training at the local police academy. For over thirty years, Royce had been a familiar figure patrolling the streets of Cab Station and taking care of its citizens.

"Hi, Deputy Darman!" Daisy said.

The big man looked up from his typing and smiled when he saw Daisy. "Well, hello, Daisy. What brings you down here? Lunch with your dad?"

"We wanted to ask him about something." She tilted her head in NT's direction, and said, "You remember NT, right? My friend from Philadelphia? He got down here a few days ago."

Darman lugged his fleshy body from the wooden chair and shook NT's hand.

"Nice to see you again, son," Darman said. "As I recall, you're a golfer like your friend here."

"Yes, sir. I love the game. Do you play?" NT was unnerved at the sight of this huge police officer and said the first thing that came to his mind.

"Nah, tried it as a kid. Too slow for me. I'm more of a rough and tumble football guy myself—that is, 'til I broke my leg." Darman picked up a pencil and snapped it in two to demonstrate the snap he had suffered. "Just like that." NT shuddered.

"Is my dad around?" Daisy asked.

"He's here somewhere, I believe. I was just about to head out for some lunch myself, but hold on, I'll check."

Darman disappeared down the hallway and returned a minute later. "I don't see him anywhere. I got a ton of paperwork to do, so I'm gonna grab me a pulled pork sandwich from Brownie's. Best in town, you know," he said, and patted his ample gut. "Is there something I can help you with before I step out?"

"Well, maybe," said Daisy. NT detected a hint of hope in her voice. "NT just found out that he had a great uncle from Cab Station who was murdered. Since he didn't know him at all, we wanted to see if Dad knew anything about the case." Daisy was more than hopeful, NT noted. She made her request sound like the most natural and innocent he had ever heard.

"Murdered? Wow. We don't get many murders around here. Do you know his name?" Darman asked.

"Clay Tyson. It happened a really long time ago," NT said.

Darman scratched his chin and nodded thoughtfully. He chose his words carefully, considering his audience, and disclosed that he, in fact, did remember the case. "It was an awful event, and your father and I investigated it together as young rookie cops. It was our first big case."

NT and Daisy walked out with Deputy Darman. He told them the case had never been solved because there wasn't enough evidence. He also said he'd be glad to tell them what he knew, but he didn't have much information to go on, given that he didn't know Clay that well. "Come back and see me later today or tomorrow." Deputy Darman turned and headed down the street toward Brownie's.

"Hey," Daisy said, "maybe we could read more about Clay where they keep the records."

NT was certain he saw a gleam in Daisy's eye. He had to admit he liked the sound of her idea. "How are we gonna find those old records?"

"Follow me," she said. The two friends rode their bikes around to the back of the station. With no one else around, they dared to peer inside the windows they could reach from the ground. Luckily, thick, overgrown bushes hid them from view.

Daisy stepped back and looked down the row of windows. "Let's see if there's a loose one here somewhere." She ran from window to window until she found one that first groaned with reluctance, then squeaked open, allowing them to gain access. Daisy crawled in first, followed by NT. Both soiled their shirts as they slipped in through years of accumulated dust and dirt.

Inside, they were greeted by towers of metal shelves filled with boxes and boxes of who-knows-what. The smell of old paper and coffee lingered in the stuffy room. Just enough sunlight filtered in through the windows to allow them to read what was written on the boxes. They were on the hunt for anything related to Clay.

"All I see are numbers on the labels," Daisy said.

Together they lugged one big box off a shelf, opened it, and saw dozens of manila folders lined upright in the box. They pulled one out and saw the name.

"Banks, Otis," Daisy read.

"Who's that?" NT asked.

"No clue." She glanced at the other folders. "This is obviously the *B* box. If they're in alphabetical order—which I guess they are—we need to go a few rows over to find the right one."

They located the *T* box in under thirty seconds and pulled it off the shelf to the floor. They opened it and thumbed through the folders until they saw the name *Tyson*.

"We found it! Yes!" NT exclaimed. He opened the folder and read to himself, mumbling the words under his breath. He was so enthralled at the find, he had completely forgotten that Daisy was standing beside him.

"Hello! I'm still here! What does the report say?" she asked.

After a second scan, he handed it to Daisy to read. "Your turn."

Police Department – Cab Station, VA
Homicide Report: 7/26/1981
Deceased: Tyson, Clayton Henry
Age: 44
Sex: Male
Race: White
Address: 6105 Briar Road, Cab Station, Virginia, 24380
Phone: (804) 646-1815
Spouse: Not married
Date of death: On or about July 23, 1981
Cause of death: Severe head trauma (blunt force), right side
Witnesses: None
Description of deceased: White male, 6'4", 200 lbs., brown eyes, brown hair
Identifying marks: 3" scar - inside right forearm; 2" circular birthmark on left calf.

Details of offense: Deceased found by juveniles on night of August 7, 1981. Larry Alexander (age 8) encountered the body of the deceased while swimming in Serenity Lake.

Report: Officers Jackson Taylor and Royce Darman were sent to the Alexander home at 10:47 that night. After questioning Larry, it was determined he did not know the circumstances of how the deceased came to be in Serenity Lake.

Officers Darman and Taylor remain in charge of the investigation.

"Wow. It's cool that Deputy Darman and your dad investigated this case," said NT.

"Yeah. I'll ask my father about it. But, it'd be more fun if—" Daisy stopped mid-sentence.

"I know that file is in here somewhere." An unfamiliar voice filtered in from the doorway. Then footsteps. Paralyzed with fear, NT and Daisy stood as still as statues.

"Hank, what was the name on that file?"

"Geez, Jerry, are you deaf? I said Jennings!" yelled a faceless voice.

"Okay, okay. I'll get it."

Jerry grunted as he pulled a box from a shelf a few rows over from where NT and Daisy were standing. He sifted through the folders until he found the one he was looking for. "I got the report, Hank," he said, then grunted again as he put the box back on the shelf. Daisy and NT heard his footsteps getting more and more distant, till finally, the slamming of the door signaled the all clear.

"Whoa, that was a little scary," Daisy exhaled.

"Yeah, no crap. Let's get outta here," NT said.

"Speaking of reports, I have ours. Let's go," she said.

NT stopped and pointed at the folder in Daisy's hands. "What? You can't take that."

"Seriously? We aren't *taking* anything. We're *borrowing*."

"You're crazy," he said.

"Oh, well," she replied and turned to the window. A minute later the two had climbed out and were speeding off on their bikes.

9

The thrill of taking the police report was alive and well in NT and Daisy, even though rain had forced them to return to Shady Acres. The storm pelted the windows with machine gun ferocity as the friends sat at the kitchen counter playing Scrabble. Judging by their hushed tones, however, they were more focused on their escapade than on the game. After an hour, they agreed they were bored.

"How about we get back to our investigation? The attic here is filled with boxes. Let's go up there," NT suggested. With the *borrowed* report in hand, they might find other important clues and information that would further clarify the story of what happened to Clay Tyson. The attic contained all sorts of photo albums, diaries, and other stuff that might be useful.

Daisy did not need to be asked twice. "Good idea!"

NT led the way up the tiny, twisty staircase to the attic. Cobwebs laden with bug carcasses hung from every beam. Dust caked the floor and made NT sneeze five times in a row. He glanced around and noticed a pile of boxes under a window. "I think I found some of Clay's stuff!"

Daisy, meanwhile, had been looking through boxes on her own. When NT turned to see what she was doing, he laughed. She had put on an oversized yellow sunhat and wrapped a lime-green scarf stylishly around her neck. She pirouetted like a model in front of a stand-up mirror then swirled from side to side as if on a runway at a New York City fashion show. NT broke into loud applause. "Bravo! Bravo!"

Not missing a beat, Daisy curtsied and spoke in a formal tone, "Thank you to all my fans. I designed this scarf and hat with you in mind!"

"Let's ask Mimi if you can borrow that stuff. It'd be hilarious if you wore it to play golf."

"Uh, no. Probably not," Daisy laughed.

NT and Daisy each carried a box into the light and sat down on the dusty floor to inspect the contents. Not much piqued their interest in the first box. They picked through knickknacks, pewter plates engraved with *CHT*, old books, and other mementos from Clay's house. NT pulled out two photo albums that lay at the bottom and set them aside.

Yellowed newspapers rested on top of the contents of the second box. NT looked closely and saw they contained pictures of Clay and his caddie, Percy "Hoot" Alexander. He dug deeper and pulled out what looked like a brochure. "1950 U.S. Open," he read.

"What's that?" asked Daisy.

"It's an actual program from the 1950 U.S. Open at Merion Golf Club in Ardmore, Pennsylvania."

NT noticed handwriting on the cover. He squinted and read aloud, "I think Kite will win. Everything is falling into place. Ben."

"I wonder what that means."

"I don't know. The only Ben I know from golf is Ben Hogan. Maybe Clay knew him?" NT flipped through the program for more information and was surprised when two ten-dollar bills fell into his lap.

"Cool! Ice cream money!"

NT ignored Daisy's comment and looked closely at the bills. They looked normal, but why would they be in this program? Did Ben Hogan give them to Clay? Who puts money in a golf program?

"Come on. Let's go to Sweetwoods. That money will come in handy," Daisy pleaded.

"No. We shouldn't use this. Don't you think it's weird that there was money in here? It must mean something to someone."

"I guess so. Maybe BB or Clay forgot they put it in there."

"Who knows. Let's take this stuff downstairs." They grabbed the photo albums and the money and headed down the twisted staircase to the den where they flopped onto the couch. NT brushed off the thick layer of dust that coated the albums.

"Just what do y'all think you're doin'?" Mrs. Josephine Walker, the part-time caretaker at Shady Acres, towered over NT and Daisy. "I just dusted this *entire* room and I'll be a chicken's uncle if I'm gonna do it again!" Mrs. Walker and her husband Spence had worked as caretakers at Clay Tyson's home. Since Clay traveled for business and was gone for long spans of time, the Walkers loved and tended to his property as if it were their own. After Clay's untimely and shocking death, Mimi asked the Walkers to help out around Shady Acres. The couple was hard pressed to say no, given their connection with BB's brother Clay. Spence passed away shortly thereafter, but Mrs. Walker stayed on. She showed up twice a week accompanied by her only companion—a gray cat named Mr. Bond, named after the famed James Bond character. Mrs. Walker was such a huge fan, she owned every James Bond movie and book. "Well?" She stood, hands on ample hips, and demanded an answer. Her tall puff of silver hair was held firmly in place by a full minute's worth of hairspray. Lively blue eyes squinted suspiciously through perfectly round lenses held in by black plastic frames.

"Sorry, Mrs. Walker," NT said. "We'll clean it up. I promise."

"Y'all most certainly will. Here!" She thrust an old dust rag at NT then eyed the albums with curiosity. "What do you have there?"

"We found these in the attic. I wanted to look for pictures of my great uncle Clay. Did you know him?" NT asked.

Mrs. Walker clasped her hands together and gave a knowing look. "Oh, Lord, child! Did I know him? My dear, departed Spence and I *loved* that man." She immediately squeezed herself in between Daisy and NT on the small couch and spread her long, flowery skirt over her knees. Daisy was reminded of an oversized tablecloth, but quickly turned her attention to what Mrs. Walker had to say.

"Did you and Mr. Walker know him well?" NT asked.

"Oh, honey, Mr. Clay was like family. Mr. Walker and I worked for him for quite a few years. He was a kind, generous man. Did you know he remembered our four children on every one of their birthdays and at Christmas? A real shame he didn't have any children of his own. But then, he was away quite a bit. We took care of his house."

"Why was he away so much?" Daisy asked.

Mrs. Walker shrugged. "I never did ask. I just assumed he was in sales or somethin' like that. He was a gregarious, funny man who enjoyed golf, reading, and being around family when he was in town. I also think he was trying his hand at being an author."

"Really?" NT asked.

"That's right. He always had this little blue notebook with him—and I mean *always*. I saw him writin' in it a whole bunch, so I once asked him about it and he said something kind of odd."

"What?" NT asked.

"Well, he was secretive about it and said he was just takin' notes and plannin' for the future. I was never sure what he meant by that, but since he was such a quiet person, I didn't press him. I could tell he didn't want to open up about it, so I let it drop."

"Could it have been a diary?" Daisy asked.

"Who knows? Maybe. I do know that he took it everywhere and kept it locked in a drawer when he was home. He kept everything nice and neat, and his routine was always the same—keys, wallet, blue book, and his lucky charm on the table in the hall."

NT was genuinely curious. "Lucky charm?"

"Yes. A beautiful piece of blue sea glass. Not dark blue, not light blue, but more like the blue a king would wear, or the color of the sea."

"How do you know it was his lucky charm?" NT asked.

"I once heard Mr. Clay tell Mr. Walker that he always had it in his pocket when he won those golf tournaments," she replied. "I'm not sure where it ended up after Mr. Clay died."

"And we didn't come across it in any of the boxes in the attic, either," NT added. "I'll ask BB and Mimi if they know where it could be."

Mrs. Walker flipped through the pages of a photo album and shook her head slowly. "Mr. Clay was one handsome devil. I sure do miss him."

NT and Daisy both tilted their heads and looked at the pictures with critical eyes, trying to see the same handsome man from those earlier years. Mrs. Walker interrupted their reverie. "Well, back at it. No more dust!" Her scolding was less severe this time around, and she winked at NT as she hefted herself off the couch. She left the room with Mr. Bond close behind.

"That's so cool that she knew Clay," Daisy commented after Mrs. Walker and Mr. Bond had disappeared around the corner.

"Clay sounded like a cool guy. I wonder where the rest of his stuff is?" NT asked.

"Mimi or BB would know, wouldn't they? Or maybe even Hoot. You should ask," Daisy said.

"I will," NT said. "Not to change the subject, but what are we doing tomorrow? Considering the club's junior championship is coming up in a couple of weeks, I need to get some serious practice in on my own golf game."

"Me too. But let's go to Sweetwoods for ice cream first." At that thought, Daisy's eyes glittered like diamonds.

"You just won't quit about the ice cream, will you?"

"So? I like ice cream." She looked out the window and saw the rain had stopped. "I have to get going. But we'll continue our investigation again tomorrow."

When Daisy had left, NT wandered outside. He heard a swish-swish sound coming from the garage and assumed his grandfather was doing some cleaning. He was right—BB was sweeping. The joke between Mimi and NT was that BB kept the garage so clean you could eat off the floor.

"What's happening, NT?"

"Nothing much. Just hanging out."

"Mimi told me about the conversation you had with her about my brother Clay."

"Yeah. He seemed like a cool guy."

"He sure was," said BB. "And he drove a really neat car. You could help me wash it if you want."

"You still have it?"

"Come on back here." BB waved NT to the back of the garage and pointed. "Clay's Jag is under that tarp."

"For real? I never knew this was back here. That means you have Clay's Jag *and* Blackie? Cool." Blackie was BB's 1937 black Cadillac LaSalle. The car had been a gift from his father years earlier. BB always said that car was one of General Motors' most beautiful cars. It was black with white-walled tires that held small, silver hubcaps lined in bright red. BB treated Blackie with utmost love and care, and drove it every year in the town's Memorial Day parade. NT and Daisy got to ride in the car on the other occasions BB drove it around town. They rode in the rumble seat, and felt like movie stars.

"Yup. I decided to keep Clay's car too. I was hoping to rebuild the engine so I could drive it. Clay loved this car so much, I would never be able to give it away. And besides, don't you think Mimi and I would look pretty cool driving around town in it?"

NT envisioned BB tooling around Cab Station in a tiny sports car with Mimi seated next to him. She would be wearing her yellow sun hat and the green scarf would be flying out behind her as they drove along.

BB carefully pulled the tarp off the car. NT's jaw dropped at the sight. He was knocked away by the car's rich green color and buff leather seats. He stood in awe at how comfortably inviting the car looked. Although the wood dashboard needed a polish, not a single scratch or mark was visible anywhere on the car. NT would gladly take care of that task.

"Wow! This car is awesome!" NT exclaimed. He walked around to the back and stopped when he saw the broken taillight. He recalled what Mimi had told him about the day Clay was murdered. "Oh."

BB saw his grandson's dismay. "I never got around to having that fixed. Something inside just wouldn't let me. You can understand that, right?" BB said. "You're going to help me wash it up?"

"Totally!"

"Go grab the bucket and a couple of sponges."

BB and NT pushed the car out of the garage and into the afternoon sunshine, where they hosed it down. "Grab a cloth and the oil. We'll polish up the seats, too. But you need to rub them in a circular motion, lightly, very lightly." BB demonstrated.

NT got in to clean the front seat and noticed the glove compartment was ajar. He opened it all the way and saw a stack of cards bundled together. "Look, BB. Old scorecards."

BB inspected them briefly and shrugged. "They're from rounds of golf Clay played. I guess I can finally toss them."

"Wait. Can I have them?

"Sure. Why not?"

NT slid out of the car. He was so engrossed in the contents of the scorecards he had forgotten to ask his grandfather about the missing sea glass.

"It's not quitting time yet, kiddo!" BB called to him.

"Oh, yeah. Okay," NT said. He set the cards safely to one side and finished washing and polishing the Jag with his grandfather. They pushed the car back into the garage and carefully placed the tarp back over it. NT could not wait to get back to the scorecards. He counted fifteen in total. The scores were excellent. The lower, the better—and these scores were low. NT examined each card closely, and paid particular attention to the stroke counts for each of the eighteen holes Clay played every round. His great uncle had carefully written each stroke count neatly inside the designated box for that hole. Some numbers were circled, which usually meant the golfer had scored a birdie on a hole. The more birdies the better, of course, because the golfer's score for each birdied hole would be one stroke under what the club said an average golfer would shoot on it. But Clay's scoring was different. Not all the numbers he had circled were birdies. And not every hole had a score filled in. NT wondered why.

The bigger question for NT was what the scorecards represented. Were they scores from some of Clay's best rounds? If Clay was defending club champ at Cascades Golf Club, he must have played a lot more than fifteen rounds. So why did he keep these cards? And why were some scores circled that should not have been? Maybe Hoot would know. NT made a mental note to ask him.

10

NT woke at nine the following morning and read Daisy's text. *"meet me in front of club at 11 2 go 2 Hardy's, k?"*

"k," he texted back. First, however, he had to get answers to two nagging questions about Clay. He pulled on golf shorts and a shirt and headed downstairs to the kitchen. The aroma of hazelnut-flavored coffee filled the air. "Morning," he greeted his grandparents. "Your coffee smells good."

BB looked up from his paper. "Morning to you, NT. Is the aroma of your grandmother's fresh-brewed coffee what got you up? I'd say you slept well."

"I sure did. That bed is so much more comfortable than my bed at home," NT remarked. "But, actually, I have a question for you both."

"What's that?" BB asked.

"Mrs. Walker told me my great uncle Clay used to have a piece of blue sea glass that he carried around as a good luck charm. Do you know where it is?"

BB answered, "I know what you're talking about, but we never did find it."

"Oh," NT responded. "She also told us about a blue book he always carried around and wrote in. Do you know where that is?" He helped himself to a bowl of cereal and a glass of orange juice.

BB scowled as he thought about it. "I know the book, but, like the sea glass, I don't know where it got to. It would be nice to have them back as mementos," he answered.

"That'd be cool," NT said.

"What's on your agenda for the day?" Mimi asked.

"Me and Daisy are going to go over to the Hardy sisters, then we're going to hit golf balls."

"Don't you mean, 'Daisy and I'?" Mimi said.

"Okay, I'll try again. *Daisy and I* are going over there. Is that better?"

"Much. What's going on there?" Mimi asked.

"Daisy has to pick up their house key 'cause she's taking care of their pig Succotash when the sisters go away," he answered.

"I see. They sure do love that pig," Mimi said.

"Yeah, I know." NT laughed. "They even take it canoeing, and it has its own life jacket."

"A life jacket? For a *pig*?" Mimi was incredulous.

"Yup. A yellow one."

"Well, at least he won't drown," Mimi joked.

"Guess not," NT replied, and he slurped down the sugary milk from his bowl.

* * *

Daisy was waiting for NT at their designated spot. "What's up?" she asked.

"Not much. You?"

"Not a whole lot. You ready to go?" she asked.

"Yeah. Let's roll," he responded.

NT and Daisy chugged on their bikes up the hill to the Hardy house. Though the house was situated barely halfway up Creek Road, Daisy and NT's thighs and lungs burned from the steep climb they had to pedal.

"My legs are killing me. Wow," NT noted.

A Letter for Hoot

"Same for me. Ouch," Daisy said, and she rubbed her screaming thigh.

The white clapboard house stood behind a horseshoe-shaped driveway located thirty yards from the road. A low stone wall separated the edge of the yard from the front porch. Directly in front of the house, pink, white, and blue hydrangea bushes displayed their full loveliness in the late morning sun. Bees drifted from bush to bush, pollinating here and there. Daisy and NT leaned their bikes against the stone wall and walked to the massive front door. Its size and black color belied the welcoming color and fragrance presented by the flower garden in full bloom. Daisy knocked three times.

"Just a minute," a voice from inside called out.

They heard feet shuffling and then chains and bolts being undone. Finally, Minnie opened the door. "Hello, Daisy. So nice of you to come by with your friend," she said.

"Hi, Miss Hardy. This is NT. He's from Philadelphia," Daisy said.

"Well, it's certainly nice to meet you, NT. I'm Minnie Hardy." She extended her hand to shake NT's. Minnie's name certainly suited her, because she stood just five feet tall. Without the floppy hat and enormous sunglasses, she looked different. Her face held happy laugh lines and kind blue eyes. NT was surprised that her hand felt so smooth and soft, and that her handshake exuded authority.

"I'm curious, what does NT stand for?" she asked.

"Nicholas Tucker, ma'am," he responded.

"Tucker. What a good English surname," she said.

"Actually, Tucker is my middle name. My last name is Tyson."

63

Minnie raised her eyebrows in surprise. "Tyson? Are you related to Marian and Willy Tyson?"

"Yes, ma'am. They're my grandparents."

"Lovely people. Good golfers, too. Please, come in. Cordie's probably out in the garden with Succotash." Minnie opened the door wide and NT and Daisy stepped into the foyer. "We can sit in the kitchen." They followed her through the house and to the kitchen. Along the way, NT snuck a peek into the large rooms. Most of them had high-backed chairs or couches that did not look at all inviting to plop down on. Thick braided rugs lay on the floors in some of the rooms.

Sunlight splashed through the kitchen windows. Minnie motioned the two friends toward a nook against the back wall. A round table and four chairs took up the entire space. On top of the table, a red vase overflowed with a bouquet of blue hydrangeas.

Minnie glanced out the window, threw it open, and belted out to her sister, "Cordie, we have company. Get in here!" NT and Daisy would never have guessed that a noise so deep and loud would be housed in such a tiny body.

The back door swung open and Cordie entered the kitchen. Her faded khakis, white shirt, and blue sneakers reminded NT of the uniforms worn by the kids at the private school near his home. Wispy, silvery curls peeked out from under her sun hat.

"Hello, Daisy," said Cordie.

"Hello, Miss Hardy."

Cordie flicked her chin at NT and asked, "Who's your handsome friend?" NT felt his face get hot just as it had that day in the caddie shack.

Before Daisy could respond, Minnie jumped in. "Cordie, you'll never guess who this young man belongs to."

Cordie cast her eyes upon NT more closely and cocked her head. After a long gaze, she responded, "I must say I don't know."

"This here is NT Tyson, grandson of Marian and Willy," Minnie answered.

A smile crept across Cordie's face. "Is that a fact? Well, it sure is a real pleasure to meet you, NT."

NT shook Cordie's hand. "Nice to meet you too, Miss Hardy." Her handshake was firm like her sister's, and her face equally warm. She held NT's hand a bit longer than he thought necessary. When she finally dropped it, she asked her sister, "Min, you give them the key yet?"

"Not yet. Do you kids have time for a glass of iced tea? I made it myself," Minnie said.

Daisy and NT nodded. "Sure, thanks."

As she poured the tea, Minnie ran through Succotash's routine—three walks a day and two feedings. "And make sure his pen is locked tightly. He's been known to escape and run wild. He means everything to us, and if he escaped and got into trouble, we'd be devastated." She sat back down at the table and took a long sip of tea.

"Key?" Cordie reminded her.

"Oh, yes." Minnie lifted a piece of string over her head from around her neck. A lone key dangled from it. "Here you go, Daisy."

In turn, Daisy looped the string over her own head to safeguard the key.

They made small talk about their upcoming trip to Myrtle Beach, Succotash, and what NT and Daisy planned for the summer. NT waited for a convenient pause in the conversation. He took advantage of the opportunity to ask about his great uncle Clay. "Uh, I have a question for both of you," he started. The sisters focused their full attention on NT. "Since you—"

"Hold on," Cordie interrupted, "Since there are two of us, call us Miss Cordie and Miss Minnie. It's easier all around, right?"

"Good idea, sister," said Minnie. "So, you were saying, NT?"

"Well, the other day I found out about my great uncle Clay for the first time ever. My grandmother told me what happened to him. I start ninth grade in September, and I have to write a paper about a relative. I know nothing about Clay and need more information about him, like what he did, what he was like. Mimi—my grandmother—suggested I talk with you. She said you knew him."

A dark cloud of emotion swept over both sisters' faces. NT and Daisy noted their reaction in the downward cast of their mouths and furrow in their brows.

"Clay Tyson. That's a blast from the past," Cordie said. Her tone could not have been icier.

"I'll say," Minnie agreed.

"How did you know him?" NT asked.

"Years ago," Cordie started, "when we were wild teenagers—if you can imagine that—a whole group of us ran around together. Clay was part of our crowd—witty, handsome, and so much fun. I remember plenty of enjoyable evenings at Serenity Lake. We'd swim, light bonfires, and tell stories and laugh deep into the night. Clay always had some wild tale to tell. Who knows if it was true? He made us laugh until our sides hurt. He was kind and patient, especially when he taught me how to play golf. Most of the girls in town were sweet on him. He could have had his pick of any one of them. But he chose only one girl, *right, Minnie*?" Cordie glared at her sister.

"Good Lord, Cordie," Minnie replied. "Are you still holding onto something that happened so long ago? It's been over forty years! I thought we put all that behind us. I was never *Clay's girl*. You know that." She rolled her eyes.

NT and Daisy swallowed and looked at each other. *This is awkward,* NT thought.

"What happened?" Daisy dared to ask.

Cordie answered, "I had been on a few dates with Clay, and when I went away to boarding school, *she* swooped right in and took him from me." Cordie's emphasis on *she* was not lost on Minnie.

"For the love of God, sister. You only went on a *few dates*. It's not as though he proposed to you. You acted like you'd ended it with him before you left and didn't seem to care about him anyway," Minnie retorted.

The kitchen fell silent and the air felt heavy with tension.

"Since you asked, we may as well finish," Minnie said. "Truth be told, we *both* fancied Clay, I more than my sister. And he managed to drive a wedge between us. But then one night, when Cordie and I were arguing about him, we made a deal."

"A deal? What deal?" NT asked. He was more intrigued by the minute.

Minnie focused her blue eyes on NT and finished with a nod. "We decided that blood was thicker than water and that no man was worth arguing over and ruining family. So, we put an end to it with Clay." A thin smile crossed her lips.

At that, NT and Daisy understood that the conversation had ended. It was time to leave.

Cordie's face brightened. "Are you all set with instructions for taking care of our baby?"

"Yes, ma'am," Daisy replied.

"Thank you. Speaking of Succotash, he needs his lunch," Cordie said.

"We'll take good care of him, I promise," Daisy said.

"Yes, I'm sure you will, dear. We'll be home on Wednesday. See you then."

All four rose from the table and walked toward the front door.

"It was nice to meet you," NT said to the sisters. "Thanks for the iced tea. Have a good trip."

NT and Daisy hopped on their bikes and rode off down Creek Road. The trip down was much easier. They headed toward Sweetwoods. After that strange conversation, they needed ice cream. And quiet time to talk.

* * *

Sweetwoods was the perfect hangout for kids. Each wall in the old building was painted a distinct color—yellow, pink, blue, or green. Small white lights lined the chalkboard menu which hung above pumps filled with hot fudge, butterscotch, caramel, and cherry toppings. The smells of the rich sauces mingled with the sweetness of the waffle cones and enticed people in at all times of day and night. NT and Daisy ordered their ice cream—butterscotch and chocolate, respectively—paid, then plopped down in a booth. Neither noticed a man sitting alone three booths down from theirs.

Daisy dug into her sundae as though it were the first, even though she managed to eat one form or another of Sweetwoods ice cream practically every day. "I can't believe the Hardy sisters kind of went out with Clay," she said, her mouth full of ice cream.

"Kind of? They *did* go out with him. But you're right. I wasn't expecting to hear that. Even weirder was when they said they put an end to it with Clay. What does *that* mean?"

Daisy paused, spoon midway to her mouth when his words registered. "Oh, my God. Do you think *they* killed Clay?" In her excitement, a blob of ice cream fell on her shirt. "Crap. Now I have to change before we go to the club," she said, and wiped at the chocolate ice cream.

"I don't know," NT said. "But that whole conversation was really creepy."

"Definitely. Totally creepy," Daisy agreed, and went back to her sundae.

NT remembered he had put Clay's scorecards in his pants pocket to show her. "Oh, yeah. Check these out." He handed Daisy the cards to study.

She flipped through the cards and her eyebrows raised in surprise. "Wow, he was really good. Four birdies on the front. That's a dream of mine." She laughed. "I guess that piece of blue sea glass really was his good-luck charm."

NT agreed and added that he wanted to locate both the lucky charm and the blue book Clay wrote in.

"You mean the one Mrs. Walker told us about?"

"Yeah. I wonder where it is. There was no mention of it in the report you stole." Daisy ignored NT's last words. NT licked the last of the butterscotch from his spoon. "I wonder why he was killed. Mimi and the Hardy sisters said everyone loved him, so why would someone do such a horrible thing?"

Daisy shrugged. "No clue. Maybe he was doing something bad?"

"Like what?"

She scraped one final spoonful of fudge from her glass before speaking. "Well, on *Law and Order* people get murdered because they're blackmailing others or they know too much stuff about bad guys," she said.

"Wow, big word—*blackmailing*. Didn't know you had such a huge vocabulary."

"Okay, Detective Tyson, why do *you* think he was killed?" Daisy leveled NT with a glare.

"I don't know. People were really mad at him? Minnie and Cordie were mad at him, right? Maybe he had a secret. Or maybe *he* killed someone." NT stopped and looked at Daisy. He sensed something was brewing behind her green eyes.

"We may never know, NT, until we find out more."

"Like?"

"Like, we still need to talk to Mrs. Cavanaugh at the library. And Hoot. And other people in town, too. Somebody *must* know something. Maybe one of them would know where Clay's book is."

NT thought about Daisy's suggestion. "Don't you think the people who knew him are really old by now?"

"Probably. Let's ask Mimi. She'd know," Daisy responded.

"Okay, and definitely Hoot, too, since he caddied for Clay. He might even know where the book is. I think we should tell him about the money we found and the scorecards. I'm going to the club for practice after we're done here. Are you coming?"

"Yeah, but I have to change first. I'll meet you there. I guess I'll finally get to meet Hoot."

NT had forgotten that Daisy had not met the old caddie. "That's right. He says he was gone a few years and just recently returned to Cascades. You'll like him. He knows BB and Mimi, and he has this cool gold tooth. He's awesome."

"Cool," she said.

Daisy and NT's conversation had perked up the ears of the man seated a few booths over. He was pretending to be reading a newspaper while listening to the friends' animated conversation. He knew he had heard correctly, which was a lucky break for him. He also knew exactly who he needed to speak to for more information. The man watched NT and Daisy leave the ice cream shop, pick up their bikes, and pedal off. A minute later, he got into his car and followed.

11

Daisy rode off to her house to change and NT rode quietly in the other direction toward the club. He thought about different things along the way, but mostly that he was glad he had two more months to spend in Cab Station. He also thought about the Hardy sisters' story about Clay and how they had come close to never speaking to each other again. That story made him think of his parents' divorce, which he did not want to do.

At the club, NT headed straight for the caddie shack, even though he knew it was against Mimi's wishes. He loved how the old place felt and had good reason to do what he was doing, including hanging out with Hoot a bit before Daisy showed up. The door was open. Hoot was getting a drink from the small fridge in the back of the shack and did not see NT approach. The creak of the floorboards made him whirl around. "Son, what're you doin' sneaking up on me like that? Gonna give an old man a heart attack!"

"Sorry. I didn't mean to scare you."

"Oh, boy. You sure got me." Hoot checked the clock.

"Yeah, I know I'm early. I wanted to hang out a little before my friend Daisy gets here."

Hoot winked and said, "You got a girlfriend, do you? Good for you."

"No way," NT said quickly. "She's just my friend. But she's really cool. You'll see."

"Well, I'm happy for the company. Have a seat." He gestured toward a chair that had four books piled on it. "Just clear that seat off."

NT lifted the books off the chair and one title caught his eye. "I have this book." He held up a copy of Hemingway's *The Old Man and the Sea.* "I have to read it for school this summer. Have you read it?"

"Yep. Many a time," Hoot responded. "I save it for every summer. I read it in between caddie loops. I did a lot of fishing as a kid and I still do when I'm not here. This story keeps me grounded in the realities of man versus nature. Even though I throw back what I catch, I like the struggle with reeling in a fish. You start it yet?"

"I read the first couple of pages. There's no action. I was kind of hoping it would be better."

Hoot laughed and shook his head. "Give it a chance, son. You can't judge on just a few pages. Summer will be over before you know it, so you may want to get goin' on that."

NT was crestfallen at the thought of summer ending. "Don't say that."

Hoot immediately picked up on NT's change of mood. "Hey, now. What's that all about?"

"Nothing." NT stared down at the floor.

"You look troubled. What's goin' on?"

NT swallowed hard, trying to decide if he should tell Hoot. Holding his feelings in made his stomach hurt.

"It's my parents. I don't want summer to end because they're divorced and I hate going back and forth between their houses. They think I'm okay with it, but I hate it." NT wiped his eyes. "Staying with Mimi and BB is way better. Sometimes I hate my parents for doing this."

"Oh, son, I'm sorry to hear that. I s'pose it ain't easy on you, goin' back and forth. Being down here with your grandparents for the summer is a good escape for you, isn't it?"

NT nodded slowly.

"You talk to them about it yet?"

"No. I don't want to upset them even more. I eavesdropped when my dad told them what was going on. I know Mimi cried a lot then and I don't want to upset her all over again."

"I understand, and that's real thoughtful of you, but your grandpappy is pretty understanding. I'm sure he'll be a good listener."

"Yeah. Maybe."

"Well, I tell you what. You can talk to me anytime you like. I'm happy to listen. I don't like seeing you down in the dumps."

"Yeah, it's really hard. I mean, Mom and Dad used to get along, but then they just started to fight. And I hated it."

"I don't blame you, NT. Life can throw some mean curveballs, but the fact that you're talkin' about it will help you work through it. And gettin' ready for the junior club champs will take your mind away from it, right? I say we get out there right now and start workin'." Hoot stood.

"That's why I'm here. Daisy and I are both going to play in the championship."

"I like that. Let's head on out to the course."

"Okay."

The wind that midsummer day was making itself apparent on the golf course. "Remember, always add ten yards to your shot distance when the wind's kicking up," Hoot instructed. "That usually means you'll want a different club than the one you'd normally use."

Overall, NT was a solid golfer, and he felt confident he would do well in the tournament. But he also knew he needed to work on certain parts of his game. He told Hoot that his drives off the tee were terrible, and that he wanted to turn the ball more to the left instead of slicing it to the right.

"Just turn your right hand over toward the left a bit when you grip the club. This should also help you gain more yards with your driver. But, remember. Improvement isn't gonna happen overnight. It'll take work and patience. Got it?"

"Yes, sir," NT agreed.

They walked up the fairway and suddenly NT heard the clanging of clubs from behind. He turned and saw Daisy running toward them, her black golf bag bouncing up and down against her back.

"Sorry I'm late," she panted. "Mom had to take Brett to baseball practice first."

"You must be Daisy. I'm Hoot. Pleasure to meet you."

Daisy flashed a grin. "Hi, Hoot. Nice to meet you too."

"Your friend here says you also signed up for junior championship," Hoot remarked.

"Yes, sir. I'm psyched for it," she answered.

"Well, I'm going to help coach young Nicholas here and am happy to help you too."

"Cool. Thanks, Hoot," she responded.

The two friends practiced for an hour before Hoot suggested they take a break. NT thought the time was right to ask Hoot for more information about Clay. "Hoot, remember the other day when you told me about my uncle Clay?"

Hoot looked at NT and Daisy out of the corner of his eye. "Mmm hmm. I do."

"Well, Mimi told me what happened, and Daisy and I have been curious to learn more about him," NT said. "We went up to the attic and found these." He pulled two ten-dollar bills out of a large side pocket of his golf bag and held them out.

Hoot focused on the money and his eyes grew round as saucers when he realized what he was looking at. He took the bills gently from NT, as if he were handling a baby bird. "Tell me exactly where y'all found these," he said.

"In an old U.S. Open program that was in a box of Clay's stuff," NT said.

Without warning, Hoot slid the bills into his own golf bag, picked the bag up, and announced, "Lesson over. We need to head to the shack."

NT and Daisy looked at each other, shrugged their shoulders, and followed Hoot without saying another word. Inside the shack, Hoot signaled for them to take a seat at the rickety table while he dug around the old lockers, muttering to himself and flinging old clothes and other miscellaneous items aside. "Aha!" he said a minute later. From deep within the locker, he pulled out a golf program from the 1950 Professional Golfers' Association Championship held in Ohio. He sat down at the table and thumbed through the pages.

NT was the first to break the silence. "What are you looking for?"

"Well, I'll be," Hoot said, more to himself than to NT and Daisy. He pulled an envelope from inside the PGA program. He opened it and NT and Daisy's eyes bugged out of their heads. Inside the envelope was a ten-dollar bill. "Clay gave me this program and told me to keep good care of it. He had me swear not to look inside it until the time was right. When you showed me that money and told me where you found it, I thought I'd been struck from above. If now isn't the right time, then..." he trailed off, shaking his head.

NT noticed handwriting on the cover of the program. It was identical to the writing on the program he had found. "Look, Hoot. There's writing on the cover. What does it say?"

Hoot read carefully, "Palmer and his caddie are looking for you. Be careful. Ben."

NT's excitement grew. "That's almost like the one we found!"

"Son, I need you to bring me the program where you found those bills." Hoot's voice was soft but commanding. "See if there are any more in those boxes too."

NT looked through the program as Hoot analyzed the ten-dollar bills and muttered to himself. "Hmm. All these bills have the same serial numbers. How's that possible?"

"Say, Hoot, do you know anything about piece of blue sea glass and some book Clay was always writing in?"

Daisy explained, "NT has to write a report about a family member, and we thought that if we found that book, we'd find out cool stuff about Clay."

Hoot looked at her with a cocked eyebrow and said, "Interesting."

"Did he keep a lot of stuff in his locker?" NT asked.

"He did, but your grandfather cleaned it out. I do remember that sea glass, though. Clay used it as a ball marker when he putted. That thing's been gone as long as

Clay has. And that book? He had that dang thing with him everywhere he went. He was always writin' in it. I asked him about it once and he said he was writing and planning for the future. He didn't look too happy about me asking, so I didn't after that. I did see him put it in his locker a few times."

Daisy got hopeful. "Really? Any idea where it is now?"

"Nah, I don't know. Maybe in his golf bag?" Hoot said.

Daisy looked at NT. "Do you know where his bag is?"

"I don't. Maybe it's at Shady Acres," he responded. "Oh, that reminds me!" NT ran out to his golf bag, retrieved Clay's scorecards, and handed them to Hoot. "I found these in Clay's car."

Hoot scrutinized the cards and added up the score on the top card. "Thirty-eight on the front nine holes. Sounds right—two over par." He flipped through the entire bunch and placed them on the table with a loud sigh.

"Look at these other numbers. They look like dates and times," NT said.

Hoot read the numbers aloud. "Six seven. That'd be June seventh. Six twenty-one and seven five, for June twenty-first and July fifth. Then eight thirty-five, eight forty, and eight fifteen. Those are times."

NT looked at Hoot. "Do you know what the dates mean?"

"Well, they could be dates he played, but I'm not a hundred percent sure." Hoot flipped through the cards again and found three more with dates and times. He noticed the dates on all six cards were exactly two weeks apart.

NT asked about something else that had caught his eye. "Did you notice only half the cards are written on?"

"Somethin' ain't right here. Clay was careful to fill out every card the same way. And I mean after *every* round he played." Deep creases formed between Hoot's eyebrows.

"He could've been in a hurry," NT offered.

"Nope. No way. Not Clay. He made sure everything was accurate and complete. Heck, if I didn't clean his clubs good enough, he'd get out an old toothbrush and finish the job!" Hoot laughed at the memory. "But still, something isn't right here." He stared hard at the cards, as if willing them to speak. "These are definitely dates and times, but why did he record them this way?"

NT had an idea. "Maybe at the library we can look up what days of the week those dates fell on."

"That's an awesome idea. Let's go!" Daisy was practically out the door when Hoot stopped her.

"That'll be tough to do today 'cause it's starting to get dark and the library might be gettin' ready to close. Your parents and grandparents are gonna wonder where you are. You'd do well to call them. Now," Hoot ordered with a wink. "I'll see y'all tomorrow. Now get on home."

"Oh, man, I forgot my phone. Do you have yours?" Daisy asked.

NT patted his pockets. "Nope," he answered.

"We need to find a phone," Daisy said.

"The Grille Room should have one. Is Lenny still the bartender there? He'd let us make a call. Maybe we can get some food while we're there too."

The Grille Room was the Cascade Club's informal dining area. NT loved the restaurant and remembered it as having dark green walls and worn carpeting, but it had received a facelift the previous summer. The walls had been painted a warm shade of red and the old carpet had been replaced with a huge, colorful rug with flecks of red, green, and blue. The towering bookcase was gone and in its place was a flat screen television mounted on the wall. The last bits of daylight peeked through windows adorned with cream-colored curtains.

Lenny was in his usual spot behind the bar. For thirty years, he had been polishing glasses, mixing drinks, pouring wine, and making the thickest milkshakes ever. He was popular among the members because he knew everyone by name and could talk about anything from golf to dogs to how much rain they would get in summer. A half-dozen club members were seated at the bar enjoying drinks and dinner. A few high pub tables stood in the bar area, a leather couch faced a wide-open fire place, and other tables were scattered about the large room to give it an informal yet comfortable atmosphere.

"Well, there's trouble," Lenny said when he saw NT and Daisy enter. He greeted them with a wink.

"Hey, Lenny. It looks so different in here," NT commented.

"We get nothing but positive feedback on the changes. I'll be right with you. I need to take care of my outside tables, especially since Mayor Hall is seated at one of them. Meanwhile, take a real close look over there," Lenny said, and he pointed to a far wall covered with pictures and plaques.

The plaques contained the names of golfers lucky enough to score a hole in one as well as the names of tournament winners, both junior and adult. NT read the list of names on the junior plaque and kept seeing the same name over and over: Tyson. His, his grandfather's, and his uncle's name. He counted and saw that BB had won the junior tournament three times, while Clay had won it five times. On the club champion plaque, Clay's name appeared five times. NT was overwhelmed with pride.

"Yo! Look at this!" Daisy pulled him from his trance.

NT turned and saw her standing at a wall adorned with photographs. He wandered to the gallery of golfers. Some of the pictures went all the way back to the 1940s. "How could they play golf fully dressed in pants, vests, and long-sleeved shirts? How could they swing a club?"

"Beats me. Imagine doing that when it was hot like it is now?" Daisy said.

NT saw Clay and Hoot in several of the photos. They were receiving the champion's trophy. In one, Clay was shaking hands with the pro with his right hand and holding the trophy in his left hand. Next to him stood Hoot with a huge smile.

"Wow! Daisy, look!" NT pointed at one picture of Clay, and Daisy leaned in to see what he was indicating. Sure enough, a small book was sticking out of the back pocket of his slacks. "Think it's the same book Hoot and Mrs. Walker told us about?"

"Maybe," she replied. "But I can't tell if it's blue. These pictures are really old."

Lenny was back behind the bar, which had since emptied out.

"Lenny, could we please use the phone?" Daisy asked. "We need to call home to let people know we're here."

"Sure," he said, and lifted the phone up from under the bar.

As Daisy dialed her number, NT's eyes fell on a golf club that was leaning against the door to the kitchen.

"Do you play golf too, Lenny?" NT asked, gesturing to the club.

"Oh, that? I did when I was a kid, but life got in the way. I like collecting the old ones, and this one has an original steel shaft—it's a real beauty. I may hang it above the door, make it my contribution to the décor." He laughed as he spoke and gave the bar another wipe.

"No one home at my house. I left a message," Daisy said, and handed the phone to NT.

NT called the house phone at Shady Acres. The line was busy and, for the life of him, he could not remember BB or Mimi's cell phone numbers.

Lenny held up a pair of menus. "Are you eating in?" he asked.

"Nah. Thanks. We're gonna grab hotdogs from the halfway house and go to the library," NT responded.

"Okay. Knock yourselves out," Lenny replied.

NT and Daisy each plucked a hot dog from the rotating grill at the halfway house and headed off on their bikes to the library. Or so they thought.

12

NT and Daisy reached the library only to find it had closed for the day.

"Duh. Check the time. The library's closed," Daisy said.

"Crap. I forgot it was this late," NT replied. "I guess we'll have to come back tomorrow. Let's go."

The friends felt a potent mix of fear and exhilaration as they rode along in near darkness. Bright stars dotted the sky and the moon shone brightly. Crickets sang their songs and the occasional bat swooped above them. NT and Daisy used the barely visible lines that edged the road to guide them as they pedaled their way home. Suddenly, headlights from behind approached. The lines were illuminated to an intense yellow. The friends stuck to the lines as much as possible to let the car pass, but it did not. NT looked over his shoulder to see who was in the car, but the beams blinded him. Unnerved, Daisy hopped off her bike and pulled it into the ditch alongside the road. NT followed suit.

The car stopped as well. A stern voice yelled out to them, "Where have you two been?" They recognized the voice as belonging to Sheriff Taylor—Daisy's father. "We've been worried sick about you! I've been driving all over looking for you, thinking the worst had happened."

"Dad—"

"Before you start to tell me you were at the club, I drove there and obviously didn't see either of you!" Sheriff Taylor stood in front of his car, glaring at NT and Daisy. "And I can guarantee that your grandparents are not too happy with you either, young man."

"Dad, I promise we were at the club. Lenny let us use the phone to call!" Daisy protested.

"Well, I've found you now, so put your bikes in the car. We're going home."

NT looked out the window as they rode along. He felt nervous about the trouble he'd be in when he got to his grandparent's.

Sheriff Taylor pulled his car into the driveway at Shady Acres. NT saw BB standing on the porch with his arms folded across his chest. That was a bad sign. He got out of the car, lifted his bike from the trunk, and approached the porch. BB waved at Sheriff Taylor, who continued on home with Daisy.

"Nicholas, we know you love riding around and being at the club. But our rule is that when it's dark, you're home. Period. Got it?"

"Yes, sir. I'm sorry.

"In the future, let us know and we'll come and get you."

"Yes, sir. I called, but the line was busy, and I couldn't remember your cell number."

NT and BB walked in and headed into the kitchen where Mimi was pouring herself a glass of water.

"What were you two doing this late at the club anyway? It's a bit dark to be playing golf."

NT thought quickly and responded, "Well, we were practicing for champs and Hoot was helping us." He felt as though he was teetering on the edge of a cliff. Should he tell his grandparents about going to the caddie shack with Hoot? About showing Hoot the scorecards and money?

"It's almost nine, which means it's been dark for nearly an hour. Maybe you should tell us what else you were up to,"

Mimi said. "I don't like you two out gallivanting around when it's dark. Your parents expect us to watch out for you, and if something bad were to happen, I don't know what I'd do. No more late nights out, understood?"

NT took the leap. "Fine," he sighed. "We talked to Hoot about the scorecards and about Clay's notebook." NT's tone was defiant. His grandmother had told him to stay away from the caddie shack, and he had blatantly disobeyed her. His defensiveness was a clear sign to his grandparents that he knew he was in the wrong, but was unable to admit as much.

BB and Mimi looked at each other, and BB scowled. "Watch your tone, Nicholas."

"I'm sorry, Mimi. I know you told me not to go in the caddie shack, but Hoot had to show us something related to the scorecards."

Mimi's look softened. She and BB were actually happy to see the interest NT had taken in learning more about Clay. "I understand you really want to get to the bottom of things, but that doesn't mean you put yourself or others in danger."

NT cast his eyes at the floor, saying nothing.

BB broke the tension. "I hope Hoot gave you some good information."

"He did."

"And, like I mentioned the other day, we'd like to have the book and the sea glass. But they seem to have just disappeared. I think Clay was planning something. He used that notebook to write down his plans. At least, that's what he alluded to."

"What do you mean?" NT asked.

Mimi said, "Well, when we asked him what he was writing in that book, he said he was just planning for the future, and when the time came, he'd share with us what he was writing. But that never happened."

"Oh."

BB agreed with Mimi. He shook his head and added, "The police weren't any help either, since they didn't know where the book was. Of all Clay's belongings I'd really love to have, that book would be it."

"Well, it's late," Mimi said. "We can continue this conversation tomorrow, fellas. I'm going to bed. Night, night."

"Night, Mimi. Love you," NT responded.

13

Sunlight crossed NT's face as he lay in bed the next morning thinking about Clay and all things related to him. He suddenly remembered he was supposed to meet Daisy at the library as soon as it opened. A check of the clock told him it was nearly eight. *I'd better get going.* He hoped he and Daisy would be successful at locating old almanacs to check the dates Clay had noted on his scorecards.

Daisy was already at the Newcomb Library when NT arrived. She sat waiting for him on the gray slate steps outside the front entrance. "It's about time you got here."

"C'mon. Let's go find Mrs. Cavanaugh."

"Shouldn't be hard, given that she's the librarian!"

Daisy wanted to check the almanacs first, but NT was bursting at the seams to find out what Mrs. Cavanaugh could tell him about Clay. He cut right to the chase and shot rapid-fire questions at her about how well she remembered Clay and what she knew about him.

Mrs. Cavanaugh smiled and responded in her soft librarian voice. She told NT pretty much what everyone else had—that Clay was friendly and popular, he traveled frequently, and he was a good golfer. NT was disappointed that she did not disclose anything new about his uncle.

"Thanks," NT said.

"You're welcome. The almanacs are in that aisle." She pointed Daisy and NT in the right direction.

They located an almanac and took it to a nearby study carrel, then each grabbed a chair and crammed into the space. They flipped to the calendars from the previous fifty years.

"This book is so old, it smells like rotten cheese!" said NT.

"Gross!" Daisy waved her hand in front of her face. "Judging by this *fragrance*, I bet no one's touched this book in fifty years or more."

NT pulled out the scorecards and organized them by date. Daisy turned to the 1981 calendar and saw that each date noted on the scorecard was a Thursday. "Think that's a coincidence?" she said. "In Nancy Drew, they talk about coincidences."

"Nancy Drew is so fake! Why do you read those books?"

"Shut up!" Daisy fired back. "Because they're fun and mysterious. Why do you like to watch *Scooby-Doo*? Talk about fake!"

"Okay, okay. You wrote down that those dates were on Thursdays, right?"

"Yup."

NT leaned back in his chair and thought aloud. "I wonder why Clay wrote down those particular dates and times?" He leaned in again and looked over the June and July calendars from 1980 and 1981. "Nothing huge happened then."

"Maybe he was going to copy those dates later into his blue notebook?"

NT slapped his forehead and exclaimed, "Oh, yeah! Duh! I totally forgot to tell you that I asked Mimi and BB about that."

"Seriously? How could you forget that minor detail?"

"Yeah, yeah, I know. They said he wrote in it all the time but he was really secretive with it."

"Do they know where it is?"

NT shrugged and shook his head. "No. And BB really wants it. I hope we can find it."

They agreed they had had enough of the library. "The Hardy sisters are back home," Daisy said. "I have to return their key by noon. Want to come with me?"

NT texted Mimi to let her know he would be going with Daisy to the Hardy sisters' house to drop off their key.

Mimi responded that lunch would be ready when they returned.

* * *

NT and Daisy climbed the steep hill toward the Hardy sisters' house. "I'm glad we won't have to ride up this hill of death anymore after today," Daisy panted.

"Me too," said NT. "That's a good name. It's a total hill of death."

They had made the ride twice daily to take care of Succotash while the Hardy sisters were away, but still struggled to ride all the way up the hill without getting out of breath. On this final ride, they discussed how they might broach the subject of Clay again without the sisters getting snippy at each other like they had the first go-around. They decided on a plan, but soon realized no plan was needed.

The sisters were lounging in their Adirondack chairs on the front lawn. True to form, they were wearing their floppy hats and sunglasses. Each sipped from a tall glass while Succotash lay curled at their feet.

"Hi, Miss Cordie, Miss Minnie," Daisy called out.

"Oh, hello, children. Come. Have a seat. Let me get you some iced tea," Minnie yelled back. Within minutes, all four were enjoying home-made sun tea in the shade of a gigantic magnolia tree.

"Yum. This is so good," Daisy said, and sat back comfortably in her chair.

"Did our baby behave while we were away?" asked Minnie.

"Totally. He's a cool little pig," Daisy answered.

"Yes, he is," Cordie agreed.

"And how is everyone at Shady Acres?" Minnie asked NT.

"They're good," NT answered.

"You stay with them for the whole summer?" Cordie asked.

"Yes, ma'am."

"I'm sure they love having you," Cordie said.

"Sister, we haven't see them in the longest time. I think it would be nice to call Marian and Willy about meeting for dinner at the club some night. You always *were* the queen of organizing everyone's social life," Minnie teased.

"Splendid idea. I'll do that when the children leave," Cordie said. "Oh, that reminds me. I'll be right back." Cordie went into the house and left the others wondering what she was doing. A minute later, she returned with a photo in hand. "We thought you'd like to see this—especially you, NT. It's a picture of your grandfather and great uncle when they were younger."

Cordie handed the yellowed photo to NT. Daisy relocated to the broad arm of NT's chair for a better look. They instantly recognized Serenity Lake. In the photo, seven teenagers—three girls and four boys—lazed on striped beach towels in the sun. They were all tanned and glowing with youth.

NT looked closely at the photo. "This is cool. When was it taken?"

"If memory serves me, it was around July 1955," Cordie answered.

"Whoa, is that BB and Mimi?" NT pointed to a handsome, dark-haired boy dressed in red swim trunks, his arm draped over the shoulders of a smiling girl.

Cordie looked over NT's shoulder. "Yes, that's your grandfather, but the girl is not your grandmother."

"Who is she?" NT asked.

Minnie responded, "Oh, that's Elizabeth Horowitz—Lizzy."

"Was she BB's girlfriend?" NT asked.

"For a while, until she moved away in the middle of the school year. We never heard from her again."

NT scrutinized the other faces and pointed to another boy. "This is Clay, isn't it?" Though he had not seen any pictures of young Clay, he was certain the boy was his great uncle. High cheekbones cast shadows down his smooth cheeks to his friendly smile. Even in a picture that old, it was easy to see Clay's dark eyes full of life, intelligence, and mischief. He was lying on the towel, propped up on one elbow, and a cigarette dangled from his mouth.

"Is he *smoking*?" Daisy was incredulous.

"We all smoked back then. It was a much different way of life," Minnie replied.

"Gross," Daisy remarked.

NT looked closer and noted, "He and BB didn't really look alike. Clay's hair was lighter and his eyes darker."

"And Clay was taller," Cordie added.

"Did BB smoke too?" NT asked.

"No. He tried it once and hated it," Minnie answered.

"Who are the others?" Daisy asked.

NT handed Minnie the photo. "Let's see," she said.

"The boy to Clay's left was Jimmy Schmitt. He died a few years ago. All those cigarettes and too much bourbon put an end to him." She next pointed to a boy with a flop of thick, blond hair that fell over one eye like a pirate's eye patch. "This boy is Bobby Hall. Well, that's what we called him before he became the almighty Mayor Robert Hall." NT wondered if the smirk on the boy's face was intentional or a mean trick played by nature.

"Oh, yeah. He was at the club last night," NT noted.

"That's him. Before that, he was City Treasurer for a long time. Being in control of the city's finances wasn't enough for him, though. He was power hungry, and when he ran for Mayor, he won easily."

"Why's that?"

"Just look at him! He's always been a real charmer and knows how to get people to say yes. Now that he's retired, he spends a lot of time at the club."

"And this cute little girl here is Miss Cordie." Minnie pointed out her sister, who sat with her legs folded beneath her and an elbow resting on Clay's side. She was clad in a tiny blue and white bikini and her smooth skin was as tan as a walnut shell. Her joyful smile radiated like the summer sun.

"And this girl next to Jimmy is Linda Powell. She was one of the smartest people I ever knew. She went to Stanford, fell in love with some guy out there in California, and never returned after college. We heard she joined some hippie commune. We used to get the occasional Christmas card, but they eventually stopped coming," Minnie said.

"Miss Minnie, why aren't you in the picture?" Daisy asked.

"Who do you think is behind the camera?" Minnie responded.

"Ah. Got it," Daisy said.

"Everyone looks so happy," Daisy commented.

"Oh, we were. Those days were golden. None of us had a care in the world. Then, a few years later, after college, we all went our separate ways." Minnie sounded sad.

"That happens when you grow up," Cordie added. "We sure missed being with everyone—especially Clay."

"Where did Clay go after college?" NT asked. "Mrs. Walker, the lady who used to take care of Clay's house, said he was away a lot. Do you know why?"

Cordie explained, "We don't really know. When we were kids, he talked frequently about his desire to travel and see the world. We told him to join the military if he wanted to travel, but he just laughed at that. So, the years went by and Minnie and I moved to other parts of the country..." She hesitated. "But we always came back to visit Momma and Daddy, usually in the summers."

NT went out on a limb. "Were you here when Clay was killed?" He thought they might know something about Clay's murder and the blue notebook.

The sisters looked at each other, then back at NT and Daisy. Minnie gave a clipped response. "We were in town during that awful time. But it was a short visit, so we didn't really see him much before his death."

"Sister, if I remember correctly, you had dinner with Clay during our visit," Cordie reminded her.

Minnie's head snapped like a bullwhip. Cordie would be dead if looks could kill. "That doesn't matter now. He's dead and that's that. *Right, sister?*" Minnie hissed.

Cordie stared at Minnie. The jovial atmosphere of reminiscing was shattered. The sun disappeared and grey clouds rolled in.

NT and Daisy knew it was time to go. "Thanks for the tea and for showing us the picture," NT said.

Minnie smiled at them as if nothing at all had happened. "You're welcome, children. Thank you for taking care of our baby."

"You're welcome. We'll see you later," Daisy said.

NT and Daisy got on their bikes and sped away, unsure of what to make of their conversation with the Hardy sisters.

* * *

The setting of a cool lunch on a wide, airy porch midsummer looked like a page out of *Home and Garden* magazine. Mimi had set a table on the porch with egg salad sandwiches, potato chips, pickles, and, of course, fresh-squeezed lemonade. "What are you up to the rest of the day?" she asked.

NT glanced at Daisy and crunched on a chip before answering as innocently as possible. "We'll probably just hang out, maybe go up to the attic and look for more stuff about Clay."

Mimi shifted her gaze between the two. She suspected they were up to something. "Like what?" The buzzing of bees filled the momentary silence.

"Um, stuff like prizes, pictures..." NT tried to sound nonchalant. "Maybe we'll find his blue notebook. Or more scorecards."

"Oh, yeah. We found old programs from his big tournaments," Daisy added.

"Old programs? I wonder why he kept them," said Mimi. She then directed herself to NT. "I doubt you'll find the book in the attic. BB and I know every item that is up there. But feel free to look."

Daisy continued, "Some of the programs have golf tips in them, and since he was champion so many times, maybe he kept them to use when he practiced."

"Hmm," Mimi said, and popped the last bite of her sandwich into her mouth. "I think your grandfather may have some old programs or pictures in his desk."

"Really?" NT's eyes lit up. He and Daisy downed their lemonade and followed Mimi into BB's office.

"Look in the bottom drawers," Mimi suggested. Just then, the phone rang. She left the room to answer it.

NT and Daisy opened the bottom drawer. They found an assortment of manila envelopes, photos, letters, and newspapers. One envelope caught their eye. Clay's name was written across the front. NT looked inside and found an old program from the Master's tournament in Augusta. Scrawled across the front were the words, "My pick is Player. Let's see if it comes true. Ben." A ten-dollar bill was taped to the inside of the program.

"What does that mean?" Daisy asked.

NT laughed at her. "Gary Player is one of the best golfers, like, ever."

"Okay, whatever. More important is that there's another ten-dollar bill. Just like in the other program!"

"Maybe Clay was betting," NT said.

"Betting? On what?" Daisy asked.

"Sometimes people bet tons of money on pro teams to win games, and there's usually some guy who writes down the amounts in a secret book. I saw that in a movie," NT replied.

"Maybe Clay was the guy writing the money amounts down in his private book?"

NT nodded. "I say we go back up to the attic and look for more programs with these weird notes."

Daisy's face lit up. "And more money for ice cream!"

NT rolled his eyes. "Seriously? Can't you, for once, think of something else?" He placed the money inside the program, then folded the program in half. He slid the program in his back pocket, but as he did so, the ten-dollar bill slipped out and floated to the floor. Neither NT nor Daisy noticed.

They climbed the attic staircase once again with the hopes of finding the blue notebook. After thirty minutes, they admitted their search was fruitless.

"It's hot and stuffy up here. Let's go," NT suggested.

"Totally. Oh, well. We looked, right?" Daisy said.

"Yeah. Maybe we'll find some other stuff later on. What time do you have to be home?"

"Around six. Why?" she asked.

"We have an hour. Want to shoot some hoops?"

"Sure," she replied.

14

Daisy shot one final basket, then said, "Game's tied. I've got to go. After what happened last night, I can't be late. My dad would freak."

NT chuckled, but knew she was right. "See you tomorrow."

Daisy rode off on her bike and NT wandered into the kitchen, where Mimi was setting the table for dinner. BB came in, and the three sat down to plates piled high with spaghetti and meatballs. NT updated his grandparents on the events of the day and excused himself when he was finished eating. "I have some school reading to catch up on."

"That's good," Mimi said. "The last thing you want is to fall behind."

The Old Man and the Sea kept NT up late. He was surprised at how the story had hooked him. Maybe because he felt sorry for Santiago, the story's main character. Santiago was a fisherman by trade, but he had gone eighty-four days without catching any fish. He was considered unlucky and, because of that, his young helper was forbidden to go fishing with him anymore. NT truly felt for the old man, who set out for sea alone on day eighty-five. NT hoped Santiago would be able to end his unlucky streak and prove the naysayers wrong. Since his parents' divorce, NT often felt isolated, and he related to Santiago's own isolation. He finally fell asleep and dreamed about lions—just like Santiago.

The next morning, NT lugged himself out of bed, splashed water on his face, and checked the golf program he had found the day before. He reread the cryptic note scrawled across the front and wondered what it meant, then flipped to the middle where he had put the ten-dollar bill. His heart stopped in his chest. The money wasn't there. He turned the program upside down and shook it. Nothing. A fist of fear squeezed his heart and his stomach felt hollow. He dressed hastily, found his phone, and called Daisy.

"Oh, my God, Daisy! Did you take the money out of the program yesterday?"

"No. Why?"

"It's not here, and with all your talk about ice cream, I thought maybe you were playing a trick."

"You're accusing me of stealing? Gee, thanks."

"Well, you wanted ice cream. So, come on. Where is it?"

Daisy heard the panic in NT's voice and softened her tone. "I swear I didn't take it. Just calm down. I saw you put it in the program. Obviously, it fell out somewhere. Did you check around?"

"No. I will."

"Okay. Tell me what you find later today. I've got to go. I've got chores to do around the house."

NT sprinted down to his grandfather's office and got down on all fours. He found nothing under the furniture or radiator. He opened the drawer where he had first found the money, but saw nothing. In frustration, he collapsed onto the floor. Something brushed against his head. He looked and saw Mr. Bond, who was staring at him with his wide green eyes.

"Mr. Bond, do you know where the money is?" NT asked.

The cat regarded NT with typical cat disdain.

"Goodness gracious, child! Why are you flopped on the rug like some old lump?"

Mrs. Walker had entered the room and bent over to plug in the vacuum cleaner. Knowing her the way he did, NT believed her capable of running the vacuum right over him. She was like a tornado when she cleaned, blowing through each room with maximum force. NT scrambled to his feet.

"I was looking for some money."

"A ten-dollar bill? I found it when I was dusting. It's on the hall table."

"Thank you!" Relief washed over NT, but it was short lived. The hall table was empty. He yelled to his grandmother. "Mimi, is BB home?"

"No need to yell. I'm right here. He just left for Foley's and the farmer's market." Foley's was Foley's Hardware Store, owned by Sam Foley.

"To buy stuff?" NT cringed when he realized he knew the answer to the question.

"Yes, of course. He was going to get the car waxed then pick up some corn. Why?"

"Nothing. I'll ask him later." NT tried to remain calm, but he put two and two together. BB had seen the money on the hall table and took it to use for his errands. NT had to find his grandfather, and quickly.

"I'm going to the club. I'll see you later," NT said, and let the door slam behind him on his way out.

15

Daisy finished her chores and her mom promptly paid her the promised ten-dollar allowance. With fresh cash in her pocket, Daisy headed to town in search of new nail polish. *Maybe purple. I'm getting tired of plain old pink.* As she rode along on her bike, she thought about how much fun she had when she and her mom painted each other's nails, one of the many girly things they did together. Unlike other girls her age, Daisy loved hanging out with her mom, who made her feel loved and special. She understood what it was like to grow up in a family of older brothers and get left out simply because she was a girl, because she, too, had only older brothers. Daisy sometimes wished her brothers could be shipped off to a desert island. Her daydreaming ended when she was about to ride past the police station but instead decided to pop in to say hello to her Dad.

Brenda was seated behind the front desk. "Hello, young lady." She greeted Daisy with her usual happy smile and hug. Daisy had known Brenda her entire life, and was always happy to see her. The woman never changed with the passage of time, and Daisy could recite her looks from memory—short, curly, salt-and-pepper hair, rectangular pink glasses atop a perfectly straight nose, and a bright smile highlighted by red lipstick.

"Hi, Miss Brenda! How are you?"

"Better for seeing you! Here to see your pop?"

"Yup. Is he around?"

"I think. But keeping track of all these schedules is tough. They're always changing, you know. Let's ask Deputy Darman."

"Hello, Daisy. How are you?" Deputy Darman said.

"Good. Is my dad around?"

"He's in a meeting right now. Something I can help you with?"

"Nah. I just stopped by to say hi before going to practice."

"How's the game? Y'all are lucky to have a nice place like Cascades club to play."

"It's fine, I guess. I have a tournament coming up, so I've got to practice."

"Good girl. I hope you win."

"Thanks. Will you tell Dad I came by?"

"Sure. He'll be sorry he missed you. Have fun."

* * *

Upon learning of his grandfather's shopping plans for the morning, NT was determined to find him and retrieve the missing money. First stop—Foley's Hardware Store. He would ask Mr. Foley if BB had been there and paid for whatever he had bought with ten-dollar bills.

NT loved walking through Foley's. The wide floor boards creaked and groaned and the air was filled with the woodsy smell of cedar chips. Unlike the large home improvement store where his mother shopped, this store felt homey and welcoming. Mr. Foley carried tools of every kind, huge clay pots for porch plants, American flags in all sizes, and aisles and aisles full of other home necessities. Mr. Foley always kept a few kites in stock. NT figured he'd buy one, to have something to do on nongolf days. He strolled by the counter, where several customers stood chatting.

"Howdy, young man!" Mr. Foley yelled.

"Hi, Mr. Foley," NT replied.

"This is the first I've seen you around all summer. Anything I can help you with?" Mr. Foley gave a big smile under his bushy mustache.

"I can wait till you're done. Are the kites still in the back?"

"Yep. A couple of aisles over, past the flags."

"Thanks."

NT moved up and down the aisles to pass time until the customers left. The first aisle held shelves of nuts and nails, all in neatly labeled plastic organizer boxes. Bolts and screws of all sizes were piled in open bins, ready for shoppers to count out however many they needed. NT loved to dip his hand into the bins and feel his fingers against the cold metal. Aisle two was full of plumbing supplies—faucets, pipe fittings, water filters, and a variety of toilet seats. When NT turned to head down aisle three, he noticed the flags in the endcap and knew he was in the right place. *Jackpot.* He saw toy trains, toy soldiers, rubber balls, even hula hoops. At the end of the aisle, he saw kites—Diamond kites and Delta kites, as well as the more common flat and box-type kites—and he was familiar with them all. He examined a neon-green Delta kite that came with a generous five hundred feet of string, thinking he and Daisy would be able to fly it at Shady Acres or Serenity Lake. His thoughts were suddenly interrupted. A man at the front of the store was yelling at Mr. Foley.

"I said now!" The man's voice was high-pitched and threatening.

NT crouched down to peek through the shelves, but saw only a sliver of faces. The goods stacked neatly on each shelf blocked much of his view. He made out Mr. Foley and the man who was shouting. NT stayed in his spot. Mr. Foley stepped away from the counter and just as quickly returned with an envelope. The man grabbed it and peered inside. With a sneer, he said, "You say some of this was used in here today?"

"Yeah. I recognized it and thought you should know," Mr. Foley responded.

"You're right, country boy, I should. You better not have told anyone else," the man threatened.

"No. But... Listen, I can't do this anymore. I'm done. The stress is killing me. I have a respectable business and the folks around here trust me. My family doesn't know and I plan to keep it that way. Please. I won't say a word to anyone." Mr. Foley was sweating.

"I guess you don't understand that you're never out. *Ever*. We've worked too hard for too long, and no matter how hard you try to get out, Foley, you never will. You'll always be part of this. *Always*."

"Not if I do something about it." If not for his usually jovial tone, anyone else would have thought Mr. Foley was full of bravado.

With the quickness of a snake, the man reached over the counter and snatched Foley by the front of his shirt. He yanked him close to his own face. "The only *thing* you're going to do about this is continue to keep your eye out for more of this," he said, then slapped the envelope across the store owner's face. "Got it?"

Foley nodded.

"Good." The man glared at Foley, turned, and left the store.

NT waited a few minutes before approaching the counter to pay for his kite. He pretended he had not heard the conversation between the two men.

"Is that it?" Foley asked. He was white as a ghost. His voice was shaky and sweat beaded on his forehead.

"Uh, yes, please," NT answered. "Oh, sorry. An orange soda, too."

"That'll be twelve-fifty for the kite."

"But I also got a soda."

"No charge for that, Nick. Always nice to see you." Foley forced a smile.

"Thanks. You too, Mr. Foley. See you soon."

NT was deep in thought about what he had observed in the hardware store and was halfway home before he realized he had forgotten to ask Mr. Foley if BB had been in earlier. *Duh. Guess I'll just have to ask BB.* NT steered his way around the shoppers crowding the sidewalk, focused on not hitting anyone with his kite. He did not hear when Daisy called out to him.

"Hey, NT!" she yelled from down the street. She pedaled furiously toward him, and tried again. "NT! Hey!" Still no response. *He's such a space cadet.* She waited till she was closer and called once more. "NT!"

He finally heard her. He pivoted around and saw her charging toward him at full speed.

"What are you, deaf?" she asked, panting. "I've been screaming your name."

"Relax." He frowned at her. "Let's go to Sweetwoods. I've got something to tell you."

The friends plopped down on their usual bench at the ice cream shop to catch their breath. A minute later, NT opened his mouth to tell Daisy what he had witnessed at Foley's Hardware but was interrupted by a low rumbling sound and the honk of a car. He turned and saw Blackie rolling down the street in their direction. BB was seated behind the oversized wooden steering wheel of the LaSalle, wearing his trademark Penn State baseball hat.

He waved and yelled to NT and Daisy, "Hey, how about some ice cream?"

NT checked his watch. Eleven o'clock. Not too early for ice cream. Daisy concurred.

"Ice cream for lunch? Awesome!" she responded.

The three sat outside and enjoyed their cold treats. NT decided the time was right to ask BB about the missing ten dollars. "Did you see a ten-dollar bill on the hall table, BB?"

"I did," BB nodded. "This morning."

"Do you still have it? I accidentally dropped it on the floor yesterday, and Mrs. Walker found it."

"Oh, I thought Mimi left it for me to buy the car wax and corn." BB reached into his wallet and pulled out two fives. "Here you go."

"It was a ten-dollar bill."

"I spent that." BB was oblivious to NT's concern about the money.

"Do you remember where?" NT asked nervously.

"At Foley's. To buy car wax." BB dug into his black raspberry and coffee cone.

NT's heart sank. Now for sure he would have to go back to Foley's Hardware to ask about the money. But it would have to wait until the next day.

16

The screaming of the sirens was so real and loud and close, it caused a painful rattling in NT's ear drums and woke him from a deep sleep. He opened his eyes, got his bearings, and realized the noise was coming from outside. He threw the window open and yelled to his grandparents who were standing in the front yard, "What's going on?"

BB responded over his shoulder, "Not sure, but the police are headed into town."

"I want to find out. Can we go?"

"After breakfast," Mimi said.

* * *

Traffic toward the town was slow along Tubman Avenue. They drove past Fatty's Bakery, Al's gas station, and the library. From a block away, all three saw the dreadful scene at once—four police cars pulled in at different angles in front of Foley's Hardware Store, their lights still flashing. NT's mouth suddenly felt as dry as a desert and his heart hammered in his chest.

"Oh, my," Mimi said. "What happened there?" She pulled the car over and parked.

"I don't know, but it sure doesn't look good," BB said.

They approached the store and saw yellow police tape across the door. One of the front windows had been shattered. Blood-speckled shards of glass littered the pavement.

A crowd had gathered and everyone was asking about the police activity. One person spoke up and asked an officer who was standing guard outside the front door, "What happened?"

"It appears someone broke in and stole several thousand dollars' worth of merchandise," the officer replied. "The safe in the back was ripped open as well. Whatever was in it is now gone."

Sheriff Taylor appeared from inside the store. He looked grim. He whispered something to the officer standing guard, who turned ashen white and nodded at the sheriff in response.

"Ladies and gentlemen, may I have your attention?" asked the ashen-faced officer.

The crowd hushed and Sheriff Taylor addressed them. "I'm sorry to inform you that Sam Foley appears to have been murdered during the course of the robbery."

NT went numb. The eggs and bacon he had eaten earlier threatened to come back up. *That can't be. I just saw Mr. Foley yesterday.*

* * *

Mr. Foley's funeral took place two days later. NT had only attended one funeral, when he was just four years old. His recollection of that event was distant. This funeral would be different, because everyone knew Mr. Foley as a long-time friend, neighbor, and businessman in the community.

The sadness inside St. Matthew's Church was palpable. Mrs. Foley and her three children sat frozen in the front pew. When NT looked at their drawn faces and glazed eyes, he felt he had been punched in the gut. His parents might be divorced and living apart, but at least they were alive. NT couldn't imagine what he would do if he lost his father.

Back at his grandparents' house, he changed clothes and threw himself down on the bed. Overcome with emotion, he wept from all the sadness and fear that had been crushing him like an elephant. He couldn't stop thinking about what he had seen and heard inside Foley's Hardware—the threatening conversation, Mr. Foley pleading, the envelope, the vicious voice of the unknown man. NT was unable to focus on any one thing because they all kept playing over and over in his head like a horror movie. He had to tell someone what he had seen and heard. He decided to tell his grandparents.

BB and Mimi were on the front porch—BB was reading the sports page and Mimi was working on her latest needlepoint project. The atmosphere was heavy with quiet sadness, and neither seemed fully focused on their task.

"I need to tell you guys something." Nerves churned in NT's stomach.

BB folded his newspaper and glanced at Mimi. "Sure, Nick. What is it?" he asked.

NT told them about his trip to the store, that he had been in a back aisle looking at kites when a strange man came in, and that the man threatened Mr. Foley, who had given him an envelope.

"You need to go down to the police station," Mimi said. "They need to know this."

"I agree. They do," BB said. "Nick, go grab my keys."

Neither BB nor NT spoke the entire ride to the station. NT was absorbed in thought and nervous about telling the police what he had witnessed. On the one hand, if his information would help solve the crime of who killed Mr. Foley, he would do it. On the other hand, what would happen if the man from the store found out he had told the police? Would NT be in danger? His stomach felt acidy and sick.

Brenda greeted BB and NT warmly from behind the front desk.

"Hello, Brenda," said BB. "My grandson and I are here to talk with Sheriff Taylor or Deputy Darman, if either are available."

"I believe the sheriff is out, but Deputy Darman is here. I'll let him know you'd like to speak to him."

A few minutes later, Darman emerged from his office. "How can I help y'all?" He looked at NT and said, "You're back again so soon?"

"Hello, Deputy Darman. This is my grandson, Nicholas," BB said. "You two already know each other?"

"Yeah," NT answered. "I met him last week when Daisy and I stopped by to see her dad."

"Brenda tells me you have something you want to talk about?"

"That's right. Nicholas has some information about Mr. Foley that may be relevant to your investigation into his murder."

"Oh, do you now?"

NT nodded. He hoped his stomach would hold out through the meeting.

"It's a real shame about Mr. Foley. He was a good man. C'mon into my office and we'll talk at my desk." Deputy Darman turned and walked toward his office. BB gave NT a gentle nudge to follow.

The deputy's desk was a mountain of paperwork and junk—folders, newspapers, food wrappers, even dirty dishes. He brushed the junk aside and miraculously found a pen and pad to take notes. "Okay, Nicholas. Start from the beginning."

NT took a big gulp then spoke nonstop for ten minutes. He recalled in detail everything about his trip to the hardware store, including a description of the man who had threatened Mr. Foley. He was exhausted by the time he finished.

Darman read his notes back to NT and asked, "Is what I've just read one hundred percent correct? It has to be before I pass it on to the sheriff." The deputy's businesslike tone intimidated NT.

NT agreed with the accuracy of the deputy's account. "Yes, sir, it is." He cast his eyes downward.

At that moment, they heard footsteps coming down the hallway.

"Sounds like Sheriff Taylor has returned," said Deputy Darman. "Sheriff? Can you stop by my office?" he yelled.

BB and NT turned to face the sheriff, who had stopped in the doorway.

"Mr. Tyson. NT. What brings you here?" Sheriff Taylor asked.

Before either could respond, Darman answered. "Well, young Nicholas here happened to be at Foley's the day before he was killed and witnessed an unpleasant situation. He relayed the whole story to me. I'll type these notes up and put them on your desk."

Sheriff Taylor turned his head sharply and looked at NT. "You were there? What time?"

"Um, midmorning, I think?" NT responded.

"Okay. Are you sure you told Deputy Darman everything you saw and heard while you were there?"

"Yes, sir. I felt bad for Mr. Foley because he seemed really upset."

"If you remember anything else—even the slightest detail—call us immediately." Sheriff Taylor turned to Darman and said, "Roy, those notes need to be typed up now, please."

"Yes, sir," Darman responded. He said goodbye to NT and BB.

Sheriff Taylor said, "Thanks, Roy. And, thank you, NT, for sharing. I saw you all at the funeral. It'll be some time before we recover from losing one of our best. But I'll figure it out—that I guarantee." He then excused himself and headed to his office.

17

A round of golf with BB, Daisy, and Hoot was a welcomed distraction for NT from the events of previous days. The warmth of the sunshine and calm of the golf course helped lift the dark clouds of the funeral and the incident at Foley's Hardware that had been hanging over him. He and Daisy walked up the first fairway together, chatting along the way. They decided to tell Hoot the latest—finding more money and another signed program, and NT's spotting of the guy who threatened Mr. Foley.

After nine holes, BB went to get a hot dog and Daisy and NT quickly poured out everything to Hoot.

Hoot let out a low whistle when he heard their updates. "Did you tell anyone else about this?"

"Yeah, BB and Mimi," NT said. "And when I told them about the scary guy from the hardware store, they said we had to tell the police. So, BB and I went down to the police station and I told Deputy Darman everything I saw."

"That's good. That's good," Hoot affirmed.

"But—"

"But what, son?"

"What if that was the guy who did it? Oh, my God. I might have seen the murderer!" NT paled at the thought.

Hoot exhaled loudly. "Stay calm, NT. We'll find time to talk later. For now, I want you both concentrating on winning the junior club championship."

Daisy added, "He's right, NT. For right now, let's just focus on our golf game."

Hoot looked at NT and winked. "Remember what I told you. Before you tee off, take that driver back nice and slow and keep it on a straight line. Keep your left arm completely straight on your takeaway and mind your grip, too. Right hand turned over a bit more. And, young lady," Hoot said to Daisy, "I want you to choke down some on your irons so you get more control. And keep that head still when putting. Y'all hear me?"

"Yes, sir," NT and Daisy answered. Hoot possessed a sharp eye for fixing the small things in a person's golf game. His skill was a definite advantage for them.

"Okay, let's get a couple of pars on the back nine. Everybody ready?" BB said, and popped the last bite of hot dog into his mouth.

"We are!" they answered.

NT stepped up to the tee and striped one down the fairway. BB complimented him. "That ball had a great shape to it, Nick."

The foursome continued their game. They were fully enjoying themselves and about to finish on the eighteenth hole when loud, vicious shouting drifted from the seventeenth fairway. Curse words sullied the peace and beauty of the day.

BB looked across to the seventeenth fairway. "What's going on over there?" Two men were embroiled in a heated argument. "Is that Mayor Hall? Who's that with him, swearing like a sailor?"

"I do believe it's the mayor, but he isn't the one screaming," Hoot responded. "It's his guest. Mayor's usually pretty level-headed."

BB scowled. "That man should know the golf course is no place for that kind of language. I'll say something when we go in."

NT listened to the argument taking place between the two men. One voice in particular caught his attention. "That guy's voice sounds familiar," he whispered to Daisy. "It's like that guy's voice from Foley's."

"Does it look like him?" she asked.

"Maybe. I can't really tell. He's far away and has a hat on. And I didn't really get a clear view of his face in the store."

"Since they'll be coming in right after us, maybe we'll see them," she said.

"Maybe. It depends how long BB wants to stay after we play. He usually gets a soda," NT responded.

"Okay, let's hope he does today."

NT and Daisy finished out the hole and shook hands with each other, BB, and Hoot. Hoot spoke to them as they walked off the green. "Nice show of sportsmanship. And good work out there today. But I saw some things that still need work. Meet me on the range tomorrow at five and we'll go over them. Got it?"

They nodded to each other and walked off the eighteenth green in the direction of the pro shop. BB set his golf bag down and worked on putting his glove, golf tees, and balls into their proper pockets in the bag. NT and Daisy dropped their bags next to BB's.

"I'll see you two tomorrow," Hoot said to NT and Daisy. Then, "Mr. Willy, always a pleasure." He and BB shook hands.

"Anyone for an iced tea or lemonade?" BB asked.

"Awesome. I'm pretty thirsty!" NT responded.

"Sure. Iced tea will hit the spot," Daisy said.

At the clubhouse restaurant, the three sipped their drinks and talked about their round. On the way out, BB stopped in the pro shop to express his concerns about the rude behavior of Mayor Hall's guest.

18

Mimi was plucking ripe tomatoes in the garden when BB and NT pulled into the driveway. BB glided Blackie into the garage with ease.

"Hi, boys," Mimi said when they emerged. "How was your golf game?"

"Great. BB played really well."

"And how did you play?" she asked.

"So-so. Hoot was with us and he gave me some pointers. He wants to coach me and Daisy some more—tomorrow at five o'clock. Is that okay?" NT asked.

"Sure. I don't see why not. That's awfully nice of him," she responded.

"I know. He's an awesome coach."

Mimi, BB, and NT enjoyed a dinner of grilled chicken sandwiches and slices of sweet tomato on the side. NT sat up for a bit with his grandparents watching television, but before long, his eyelids sagged, so he bid them good night and went upstairs to bed.

* * *

NT spent the next morning helping BB and Mimi with chores around the house. After lunch, he did some more reading for school, but by two o'clock he was ready to get outside. He headed out on his bike to Daisy's house, even though they had three hours till their appointment with Hoot. He was ready to get back to his search for Clay's lost notebook. So lost in thought was he about the notebook, he didn't hear the sound of a nearby car starting its engine. Nor did he notice when the car followed him almost the entire way to Daisy's. The driver of the car had an inkling where NT was headed, so he stopped following when NT turned onto Daisy's road. He pulled off to the side and waited.

Daisy and NT plopped into the lounge chairs on Daisy's back patio and talked about the junior club championship and their chances of winning, about Hoot's coaching suggestions, and about all things related to Clay.

Daisy wondered aloud, "Okay, so far, we've found a bunch of ten-dollar bills, scorecards with dates and numbers, and old golf tournament programs signed by some guy named Ben. Do you think any of this stuff has to do with Clay's murder?"

NT shrugged. "Who knows? It's kinda like his blue notebook. I mean, that could have something to do with his murder, right?"

"I guess," Daisy said. "But we may never know unless we find it. Think. Think. Who would know where it is?"

"I already asked Mimi, BB, and Hoot, and they don't know."

"Who else is there?"

"Other people at the club? Other caddies? What about Lenny?"

"That would be a stretch," said Daisy.

NT slapped his forehead and blurted out, "Wait! Today's Wednesday, right?"

"Yeah. Why?"

"Mrs. Walker doesn't come over on Wednesdays or Sundays."

"So? What's she got to do with this?" NT rolled his eyes. "What?" Daisy wanted to choke him.

"Since we have hours 'til we see Hoot, let's go over to her house. She's the one who told us about the sea glass and the book in the first place. We never asked her if she knows where they are."

"That's right. We didn't. Do you know where she lives?" Daisy asked.

"Yup. Not far, and there are no hills of death like on the way to the Hardy sisters," he responded.

"Thank God."

The driver of the car watched as Daisy and NT pulled out of Daisy's road. He started the car and followed them from a distance. Fifteen minutes later, the two friends were standing in front of Josephine Walker's house. "Reminds me of that creepy candy house in *Hansel and Gretel*," Daisy observed.

"Ooh, you're right. Look at it."

The house was the color of gingerbread and sat close to the curvy lane that ran past. Crepe myrtle trees lush with pink and white blooms stood on either side of the house. Pale blue window trim framed the six front windows, and the front door had been painted a purple lilac color. The white scalloped edging that hung along the roof line reminded NT of icing.

Crooked stone steps led them onto the dust-covered front porch. Firewood was stacked neatly in one corner, and a wooden rocking chair with two missing back rungs rested next to the front door, its blue seat cushion covered in cat hair. The porch groaned with each step Daisy and NT took toward the door. They knocked and waited thirty seconds with no answer. Daisy peered through a window, but saw nothing in the darkness. Just then, Mrs. Walker's cat, Mr.

Bond, jumped onto the inside window frame, nearly causing Daisy to jump out of her shoes. "Oh-my-God-oh-my-God!" she shrieked.

A voice from around the corner of the house yelled, "Who's there? Get off that porch!"

NT and Daisy recognized Mrs. Walker's voice and scurried to the side of the house where she was watering a patch of sky-high sunflowers.

"Stay off that porch. It's so old and rotten, it'll swallow you whole! What are y'all doin' here anyway? Social call? Spyin' on me?" She gave them a wink.

"We came over because we wanted to ask you some questions," NT said.

"Oh, yeah? Like what?" Mrs. Walker eyed NT and Daisy with suspicion.

"Nothing bad. Just that... well... remember the other day you told us about Clay's notebook?"

"I do."

"We were wondering if maybe you knew where it was."

Mrs. Walker scratched her chin with pink fingernails. "I tell ya what. I was just fixin' to get some chicken salad and sardines from Wink's Deli. This ole hip of mine has been giving me fits. If y'all go for me, I'll answer whatever questions I can."

NT looked at Daisy who nodded vigorously and said, "Sure."

Mrs. Walker dug into the deep pocket of her voluminous sundress and pulled out a crinkled wad of cash. She peeled off a few bills and handed them to Daisy. "See ya in a bit."

Daisy and NT rode off on their bikes and the mysterious driver followed them at a safe distance. He stopped and hung back when he saw Sheriff Taylor approaching in his car from the other direction. He watched the interchange between them.

From his open car window, Sheriff Taylor asked NT and Daisy where they were headed.

"Wink's. To get lunch for Mrs. Walker."

The sheriff's next question made them stop short. "What were you doing in the archive room the other day?"

A rush of blood roared in their ears. NT and Daisy were speechless.

"Before you try to make up some silly reason, I also know you were seen holding a folder on your way out. Do you care to elaborate?"

The friends froze in place, their eyes downcast.

"Daisy? NT?"

"Uh, yeah," Daisy answered. "But we're gonna return it, Dad. I promise!"

"Listen to me, both of you. You have no business being in the archive room. What on earth were you thinking when you took an official police report? Or maybe you weren't thinking at all." His glare would melt rocks.

"We wanted to know more about NT's Uncle Clay," Daisy said.

"Well, there are better ways to do that than sneaking into the archive room and removing police property. You will return it to me tonight when I get home, understand?"

"Yes."

"And you will *never* step foot in the archive room again."

"Yes, sir," Daisy said in a soft voice.

"Yes, Mr. Taylor," said NT.

"Now, go get Mrs. Walker's order." His tone was still gruff. Before driving off, he gave one final warning. "And you best behave yourselves from now on."

Without a word, NT and Daisy climbed back on their bikes and pedaled their way to Wink's.

"Who do you think saw us?" NT asked.

"No clue," Daisy said. "I'll give the folder back to my father later."

The brass bell that hung on the door tinkled when NT and Daisy entered Wink's. Inside, they were greeted by the smells of vinegary pickles, pungent oregano, and fresh-sliced onions. They wandered around and found the chicken salad and sardines Mrs. Walker wanted.

At the register, Wink's owner Pete asked, "I suppose this is going to Josie Walker?"

"That's right," Daisy replied, and paid for the two items.

NT stood waiting by the door. Across the street, he saw Deputy Darman, who had gotten out of his patrol car in front of Fatty's Bakery. Darman popped the trunk open and went inside the bakery.

"What's going on?" Daisy asked.

NT jerked his head to where Darman's car was parked, and said, "Look."

Darman exited the bakery and looked all around. He pulled what appeared to be a large, squarish bag from the trunk of his car and went back in the bakery. He came out a minute later, munching on a doughnut.

"What the—?"

"Yeah, that's weird," Daisy said. "Let's drop this stuff off to Mrs. Walker, see if she knows where the notebook is, then come back. Maybe he'll still be here."

"Okay, but let's hurry," NT said.

In their concern about getting back to Mrs. Walker's house, they were once again oblivious to the car that tailed them. They turned into her driveway and the car kept going, but stopped and parked farther down the lane. The driver was patient and would wait for as long as it took.

Mrs. Walker was no help in telling them the whereabouts of Clay's notebook. "I haven't seen it in years. Why don't you ask your grandparents?"

"I already did, but they don't know where it is either."

"I see," Mrs. Walker said. "I'll keep racking my brain, but I'm not sure I'll be much help." She glanced at her watch and noted, "Well, kiddies, time for lunch. Mr. Bond becomes disgruntled if his sardines aren't put out on time. Silly old cat."

They walked toward the front of the house. Mrs. Walker opened the door, thanked them, and said she'd see them soon.

"You're welcome. See you again at Mimi and BB's," NT replied.

"Bye, Mrs. Walker," Daisy said.

Mrs. Walker nodded and entered her house.

Just as Daisy hopped on her bike, her phone buzzed. "Oh, wow. My mom just texted me. She says I have to get home to help with dinner."

"I have no clue what time it is, but I guess I better get home too," NT said.

"Tomorrow we can go back into town and see if anything else *suspicious* is going on," Daisy suggested.

"I like the way you think," NT answered.

They rode together for most of the way home until Daisy turned onto her road. "Text me when you get up," she yelled over her shoulder.

"Okay. See you tomorrow," NT yelled back, and he picked up speed on his own bike as he headed toward Shady Acres.

19

NT's brain kicked into high gear in the middle of the night. He normally slept like a baby, but the frustration at his and Daisy's lack of progress at better understanding the mystery of Clay made him toss and turn till he finally woke up. The bright orange numbers on the clock glowed in the darkness. *3:37. That's all? Geez, I wish I could call Daisy right now and talk to her.* NT rolled over and stared out the window into the night. His eyes focused on the brightest stars in the sky. *Some people count sheep. I'll count stars.* Within minutes, his mind calmed and he drifted back to sleep.

The next morning, NT was still unable to shake the frustration he had been keeping bottled up—until then. "First, no one told me I had a great uncle who was murdered. Second, no one knows who killed him. Third, no one knows where his stuff is! How can things just disappear? God!" he yelled.

Daisy was taken aback. "Wow. You're really mad. Just because the people we've talked to don't know where the notebook is doesn't mean it's totally gone," she reasoned.

"Yeah, but—" he began. Just then, something across the street at Al's gas station diverted NT's attention. Deputy Darman and Al were on the sidewalk having a conversation. Darman opened the trunk of his car and hoisted out a golf bag, which he handed to Al. The men nodded at each other and Al disappeared inside his garage, golf bag in hand. Darman got in his car a moment later and drove away.

"What's he doing with a golf bag?" Daisy asked. "Didn't he tell us he hates golf?"

"I don't know, and you're right. He did," NT responded.

"Let's go find out," she said, and walked her bike across the street to Al's.

"Wait! You can't be so obvious!"

"I'm not gonna be. Trust me," she responded, but NT wasn't so sure.

The cavernous garage stank of grease and oil. Ten cars were raised on lifts waiting to be repaired. Fan belts, tires, and discarded car parts littered the floor. The golf bag was standing in the corner near the office.

Daisy called out to Al, who popped up from under the hood of a car, almost knocking his trucker's hat off his head.

"Hi, Daisy. What's up?"

"My bike tire is getting flat and I was wondering if you could fill it."

"Sure. Hang on." Al wiped his grease-covered hands on an orange rag then disappeared into the back.

Daisy jerked her chin to where the golf bag was standing. "Quick! Check the golf bag," she whispered.

"What? Why?"

"Just do it!"

NT did as he was told. He hoisted the bag up with a groan. The weight of the bag got his attention. "Whoa. This is heavy. I wonder what's in—"

"Here comes Al!" Daisy hissed. NT set the bag back down and pretended to be looking at the elevated cars.

Al reappeared with a pump and took care of Daisy's bike tire.

With all the innocence she could muster, Daisy said, "I didn't know you played golf, Al."

"Huh? What makes you say that?"

She pointed to the bag in the corner.

"Oh, those. I don't. They're for my nephew Johnny. He's comin' to visit and I borrowed them from one of Deputy Darman's buddies. Johnny's a pretty good player." He gave the bike tire one final squeeze. "Fine now."

"Thanks," she said.

"Say hi to your pop for me," Al said, and tipped his hat.

"I will. See ya!"

From Al's, NT and Daisy headed to the club. They talked about everything they wanted to tell Hoot, including what they had just witnessed in town between Al and Deputy Darman. Daisy said, "I guess it's possible Al has a nephew who needs clubs to use while he's here."

"Yeah, but that doesn't explain why the bag was so heavy," NT said.

A shiny stretch limo was parked at the main entrance to the club. "That car's huge," Daisy said. They were intrigued and stopped to see if anyone was in it.

The driver-side door opened and out stepped a barrel-chested driver, who opened the back doors of the limo. Three men slid out. Two were so tall they dwarfed the third man by at least six inches. They were dressed in dark suits and looked all business. A fourth person exited the vehicle—Mayor Robert Hall. The driver popped the trunk, hauled out four golf bags, and placed them on the rack. The mayor gave Daisy and NT a quick wave.

"Guess they're going to play some golf," Daisy said.

"I guess so. Let's go find Hoot."

Lenny came out of the clubhouse. "What are you two doing here so late in the day?"

NT spoke up quickly, "We're here to practice and maybe eat dinner later." He ignored the part about him and Daisy meeting with Hoot to have a serious talk.

"Have fun. Gotta run, kids. Have to get those bags that were just dropped off. The mayor and his guests are pretty important, so I can't let their bags sit there too long."

Daisy wrinkled her nose and said, "But you're the bartender. Where are the caddies?"

Lenny snarled back, "It *should* be one of the caddie's jobs. I've certainly got enough of my own work to do." He headed off to the parking lot to take care of the VIPs.

NT and Daisy went into the pro shop. Head pro Gates was at the desk checking the next day's tee sheet. They asked if the bigwigs with the mayor were pros.

Without looking up from his work, Gates said, "No. They're just some political pals of the mayor's. Why do you care?" His tone was gruff and abrasive as usual.

"Oh. They came in a huge limo, so we thought they were. It'd be cool to have pros here," NT said.

"Nope," replied Gates. He set the tee sheet on the counter and rubbed his eyes. "Anything else you want to know?"

"Uh, no. Thanks. We're gonna go practice," NT said.

"Well, you'd better get to it," Gates said in his clipped manner.

NT and Daisy couldn't leave the pro shop fast enough. "God, what's his problem?" Daisy said.

"Who knows. He's always mean. Maybe he hates kids." NT responded.

"Ya think?" Daisy retorted.

Hoot was ready and waiting for them as promised. He pointed to the range and said, "Let's go." He had set up a series of stations for Daisy and NT to run through to practice different golf shots. Daisy saw what Hoot had prepared and spoke to NT out of the side of her mouth. "I guess he was serious about practicing."

"Okay, you two. Get out your wedges and seven irons. It's time to work." NT and Daisy pulled out their clubs as Hoot continued. "Here's the plan. First, you'll chip twenty balls as close as you can to those baskets—or in 'em." He pointed to two baskets turned upright about fifty yards out in front of the stations. "After that, another twenty balls each onto that green." He pointed to the target green. "Then you'll finish with some putting drills. Got it? When we're done, we can head to the shack to talk. That is, if I am satisfied with your work here."

NT and Daisy completed their drills under Hoot's watchful eye. The hour-long practice session flew by. Hoot was so pleased with their efforts, he decided to reward their diligence. "Whichever of you lands a shot from the sand bunker closest to the cup gets a sundae from Sweetwoods."

Both the competition and the prize set Daisy into high gear. "You *know* I'm gonna kick your butt in this game, right?" she said to NT.

"Yeah, right. Dream on," NT responded.

At the end of the game, Hoot tallied up the points. Daisy was right, she beat NT handily.

"Maybe I'll share when we go. *Maybe*," she teased.

"I'll believe that when I see it," NT answered, then turned to Hoot, "How'd we do?"

"Y'all did good. Let's go."

Inside the caddie shack, they joined James and Lawrence, who had finished caddying for the day.

"Did Hoot work you pretty good today?" Lawrence asked.

"He sure did," Daisy said. She jerked her head toward NT and added, "And I got a free sundae by demolishing him in a game."

"Good girl," Lawrence said. "My pa really knows how to work his students."

"Your pa?" NT and Daisy looked back and forth between Hoot and Lawrence.

"That's right," said Hoot. "Larry, here, is my son. I brought him up into the good life of workin' all day at his favorite game."

Daisy and NT smiled at the thought.

Lawrence continued, "Hoot said y'all are on the hunt for a book that used to belong to your uncle Clay. Did he mention that James here knew him pretty well too?"

NT looked at James and asked, "Really? Did you spend a lot of time with him?"

James began, "Yep. Sure did, over the years. He always made time to talk with the staff members who worked here. He treated everyone like family. He was a real workhorse, too. I don't know if you know this, but he was on the House Committee here at the club—you know, to keep Cascades running and successful. And he poured the same energy and time into his golf game. Before a match or a tournament, he'd stay on the range 'til the sun sank from the sky. I'd often be here late myself—past nine—fixin' members' clubs or whatever, and we always shot the breeze about things."

"Like what?" NT asked.

"Well, one night after he finished on the range, we were talkin' about the club and he asked me if I ever heard any noises comin' from the basement of the locker room late at night. He knew I was there most evenings, so I didn't think anything weird about what he asked. I told him that I did indeed hear noises comin' from down there. I said I didn't think much of it 'cause this place is old and I assumed it was the old boiler actin' up or water runnin' through old pipes. He asked me to describe the sounds. I said they were loud bangs and thunks. The thunks sometimes repeated, one after the other. I remember a hissing noise too. After I told Clay all this, he nodded and wrote all that down in a small notebook—"

NT interrupted James. "A notebook?" He looked at Daisy.

"Yep, a small blue one. Why?"

"Because everyone we've talked to about Clay said he had a blue notebook he took everywhere with him, and we want to find it. BB—my grandfather—would really like to have it as a memento from his brother. Do you know where it is?"

James felt the hope in NT's question. He hated to disappoint him. "Sorry, son. I don't." NT sighed deeply in response. "Anyway, I told him it was real smart to take notes and he said it was his job to report things like that to the other committee members. I asked him if he knew that Lenny the bartender was also a good handyman and maybe he could fix the noises. But then—" James stopped mid-sentence.

"What? What were you going to say?" NT asked.

"Only that I don't think he ever got the chance to ask Lenny, 'cause, well, you know why. I'm sorry, son," James's dark eyes glistened. He added, "I don't think he'll mind if I tell you, but Lawrence here was the young boy who found Clay's body in the lake."

NT and Daisy's eyes grew wide. They looked at Lawrence, who only nodded and let heavy silence fill the air. NT was speechless. In his head, he was putting two and two together. In a soft voice he asked Hoot, "Have you heard weird noises too?"

"Actually, NT, I have—and Clay also told me that he heard 'em."

"Really? What did he say?" NT asked.

"He told me he thought they were coming from the basement of the locker room," Hoot said.

"Didn't you ever go down and see what it was?" NT questioned.

"Nah, not me. I mentioned it to Lenny, too, since he can fix anything, like James said. And I figured he might know, since he's been here 'bout as long as I have. He said it was probably just old pipes and the boiler. An old club like this has lots of clunky old parts. Kinda like my old body!" Hoot joked.

"Did Lenny fix whatever it was?" Daisy asked.

"He did, 'cause I don't hear the noises as frequently as in years past. They're still there, but at least Lenny fixed it as best he could," Hoot responded.

"Well, that's all fine and good, but we still don't know where the notebook is," NT said. He was despondent.

"That's true," Hoot said with a nod. "But I believe it'll turn up. As my old granddaddy used to say, 'Sometimes the obvious is right under your nose, but you just can't see it 'cause you're lookin' too hard.'"

NT considered Hoot's words. "Does that mean that we shouldn't keep looking for it?"

"You can, but maybe take a break from it. Think about winning the junior championship. After all, you and Daisy did some good work today on the range. Now, it's time for you to head home before it gets late." Hoot stood and the others followed his lead. He gave his final advice to NT and Daisy. "Remember, focus on your golf game. Things have a way of working out."

Everyone made their way outside. Daisy and NT thanked Hoot and said their goodbyes, then decided to head to Daisy's house. She said her father would be home and they could ask him if he knew anything about the notebook.

NT had taken Hoot's suggestion to heart. "Yeah, but didn't Hoot just say to give it a rest?"

"NT, listen. It's not gonna hurt to ask him, is it?"

"I guess not," NT said, and off they went to Daisy's house.

* * *

As Daisy expected, her father was relaxing on the patio. "Hey, Dad!"

Sheriff Taylor set the book he was reading on his lap. "Howdy. What are you two up to?"

NT filled Daisy's father in on the story of Clay's missing blue notebook and he raised his eyebrows in surprise. "Now, why would you want to know about your uncle Clay's notebook? You sound like a couple of detectives."

"Well, for school next year, I have to write a report about a family member, and since I don't know a lot about my great uncle, I picked him. BB knew from Clay that he wrote stuff in the notebook, and I thought what he wrote could tell me more about him. Maybe it's in the evidence room?"

Sheriff Taylor chuckled at NT's suggestion. "Nice try, NT, but I don't think so."

"Well, my grandparents and other people say he was always writing in that book. BB even said that when he asked Clay about it, Clay was really secretive and said something about planning for the future."

"Yeah, Dad. We saw the notebook in one of the old pictures of Clay that's hanging in the Grille Room. It's in his pocket. You should look," Daisy said.

"Interesting. I'll tell ya what. When I head in tomorrow, I'll check out the evidence room. But off the top of my head, I don't recall seeing any evidence like that. The police did a thorough job collecting any and all evidence at the time. There wasn't a whole lot though. Whoever killed your uncle Clay cleaned up pretty well." And with that, Sheriff Taylor picked up his book, signaling the end of that conversation.

20

Cascades Golf Club was closed every Monday for maintenance. NT and Daisy welcomed the break from golf, as they had made plans to go on a rafting expedition on Martin's Creek. They were going to use an old army raft BB kept in his garage. BB, who insisted on still doing things the old-fashioned way, had used an old hand pump to inflate the raft. NT thought it took forever to get the job done.

Daisy showed up late morning and immediately suggested to NT that they head to Al's convenience store to buy lunch. "We can get spicy chips, beef jerky, and those cream-filled cakes you like, plus soda to wash it all down." Daisy's plan was smashed when Mimi hefted a picnic basket onto the kitchen counter.

NT lifted the basket and nearly popped out his shoulder. "Wow! This weighs a ton, Mimi." He looked inside and found chicken salad sandwiches, pickles, potato salad, chips, and lemonade, all nestled around three separate ice packs.

"Well, if I left the lunch menu up to you two," Mimi said, "Al's would be completely cleaned out of all that junk food you love so much!" She winked at them and added, "Have fun!"

Lucky for NT and Daisy, Martin's Creek was a short walk down the field from BB and Mimi's house. They placed their lunch inside the raft then carried the raft to the water. The creek was calm, perfect for leisurely rafting and lunching. They drifted down the creek in the direction of the club and saw holes sixteen, seventeen, and eighteen along the way.

"The seventeenth hole is so hard. I can hardly get on the green in three," Daisy commented.

"Eighteen's hard too. I've hit a ton into the stream at the bottom of the hill there," NT responded. "When we play tomorrow, I'm gonna smack the ball across."

"Yeah, sure." Daisy turned her face toward the sun. "Listen," she said.

"To what?"

"Exactly. To nothing. Just birds chirping their songs and water lapping against the sides of the raft."

At that moment, the quiet was assaulted by a deafening squeal.

"What the—" said NT.

Crashing through the bushes along the creek's edge came Succotash, relishing in another escape from his pen.

"It's Succotash!" said Daisy.

The friends watched first with amusement then horror as the little pig dashed down the bank and sprang into the water. His pink head was barely above the surface and he bobbed like a buoy. He snorted and squealed even louder than the first time.

"Oh, my God! Can pigs swim?" Daisy screamed. "We have to save him!"

They paddled upstream to the shrieking pig. Luckily, the soft current pushed Succotash in their direction. NT leaned over and plucked the pig from the water.

"You saved his life, NT!"

"*Succotash*! Where *are* you? Come to Momma!" Cordie Hardy's panicked voice sliced through the woods.

"Oh, hush, Cordie. He's probably munchin' on those raspberry bushes he loves so much!" yelled Minnie.

The sisters, in their signature straw hats, ducked and dodged branches as they weaved their way through the trees toward the creek. NT and Daisy waited till they reached the bank. Minnie saw the raft first, then spotted NT holding Succotash. She smiled. "Look, sister!"

"Don't worry, Miss Hardy," NT called to her. "We have him. I guess he got hot and wanted to take a swim!"

Cordie waved frantically. "Oh! Poor little baby! Come to Momma!"

"That little rascal!" said Minnie. "We'd better check the lock on his pen. If he escapes again, he'll end up as a nice slab of bacon at John's butcher shop."

NT slid out of the raft with Succotash in his arms, then waded to the bank where he handed the soaked pink swimmer to its owners. "Yeah, you definitely want to check the pen, or get a new one."

Cordie took Succotash from NT and kissed the pig on the head. Succotash snorted in response.

"Bless you, children," she said. And *you*, you naughty pig, *you* stay in your pen. Understand?"

The sisters thanked NT and Daisy again and headed back home. Tranquility returned to the creek and the friends ate their lunch in comfortable silence. The chicken salad was fresh and the lemonade cold and sweet. They drifted down the creek, lost once more in the soothing sounds of nature.

After ten minutes of silence, NT spoke. "If that blue notebook of Clay's was so important, why doesn't anyone know where it is?"

Daisy rolled her eyes. "And here I thought you were just enjoying the sights and sounds of mother nature."

"For real, Daisy. If you had something valuable at home, where would you hide it?"

"We know Clay was a neat freak, right? He had it with him all the time, so it couldn't have been thrown out."

"Right. That's what I'm thinking."

"Well, I would hide something valuable behind a clock or in a secret drawer somewhere. That's what happens in *Nancy Drew*."

This time it was NT's turn to roll his eyes. "Seriously. Her again?"

"Yes. She's very insightful."

"Okay, okay, Miss Big-Word Daisy. I just don't believe that notebook is gone. Someone *has* to know where it is." NT sighed heavily. "And, you know, think about it."

"About what?"

"Everything. There's lots of unanswered questions."

"Like what?

"Like, how did Clay end up in the lake? What's with the ten-dollar bills and the guy named Ben? How did the taillight on Clay's car get broken? And, if that notebook was so important to him, he wouldn't let it just be thrown out, right?"

"Probably not," Daisy replied.

They ended their conversation with more questions than answers and decided it was time to paddle back upstream. After what seemed like an eternity paddling, they finally reached their starting point. They left the raft out to dry and went to find BB. He was on the porch with Mimi, engrossed in a game of Scrabble.

"Hi, kids," said BB. "Everything go okay?"

"Yeah," replied NT. "Other than saving an escaped pig from drowning."

"Not again," Mimi said. "Those sisters need to get a better pen for Succotash."

"That's what we said. If it's okay with you, we're gonna head into town."

"That's fine. Just don't be late."

NT and Daisy decided to visit the police station to see if Daisy's father had located the notebook in the old file. They greeted Brenda on their way in. "Hi, Miss Brenda. Is my dad here?"

"Hello, Daisy, NT. I just saw him. Go on back."

Sheriff Taylor was sitting at his desk. Unlike Deputy Darman's, his was immaculate and nothing was out of place.

"Hi, guys. I think I know why y'all are here."

"Did you find the book, Dad?"

"Bad news. I did not."

"Oh," said NT.

"Your grandparents don't know where it is?"

NT's voice reflected his heavy disappointment. "I already asked them. They don't. But, I was wondering…"

"About what?"

"Can you answer some other questions about Clay?"

"I'll certainly try. Go ahead."

"Well, for starters, do you know how he ended up in the lake? What was used to hit him?"

Sheriff Taylor rubbed his hands together, sighed, and responded, "You sure you aren't trying to take my job?" He laughed softly.

"No, sir. More than anything, I just want to know what happened to him. I'd really like to know what you have to say."

"Okay. You ready? It's not pleasant."

NT gulped. "Yes, sir."

"Our police report stated that whoever hit Clay in the head also tied him up and threw him in the lake. As I explained earlier, evidence was collected, but there wasn't much. At the time of his murder, his golf bag was in his car and his wallet was in the glove compartment, along with some scorecards. Believe me, this case has gnawed at my gut for years. Someday I will figure out who killed him. As for the weapon used, it was something heavy, like a bat or a wrench or a hammer."

"What did you do with his stuff?"

"I gave the wallet and golf bag to your grandpop."

At those words, NT's hopes were deflated. He sighed and shrugged his shoulders. "One more question."

"Shoot."

"Why would anyone want to murder him?"

Sheriff Taylor leaned forward on his desk, looked NT directly in the eye, and said, "That, young man, is the million-dollar question."

21

"That, young man, is the million-dollar question." Sheriff Taylor's words echoed in NT's head. Daisy's father was right—why Clay was killed *was* the million-dollar question. Everything NT had heard about Clay was positive. If he was such a great guy, it made no sense that he was killed. Obviously, though, someone did not think Clay was so great. NT was convinced the answers to the mystery surrounding his great uncle lay in his blue notebook. After all, nobody knew what Clay wrote in the book, and he was always evasive when telling people about what it contained. *Where is it?* NT wondered.

NT arrived at Shady Acres and steered his bike into the garage, where he rested it against a side wall. The smell of fresh-baked cookies had wafted outside, so NT headed straight to the kitchen for a snack. He made small talk with Mimi about his day, after which she mentioned the end-of-year summer party at the club would be in a few weeks. NT looked at the calendar on the wall and was shocked to see the end of July was fast approaching. The junior club champs were just ten days out, and then he'd have only two more weeks at his grandparent's before returning home. NT munched quietly on a third cookie and his mind wandered. *Not that it's an actual home. I'll be going back to the world of two houses, two toothbrushes, two beds. I hate having two of everything.* He pushed those thoughts aside and thought about Clay. He was dismayed that time was running out and he and Daisy weren't any closer to finding Clay's blue notebook. It had to be some place. But where?

* * *

Rather than staying home for dinner, BB, Mimi, and NT dined at Wellie's. NT loved Wellie's and thought their cooking was delicious. The massive amounts of food they served and the plates the servers balanced on their trays would impress even the biggest, hungriest lineman on a football team. NT gorged on nachos and sticky ribs with fries. Two sodas helped wash it all down. Mimi and BB opted for healthier choices—salads and sandwiches.

"How have the practice sessions with Hoot been going?" Mimi asked.

"They're really fun. Hoot knows his stuff. He makes practicing seem like a game."

"You know, your grandfather and Uncle Clay won several junior titles when they were your age."

"I know. Me and Daisy saw pictures at the club."

"Daisy and I," Mimi reminded.

"Is your game in top shape for the tournament, NT?" BB asked.

"For the most part. There're still some things I need to work on. Is it okay if I go over to the club tomorrow?" NT asked.

"Sure," said Mimi. "Oh, Willy, I forgot to mention. Cordie Hardy called and wanted to know if we were free for dinner tomorrow night. I told her yes and that we'd meet them on the patio at seven."

"Oh, boy, the Hardy sisters," BB said. "They're somethin' else—fun to be around, but that Minnie sure can talk."

"Be nice. You've known them a long time," Mimi said.

"Yeah. They showed Daisy and me a picture of you from like, forever ago," NT teased.

"Did they now?" BB asked.

"Yeah. It was you, Clay, a couple of girls, and the mayor. I think it was taken at Serenity Lake?" NT said.

"Hmm, that must be really old—probably when we were seniors in high school or just graduated," BB replied.

"Oh, and you were all smoking!" NT remembered.

"That was a dumb habit. I stopped cold turkey soon after that," BB said.

"Did you ever smoke, Mimi?"

"I admit, I did try it—only once. It made me gag."

"I don't recommend you try it, young man," BB said.

"No way. It's gross."

They finished dinner and shared two desserts among the three of them—carrot cake and chocolate mousse. Back at home, NT was exhausted and stuffed, and when his head hit the pillow, he slept a rock.

* * *

The next morning NT woke at eight thirty and read a few more chapters in *The Old Man and the Sea*. The more he read, the more he liked the story, including Hemingway's style of writing. It was simple, clear, and had just the right amount of detail. NT especially liked that Hemingway left enough room for readers to paint their own images of his characters. After three chapters, however, NT's mind drifted to golf and he decided it was time to get up, have breakfast, and head to the club for practice.

Mr. Gates was in the pro shop, organizing boxes of golf balls. NT asked him to tell Daisy he'd be at the practice range in case she showed up.

"What am I, your personal message service?" Gates snarled.

"Sorry," NT responded. "I didn't mean—"

"Yeah, yeah, if she shows up," Gates said. "Just keep it down. The mayor is down there with a couple of guests and he gets priority at the range," Gates warned. "Oh, and another thing. What are you doing hanging out in the caddie shack?"

The blood drained from NT's face and his throat felt like sand. This was the last thing he expected to hear. "Uh..." he stuttered. *Oh no, oh no.* He was flustered but had to come up with a good excuse—quickly. "I, uh, wanted to ask Hoot about my great uncle. And, uh, we're also reading the same book. I just wanted to talk to him about that stuff."

Gates challenged NT. "Oh, really? Why would Hoot know about your uncle?"

"He caddied for him and they were friends," NT felt sweat pop on his brow.

Gates eyed him. "If I were you, I'd find somewhere else to talk to Hoot. Got it? If I see you in there one more time, you won't like the consequences."

"Okay." NT left in a hurry before Gates could bark at him again.

On the range, he began his practice with his favorite club—his nine iron. He hit a few half-shots to get his body warm and ready to swing. The course was firm, so NT knew he'd be able to bump and run short shots up to the pin if his ball didn't land on the green on his approach shot. A good nine-iron shot could make or break his score on a hole. Click. Click. Click. One after another, he hit balls to the same spot. He made sure to keep his head still and behind the ball.

Satisfied he had mastered the short shots, NT moved to his six iron for full swings. He fixed his eyes on the red flag about one hundred and forty yards out. He took his stance, looked at his target once again, and let the ball fly. He pulled it a bit left, but that was fixable. *Check your feet,* he said to himself. He lined up another ball, checked his stance, and drew the club back. Right at impact, he heard it—not the click of the club against the ball, but the unmistakable voice of the man he had seen at Foley's Hardware Store. The shrill voice pierced his ears. NT looked to where the mayor and his group were standing. He heard the man's voice again and his skin crawled. He squinted and blocked the sun with his hand for a better view. He counted at least ten men but was unable to see their faces because most were wearing baseball hats. Nonetheless, NT was one hundred percent certain the voice he just heard was the same one he had heard that horrible day at Foley's. And from the fairway the day he and Daisy played golf with BB and Hoot.

The mayor herded his guests off the range. He noticed NT looking his way and waved to him. NT waved back and watched the men file into their golf carts. He pondered what to do. Instincts told him to wait until they were gone and then find Hoot. He had to tell someone, and he trusted the old caddie.

After the group drove off, NT made his way to the caddie shack. He made sure the coast was clear before tapping on the red door. The last thing he needed was for Mr. Gates to see him anywhere near the shack. He heard the floorboards creak from inside. NT prayed it was Hoot. His prayers were answered.

"Well, hello there, Nicholas. You come for some more pointers?" Hoot's smile settled NT's racing heart.

"Maybe later, Hoot. I really need to talk about something else."

Hoot could tell it was serious. He shuffled NT into the shack. "Have a seat. What's on your mind?"

NT first told Hoot about his unpleasant conversation with Mr. Gates. "He's always mad about something or other."

"Well, I understand his concern. He and I are on good terms, so I'll talk to him, okay?"

NT nodded then told Hoot about the voice he had just heard on the range. "It's the same one I heard in Foley's Hardware. And from the other day when we played. Remember those noisy men?"

"I sure do, son. You certain?"

"Yes, a hundred percent. It was definitely him."

"What'd he sound like?"

"His voice was high-pitched and sharp, kinda like a cartoon character would have."

"You see what he looked like?"

"Not really. The men all had hats on and they were at the far end of the range. But I'll never forget that guy's voice."

Hoot stroked his smooth chin, deep in thought. "Could you see if they were tall? Short? Skinny?"

"Yeah, some of them were, like, pretty tall, but the others were normal height, like you and BB."

"Well, I'm glad you told me. I think Sheriff Taylor needs to know. As far as I know, they don't know yet who

145

murdered Mr. Foley, and if what you said is right, Sheriff needs to know."

"Oh, wow."

"Son, you need to tell the authorities and your grandparents."

"I already told them I was at the store the day before Mr. Foley was killed. Isn't that enough?"

"You did the right thing by telling them about that. But this is important too. The man you heard here may not be the same man as in Foley's, but the police need to know anyway."

NT became fearful. "What if it *is* the same guy? What if he did kill Mr. Foley? What if he finds out I'm the one who told the police?" His voice rose with each question.

"Calm down. It's okay. It's okay. You are simply reporting something you heard. That man will never find out you said a word."

"But what if he does? What if he comes after me or BB or Mimi?" NT countered with panic.

"Stay calm," Hoot ordered. "That's the only way you keep your brain clear." He knew NT was frightened, so he related to him another way. "Do you think Santiago in *The Old Man and the Sea* panicked when he was out to sea by himself?" NT looked at Hoot but said nothing. He was thinking. "Speaking of Santiago, how much have you read in the book?" Hoot asked.

NT came around. "Santiago's in a bad way. His hands are cramping and he has no water. I don't know how he'll get the fish in if he can't grip the lines."

"Santiago is a tough old man with the wisdom to figure it out."

"Santiago's kinda like me."

"Really now. How 'bout you tell me what you mean by that. After all, he's an old man and you're a kid."

NT had been thinking about the parallels between his life and the old fisherman's. He spoke in a firm tone. "He lives in two places—the ocean and his hut. So do I. I go back and forth between two places—my mom's and my dad's—and I hate it. I don't get why they had to get divorced. I don't want to go home, Hoot. It sucks."

"I'm truly sorry for your trouble, Nicholas. I can imagine how difficult that is on you." Hoot steered the conversation back to the book by asking how else NT thought he and Santiago were alike.

"Well, he's looking for something—a fish—just like I'm looking for Clay's missing book. BB said he wanted it, so I'm going to keep looking for it, even though you said to give it a rest. I can't. I really want to find it."

Hoot rubbed his chin again. "I understand," he said in a low voice. "I'll help all I can."

NT looked at the clock. "I have to go. I told Mimi I'd be home this afternoon." NT stood to leave, then turned back to face the big caddie. "Thanks, Hoot."

"Anytime, son. My pleasure. Remember, tell your grandparents about what you heard on the range."

NT said he would. Hoot's words comforted him and gave him confidence. At the door, NT asked, "Are you done for the day?"

"Yup. I got some straightenin' up to do here, then I'll go home."

"Okay, I'll see you tomorrow."

"Yes, you will, Nicholas. Yes, you will."

22

NT knew Hoot was right. He had to tell his grandparents about the voice on the range. Back home, he found BB and Mimi watching television in the family room. Without saying a word, he picked up the remote and muted the TV.

"Hey now," said BB. "What's that about?"

"I need to tell you something."

"What's going on?"

NT relayed what he had seen and heard on the practice range. BB and Mimi exchanged glances, and BB asked NT if he was sure it was the same person. NT was emphatic that it was.

"There's only one thing to do." NT and Mimi watched as BB picked up the phone and called the police station. "Brenda, Willy Tyson here. Is Sheriff Taylor in?"

"Yes. He's in his office."

"Would you relay a message that NT and I will be there in fifteen minutes? We have some important information to tell him."

* * *

At the station, Sheriff Taylor and BB listened intently to NT's story about the man with the high-pitched voice. The sheriff interlaced his fingers and rocked back in his chair, digesting what he had heard. "Son, are you certain it's the same voice?"

"Yes, sir. One hundred percent."

"How can you be so certain?"

"Because it reminds me of that guy in one of my favorite movies."

"Excuse me?"

"*My Cousin Vinny*. The guy who plays Vinny. Him."

Sheriff Taylor cocked his head. "Who?"

BB interjected with a chuckle. "Oh, Vinny. Joe Pesci played him, remember?"

Sheriff Taylor squinted and nodded. "I suppose I do, yup. Joe Pesci—a short guy with a high-pitched voice."

BB added, "Marian and I saw that movie when it first came out. Loved it."

"I remember the movie. Never saw it, but I do know the actor NT's referring to," Sheriff Taylor said. "What did the man on the driving range look like?"

"I wasn't really close enough to see."

"But it was definitely this man, the one with the Joe Pesci voice?"

"Yeah. A bunch of men were hitting balls then left to play."

"Thank you for coming down here to tell me. If that's all, I'll walk you out." The sheriff stood and shook hands with NT and BB. After they left, he went back to his desk, noted down what NT had told him, and decided to drive to Cascades Golf Club to talk to Michael Gates. If the mayor checked in his guests, he would have done it at the pro shop, which meant Gates would have a list of everyone's names. First, though, Sheriff Taylor took a minute to reread Deputy Darman's notes regarding NT's description of what he had witnessed at Foley's Hardware. He read carefully, but the description of the man was missing. *Where are the notes on*

NT's description of the man he saw? They must still be in Darman's office.

Sheriff Taylor went to Darman's empty office and glanced at the messy desk. He didn't like looking through people's things, but this situation was different. He shuffled a few papers around and found nothing. He next tried the filing cabinet but it was locked. Knowing Darman, he had two keys—one with him and one hidden somewhere nearby. Sheriff Taylor started his search by running his hand behind the file cabinet—a logical place to hide an extra key. He felt something taped to the back—an envelope. *Aha. Got it.* He removed the envelope and noticed it was larger than one that would hold only a key. Inside the envelope, he found a stack of paperwork and no key. A glance told the sheriff he was holding notes from Darman's conversation with NT. Sheriff Taylor read the pages three times. *Why aren't these pages with the rest of Darman's notes? Why are they hidden inside an envelope and taped to the back of a filing cabinet?*

Sheriff Taylor pushed those thoughts aside and left for the club. He thought about Darman as he drove. He knew better than to be immediately suspicious of his deputy, but tried to make sense of the discovery. Did Darman put the notes there so he'd remember exactly where they were? After all, his desk was a disorganized mess. In the thirty years Sheriff Taylor had known Darman, he knew Darman occasionally operated in unconventional ways and had interesting methods of doing things, some of which added a new perspective when solving crimes. *Darman must have a reasonable explanation as to why his notes were in an envelope taped to the back of his file cabinet.*

Sheriff Taylor drove up the main drive of Cascades Golf Club and recalled Daisy's words about a photo of Clay with his notebook. He would make the Grille Room his first stop. Inside, he examined the pictures and found the one Daisy had mentioned. Sure enough, a small book was sticking out of Clay's back pants pocket.

"Hello, Sheriff. Day off for some golf? Can I get you something?"

Sheriff Taylor turned around to see Lenny behind the bar polishing glasses.

"Hi, Lenny. Nope, no golf today. I'm on the clock, but I'll take a soda to go. Thanks."

"Here you go."

Sheriff Taylor took a sip of his drink and looked around. He took in the new décor and thought the improvements looked great. *I'll have to bring the family here for dinner. They enjoy the outside dining.* "It's looking good in here, Lenny. Thanks again." He headed to the pro shop.

Gates was surprised to see the sheriff, but when he heard the reason for his visit, he cooperated and retrieved the tee sheet. He ran his finger down the list, located the mayor's name, and handed the sheet to the sheriff, who skimmed the list. *Nicholas was right. The mayor did bring a group of men to play—eleven in all.* He jotted down the names from the list on a separate sheet of paper. One in particular caught his attention.

"Everything okay?" Gates asked.

"For now, yup," the sheriff replied.

* * *

After Nicholas left, Hoot sat back down at the table and glanced around the shack. Over the years, its walls had heard countless secrets, stories, and jokes. Hoot did his best thinking here, and ever since Nicholas first learned about Clay and how he was murdered, Hoot's memories of that horrible event had been stirred. An old wound had been opened and all the pain of that dark time crashed down on him. That it remained unsolved made Hoot sick to his stomach. Clay deserved better than that.

The sun was beginning to drop in the sky. It was time to head home. Janie would have dinner ready and waiting. Hoot slipped his red caddie bib over his head and hung it in his locker. He looked up at the bookshelves overhead. He was just about finished *The Old Man and the Sea* and needed another book. He fingered the spines of the books on the first two shelves and pulled out a few to read the summaries. He returned them, uninterested. The brilliant vermilion color of a book on the third shelf stood out. Hoot pulled it down and read the synopsis. *Hmm. This looks interesting. A soldier who fights in WWII and survives a series of horrendous predicaments.* Hoot flipped through the dusty pages to learn more. A yellowed envelope stuck between the pages caught his eye. Three letters had been handwritten in the bottom left corner—*PRA*. He inhaled sharply and looked again. He had no doubt about whose initials they were—his. *Percy Robert Alexander.*

He opened the envelope, uncertain what he would find. The letter shook in his hands as he read.

July 20, 1981

Dear Hoot,

You are one of the finest men I have ever known. You are a deeply trusted and respected friend, someone whom I trust with my life. It is for that reason that I now burden you with an enormous responsibility. I need you to complete one last job for me—get my blue book. Never can it fall into the hands of the wrong person. Till now, I have kept its location secret.

I constructed a small drawer under the base of my locker. It is there you will find my book. I know you will know what to do with it. My hope is that it won't be too late. My thanks will be with you forever, even after I am gone.

Eternally,
Clay

Hoot was speechless. A voice from the grave—that of his beloved friend. He blinked away the tears. Clay had entrusted Hoot with this secret, one that lay silent and unknown to Hoot or anyone else for thirty years. It was now up to him to help his friend. Hoot put the envelope in his pocket, hung up his hat, and turned off the lights on his way out the door.

* * *

Sheriff Taylor returned to the police station after his visit to Cascades. He went straight to his office and closed the door. He needed to think about what he had discovered in Darman's office and the name he had read on Gates's tee sheet. A voice inside his head was telling him things he didn't want to hear about his friend and partner. He desperately wanted to believe Darman had a good explanation for hiding his notes. He would try to find one. He went back into Darman's darkened office and, against every ethical thread in his body, slid open the first two drawers of his desk. Nothing but pens, pencils, straws, and paper. The third drawer was locked.

"Can I help you with something, Sheriff?" Darman was standing in the doorway with a serious look on his face.

Sheriff Taylor played it cool. "Oh, good, you're here. I was looking for those notes regarding what Nicholas Tyson told you about the man at Foley's Hardware. Any chance you have them?"

"I do, but not in there. I keep the important stuff in the file cabinet."

"Good idea."

Darman unlocked the cabinet and pulled out the file.

"You lock your desk drawers too?"

"I keep my ammo in there," he answered curtly. "Here," he said, and handed Sheriff Taylor the file.

The sheriff flipped through it and remarked, "Thanks. The sheet with the description of the man in question seems to be missing."

Darman's response was edgy. "Hmm. Really? It should all be there, Sheriff. You know I take meticulous notes. Maybe you should look again?"

"I am not questioning your note-taking skills—they're impeccable. I just don't see the description." He sifted through the notes and said, "Nope, I don't see it. Maybe you accidentally left it out?"

"Not possible. I do my job thoroughly and it was all there," Darman countered.

"I am not suggesting otherwise. I'm simply saying part of the report is missing. You could've misplaced it."

The air was tense with a cloud of mutual suspicion. The two men stared at each other.

"Look, Sheriff, if it ain't there, I don't know where it is."

"Well, I highly suggest *you* look again." Sheriff Taylor glared at Darman as he left the small office.

23

NT crashed hard and fell into a long, deep slumber. He'd had a long day. His energy was spent after speaking to Hoot and Sheriff Taylor about the man on the range. The next morning, he woke up later than usual but felt renewed and refreshed.

He made his way to the kitchen where Mimi and BB were sipping coffee and happily discussing their plans for the day and evening. Mimi said she was going to the grocery store and the drug store, then joining a few girlfriends for lunch in town. BB was off to an eye doctor appointment then to hit balls on the range.

"Do you want to join me at the range, NT?" he asked.

"Sure. But I may hang out here for a while first. I need to read some more."

"Are you enjoying the book more than you thought at first?" BB asked.

"Yeah. Santiago's a cool guy, for someone really old," NT joked.

"Careful about who you're calling old!" BB teased back. "I'll text you when I'm leaving the doctor's office, then you can meet me on the range."

"Speaking of the club, Nicholas," Mimi said, "we're meeting the Hardy sisters at seven for dinner. If you'd like to invite Daisy, that'd be fine with us."

"Cool. I'll text her."

* * *

Members enjoyed Friday nights at Cascades Golf Club, as it was the most popular night to have dinner there. A jazz trio played on the crowded porch, kids participated in lawn games, and Chef Allison created tasty dinners to tempt even the most discerning diner. The biggest and most popular part of Friday night dinners was, by far, the ice cream sundae bar. Weekly, the bar offered five different flavors of ice cream with all the fixings—hot fudge, caramel sauce, candies, and whipped cream.

NT and Daisy had devoured their cheeseburgers and excused themselves from the table where BB, Mimi, and the Hardy sisters sat contentedly listening to the music. The friends moved to the ice cream bar where they created towering sundaes that were sloppy and delicious at the same time. NT pointed to the garden wall that bordered the driveway near the upper parking lot. "Let's go sit over there," he said. A minute later, he and Daisy were digging into their desserts with delight.

They heard snippets of conversation floating down from the lot, but were more occupied with dessert than with the voices, and thought nothing of the chatter. Then one of the voices got loud. The person sounded angry. Curiosity got the best of NT and Daisy, and they crept up the driveway, pressed close to the wall. They stopped and crouched behind a parked car where they took in the scene and the conversation. Against the setting sun, they saw the silhouettes of two men standing next to the bag drop. The men were pointing to three golf bags propped up there.

"How much in each?" one man asked. "The regular? It'd better be." The man's voice sounded threatening and NT's ears perked up.

Could that be? he wondered. *No. No way.* NT shook his head as if not believing his ears. *But it is—it's the voice from Foley's Hardware!*

The second man responded with an edge in his voice. "Yeah, I stayed late last night to fill the order."

"That sounds like Lenny!" Daisy whispered.

NT was afraid they would be discovered. "Shh!"

"Okay. Pickup is in ten minutes," said the Joe Pesci voice, and the man glanced at his watch.

"It's all there," said the man who sounded like Lenny. "I gotta get back. I don't need no one noticing I'm gone."

"Right. I'll be in touch," the other man said.

"Daisy, I swear that's the guy from Foley's," NT whispered. "That's definitely him!" They watched the man get into a car and drive off.

The other man checked his surroundings then hustled inside through a kitchen door located on the side of the clubhouse building.

Daisy said, "And that other guy is definitely Lenny! What is going on?"

NT was dumbfounded and said nothing.

"We should look at those bags," Daisy said, and started toward the bag drop.

NT grabbed her arm. "Wait! We can't let anyone see us."

"Fine."

They looked around and felt confident everyone was still packed inside the restaurant and on the porch eating ice cream. They dashed to where the bags were standing and unzipped the side pockets. They almost fell over in shock at what they found. Inside every pocket and pouch of all three bags were neat stacks of cash. NT and Daisy looked at each other in disbelief, terrified at their discovery.

"Whoa! I've never seen so much money! What's up with this?" NT breathed.

"No clue, but I sure could buy a lot of ice cream with it!"

"Very funny. This is so—" He didn't finish his sentence. Bright headlights swept across the parking lot. He grabbed Daisy's hand and said, "Quick! We have to hide!"

They squatted behind another car and peeked over the hood. The unfamiliar car swung into the lot and stopped at the rack where the golf bags were standing. For a full minute, there was no movement from the car. Finally, the driver got out and glanced around.

NT and Daisy's eyes went wide with astonishment upon seeing the man who exited the car. NT immediately signaled "shh" and Daisy clamped a hand over her mouth. The only sound they heard aside from the crickets was the crunch of the driver's shoes on the gravel. NT and Daisy crouched motionless and watched the man unzip the bulging golf bags and look at what they contained. With a smug smile, the man hoisted the bags into the trunk of the car, got back in, and drove away.

NT and Daisy stared at each other. NT was the first to speak. "Oh my God! Holy crap! Is that who I thought it was?"

"Totally. What the heck is going on?"

"I have no idea, but it can't be good."

"Hardly," agreed NT.

"What is *he* doing with those golf bags? Maybe we should—" Daisy started, then stopped.

From across the parking lot they heard the distinct snap of a branch. They looked into the inky darkness, but saw nothing.

"That came from the tenth tee box," said NT.

"Oh my God! Something, or someone, is over there," Daisy whispered.

"This is totally creeping me out. Let's go back," NT said.

They timed their return perfectly, as BB and Mimi were saying good night to their friends.

24

NT flopped down on his bed, looked up at the ceiling, and tried to process what he and Daisy had seen earlier that night. He wanted to text her, but it was late. He opened *The Old Man and the Sea* and read a few pages before sleep eventually overcame him.

Having slept in the day before, NT got up earlier than usual the next morning—even before Mimi and BB. He left a note telling them he had gone to the club. After the events of the night before, he was bursting at the seams to tell someone. And that someone was Hoot. He sped to the club through the warm morning air, hid his bike in the trees near the caddie shack, and knocked on the red door.

"Nicholas, it ain't even nine o'clock yet. What're you doin' here so early on a Saturday morning?" Hoot knew something had to have happened.

At the table, NT told Hoot what he and Daisy had observed and the money they had found in the golf bags the night before. Hoot couldn't believe his ears.

"This is serious business, Nicholas. For now, don't you and Daisy tell anyone. Let me think on what to do. Got it?" NT nodded. "All right, then. Larry and I are carrying for Mayor Hall and his group today. We'll talk later, son." Hoot stood, walked to the door, and opened it for NT.

"Thanks, Hoot."

Hoot closed the door behind NT. Inside the shack, he picked up the phone and called the sheriff. Deputy Darman answered. "Sheriff's not in. Can I help you?"

"I'll try back later," Hoot said. Darman pushed, but Hoot thanked him and hung up. He made his way to the range and watched the mayor and his group warm up. Judging by how well—actually, how poorly—some of the men were swinging, Hoot knew it would be a long round. But, money was money, and the mayor usually tipped generously.

"Gentleman, we are on the tee," Hoot informed the group as their tee time approached.

"Ready, fellas?" the mayor called out to his group.

"You ready to lose some money, Mr. Mayor? Ten bucks a hole?" That last voice cut through the others to reach Hoot's ears. Hoot looked up and saw the source of the high-pitched, squeaky voice. He saw a small, tightly built man with the face of a rat. His gelled dark hair looked like a seal's coat, all slick and greasy. Looks aside, Hoot was stuck on the man's voice—high-pitched, squeaky.

"Yeah, okay, Tony," responded the mayor. His tone was arrogant. "You willing to put your money where your mouth is?"

The man the mayor called Tony laughed. The sound reminded Hoot of a machine gun. Tony reached into his pocket and pulled out a wad of cash. He waved the bills at the mayor.

"Just got these, and am happy to add more from your pocket," Tony squeaked. Tony was the same person Hoot, BB, NT, and Daisy had heard yelling obscenities on the course the day they played a round together.

"Let's let our clubs do the talkin'," Mayor Hall said, and he lit a huge cigar to kick off their round.

* * *

At the same time NT was telling Hoot about the previous night's events, Daisy was attempting to tell her father. But she wasn't having much luck. The breakfast table at the Taylor household was not the best time to have important conversations, especially when all three of Daisy's brothers teased her relentlessly.

"Dad, last night, me and NT saw somethin' weird," she started.

Daisy's oldest brother jumped in before Sheriff Taylor could respond. "You and your little boyfriend were on a date?" He stuffed a spoonful of cereal into his mouth.

"Shut up! I wasn't talking to you, jerk!" she yelled back.

"Did he take you for a big night out at Sweetwoods?" middle brother Brett taunted.

"You're so obnoxious!" Daisy threw her toast at him.

"All of you, stop. Leave your sister alone," Mrs. Taylor admonished. "It's too early for this kind of bickering."

Sheriff Taylor pushed his chair back to get up from the table.

"But, Dad, wait. I have to tell you what—"

"Sorry, sweetheart. Runnin' late. We'll talk tonight when I get home." He holstered his gun and took a final swig of coffee. Then he kissed his wife on the cheek and left for the station.

Daisy's sigh conveyed her disappointment. No one ever listened to her. Having three older brothers was horrible, most of time anyway. She couldn't wait for them to go away to college, but that was a long way off. She finished her breakfast and told her mother, "I'm going to the club." The door slammed behind her as she raced out of the house. She pedaled furiously. Her brothers had gotten her blood boiling so badly, it felt good to pump the pedals and work off her anger. *I have no idea why Mom keeps telling me that one day I'll be thankful for my brothers.* Yeah, right.

Daisy found NT in the chipping area practicing bump and run shots with his pitching wedge.

"Hey, NT. Looks like you've been here a while. What's up?"

"Not a lot. I can't stop thinking about what happened last night."

"Same here. I tried to tell my dad, but my idiotic brothers were being pains and then dad had to leave to go to work. I hate them sometimes."

"I told Hoot."

"You did? What'd he say?"

"He just said for us not to tell anyone and that he'd think on what to do."

"Okay. We should find him later." Daisy pointed to the three sand traps nearby and said, "Since I can't seem to get out of sand traps, I'm gonna go bury myself in there. Come get me when you're done."

NT and Daisy alternated their short game practice between chipping and sand shots for an hour. NT had not yet had breakfast, so in time, his stomach was knocking against itself with hunger. "Let's go to the Grille Room. I'm starving."

On their way, they detoured into the pro shop to see if the tee times for the Junior Championships had been posted. Pro Gates was at the desk as usual. "Do you have the tee times for the championship ready?"

"Tee times?" he barked back.

NT was still not used to this man's gruff ways. "Yeah," he said in a meek response. "Champs are in a few days and we thought maybe you had the times ready."

Gates glared at them. "I'll try. But I've got a ton of work to do before that. Maybe they'll be posted later today or first thing tomorrow. Got it?"

NT and Daisy walked out of the pro shop with slumped shoulders. They had hoped to learn their start times.

"He's always in the worst mood," Daisy remarked.

"I know. He scares me," NT responded. "It's like he doesn't have time for us kids."

For a Saturday morning, the Grille Room was nearly empty. A few people were enjoying a late breakfast or early lunch. Lenny was nowhere to be found.

"I wonder where he is," Daisy said. "I'll look on the porch. Maybe he's out there."

NT looked up and down the bar for a bowl of pretzels and mixed nuts that Lenny put out for the patrons to munch on with their drinks. He saw a bowl at the far end of the bar and went to get a handful of the snacks. As he tossed them back, his eyes fell on the old golf club Lenny had said he was going to hang above the door to the restaurant. The club stood leaning against the wall, its leather grip now turned a dull, dark brown. NT stepped behind the bar and lifted the club. Its solid steel shaft made the club heftier than the clubs NT was used to. He observed the club was made by Titleist, then turned it upside down and saw a small 7 engraved into the toe of the club. The grooves on the face of the club were so worn they were barely visible. This club had clearly smacked a lot of balls.

Just then, the kitchen door to the bar swung open and Lenny walked through. He was wiping his mouth and saw NT with the golf club. "Hey, what're you doin' with that club?" he asked.

NT's face burned. He knew he should not have gone behind the bar. "I just wanted to see it up close."

"Okay, but be careful with it. I've had it a long time and it's pretty special to me."

"Yeah, I remember when you first told us about it. It's pretty cool, for a club. An old seven iron," NT said.

"That's right. Y'all want something to eat?" Lenny asked.

"Can we get a turkey club with chips? And two sodas, please?"

"Comin' right up," Lenny answered, and he returned to the kitchen to place their order.

NT and Daisy wandered to the wall of plaques and pictures and stopped in front of one photo of Clay they hadn't looked at previously. NT leaned in close and saw a small notebook in Clay's pocket. NT knew it was *the book*. Where was it?

25

After Mayor Hall's marathon six-hour round of golf, and a long day in general, Hoot sat resting in the caddie shack. He replayed the events of the day as he caddied for the mayor and his group, and focused especially on the man called Tony. Hoot concluded that Tony was the man NT had heard in Foley's Hardware Store. Hoot had never heard a human being talk so much. After two holes, he thought his ears would bleed from Tony's nonstop yammering.

Hoot's thoughts turned to Clay's letter, which he now carried with him everywhere. He pulled it from his wallet and read it again. *When the time is right, I'll go see Clay's secret drawer for myself.* The golf course would not shut down for another couple of hours, which meant he would not be able to dig around the men's locker room without raising suspicion till then. To pass the time, Hoot decided to revisit Hemingway's Santiago and the magnificent, yet tragic, marlin the old fisherman had hooked.

* * *

Hoot entered the darkened men's locker room and walked straight to the back where Clay's former locker used to be located. It was in a row of other old, unused lockers. Along the way, Hoot noticed the exit sign above the back door was not lit. A security light from the bathroom cast a dim light in the locker area. *I'll need to report that to maintenance.* Even with the lights out, Hoot knew his way around the locker room like he knew the back of his hand.

He and Clay had had many heartfelt conversations there after hours when no one else was around.

The locker room was deathly quiet and eerie. The silent stillness enveloped Hoot. At once, he became conscious of his heart thudding against his chest. *What's that all about? I've been down here hundreds of times. I got nothing to be wary of.* Abruptly, his attention shifted to the distant sound of voices, then bangs. Hoot stopped dead in his tracks. More muffled voices and bangs. *What the—?* The noises emanated from behind a concrete wall near Clay's old locker. Hoot sat down on a bench against the wall and pressed his ear up against it. He thought back to when Clay had told him about the noises he had been hearing. A dull thumping sound drowned out the voices, so Hoot could not make out the exact words. His instincts told him to check Clay's locker and get out. Quickly.

He started toward the row of empty lockers, and mumbled to himself, "Clay did hear somethin' goin' on down here. Maybe if I had listened better, he'd still be—"

"Still be what?" A familiar voice sliced through the darkness of the locker room, catching Hoot unawares. Had he been watching Hoot the entire time? Hoot felt his scalp tighten and his heart skip a beat. A man approached. Hoot heard him smacking something in the palm of his hand. With the quickness of a cobra, the man shoved Hoot against the lockers and pressed something cold against the soft part of his throat.

"I asked you a question. Gimme an answer!" the man hissed, and nudged his weapon closer against Hoot's throat.

Hoot gasped, "—alive."

The man leaned in so closely that his nose was almost touching Hoot's. "Well, guess what, *caddie boy*. He ain't." Hoot was disgusted by the smell of the man's onion and salami breath. "You'd be real wise to keep your mouth shut, ya hear? You wouldn't want nothin' happenin' to your family now, would ya, especially your pretty wife Janie."

Hoot struggled for air, the room started to spin, and he was seeing double. Upon hearing the man's words, however, he regained his strength—whether from fear or anger, he did not know—and smacked the weapon away. "How dare you threaten me and my family! They'll find you. Mark my words."

The assailant grabbed Hoot by the throat and squeezed hard. "You tell anyone about this, and your family will be buryin' you, understand? I'll be watchin' you—your every move. Got it?" The man threw Hoot to the ground. On his way down, Hoot slammed into a wooden bench. Pain bolted through his shoulder. Bile rose in his throat. He lay on the floor taking in deep breaths. The squeaky squish of the assailant's shoes on their way out of the locker room was the only sound Hoot heard. He didn't know how long he was on the floor, but he rolled over gingerly onto his good side and sat up. He rubbed his aching shoulder and cleared his head. As he processed what had happened, he got angrier by the minute. Even though he had to take the man's threats seriously, Hoot vowed to not let him get away with what he had done. Carefully, Hoot got to his feet, opened the door, and stepped into the darkness of the outer hallway.

26

Sheriff Taylor took most Sundays off. Today was different. He was at his desk bright and early. Sleep had eluded him the night before because he was consumed with thoughts of Darman and what he had discovered behind the filing cabinet. He read through his messages and saw the one from Percy Alexander. Percy had called on Friday and left word with Darman that he'd call the sheriff back later. This piqued the sheriff's curiosity. *Why would Percy be calling me? Daisy had better not have caused trouble at Cascades.* He set the message aside. For now, he had to plow his way through the pile of paperwork that awaited him.

After three hours of mind-numbing work, the words all swam together. Sheriff Taylor helped himself to a stretch and a big glass of water. He looked out the window and noticed Darman's patrol car was not parked in the lot. He picked up the phone, dialed the number of the club, and asked to be transferred to the caddie shack.

"Caddie shack. James speakin'. How can I help you?"

"Good morning. This is Sheriff Taylor. I'm returning a call I received from Percy. Is he available?"

"Howdy, Sheriff. Hoot's not around. He just left to get some lunch. Can I give him a message?"

The sheriff hesitated. "Ah, no, James. That's okay. I might swing by later. Thanks, though."

"You're welcome. Enjoy your day now."

"You too."

Sheriff Taylor's rumbling stomach told him he hadn't eaten since the plate of scrambled eggs and toast hours earlier. The thought of breakfast reminded him that Daisy had wanted to tell him something the day before. He felt guilty he had not been able to listen to her at the time. *I'll catch up with her later.* For now, though, a sandwich from Wink's would quiet the rumblings in his belly. He got into his cruiser, drove into town, and entered the deli.

"Howdy, Sheriff!" said Peter from behind the counter. "What can I get you?"

"Hello, Pete. I'll have one of your famous chicken salad sandwiches, two pickles, and a bag of chips. Oh, and a sweet tea from the fridge."

The sheriff sat in his parked cruiser to eat lunch. Tubman Avenue was alive with shoppers and tourists enjoying a lovely August afternoon. Sheriff Taylor felt a swell of both pride and love for the town and its citizens, especially given how hard he worked to protect and serve. Thoughts of Darman entered his head. Darman had been a supportive and upstanding public servant to the residents of Cab Station for over thirty years and it made no sense to Sheriff Taylor that Darman would lie to him.

The sheriff recalled when he was voted into the job. Darman had also wanted to be sheriff and was confident at the time that he'd be elected. The vote for Sheriff Taylor, however, had been unanimous. *Was Darman bitter over that?* In the end, Darman appeared content with his appointment as deputy sheriff. Regardless, Sheriff Taylor had to figure out a way to get to the bottom of the matter, which meant risking their friendship. But the safety and well-being of the people of Cab Station were the sheriff's priority, a vow he had sworn to uphold thirty years earlier.

"Sheriff Taylor!"

At the sound of his name, the sheriff looked up from his lunch to see who had called him. The shout had come from across the street.

"Sheriff!"

Hoot stood waving at him from across the street. Sheriff Taylor finished the last of his sandwich and climbed out of his car. Hoot crossed over and greeted him with a handshake.

"Percy," he said. "Good to see you."

"Afternoon, Sheriff. Got time to talk?"

"Sure do, Percy," he responded. "I saw that you called me. I got tied up yesterday but was hoping to catch up with you today. What's up?"

"Thank you. But, first things first. Please call me Hoot. All my friends do."

The two men sat down on an empty bench underneath a row of big-leaf magnolia trees that were still in full bloom.

"What's on your mind, Hoot?"

Hoot cleared his throat and shared with the sheriff the circumstances under which he had found Clay's letter in the caddie shack. He next told the sheriff about being assaulted in the locker room.

Sheriff Taylor let a few beats of his heart pass before responding. He asked, "You sure about all that?"

"Yes, sir. Unfortunately, it's all true."

The sheriff nodded slowly as acknowledgement of the gravity of the situation. "Thank you for telling me."

27

NT and Daisy ate lunch at what had become their second favorite spot after Sweetwoods—on the wall bordering the driveway at Cascades. From their vantage point, they spied all the goings-on at the club, such as who was teeing off with whom on the first tee box. They also saw when head pro Gates stepped out of the pro shop, which gave them time to run inside and avoid him altogether. The wall was also a prime spot to eavesdrop on the diners seated on the porch above them. Some of their conversations provided endless entertainment.

"What do you want to do now?" NT asked.

"I don't know. Get ice cream?" Daisy responded with a cunning smile.

"I can't. I'm way too full from lunch." To prove just how full he was, NT belched out loud.

"Ex-*cuse* you!"

"Yeah, yeah. It's not like you've never heard a boy belch before."

"True," Daisy said with a nod. "Let's go back to your house and shoot hoops or something. The only thing is, I want to get home before my idiotic brothers do, so I can talk to my dad about what we saw the other night in the parking lot. I still can't believe who we saw pick up the bags. Totally weird."

"I know."

They hopped on their bikes and hugged the hedges along the drive on their way out of the club to avoid the traffic coming and going. A stretch limousine turned in from the road, but NT and Daisy were on a curve and did not see it. The limo seemed to appear out of nowhere. NT tried to steer clear to avoid colliding with it, but he was too close. His tire hit the side door with a solid bang. Daisy, who was right on NT's tail, was unable to stop in time and crashed into NT. The limo stopped.

"Oh, crap!" NT yelled.

"Sorry!" said Daisy. "You stopped so fast! Are you okay?"

The soft buzz of the limo's side window opening caught their attention.

"What are you kids doin'? You just crashed into the mayor's limo! Watch where you're goin'!" NT recognized the man right away—not by his mean, rat-faced looks, but from the sound of his voice. It was high-pitched, squeaky, and dripped with venom. It was the same voice from Foley's Hardware Store, the same voice from the practice range. Fingers of fear tickled the back of NT's neck. The man looked up from lighting his cigarette and stared at NT with black, rodent-like eyes.

A pleasant voice from inside the limo spoke. "Tony, take it easy. They're just kids and meant no harm. It was an accident, I'm sure." That voice belonged to Mayor Hall. He stretched his head to look out the window. "Is anyone hurt?"

"Uh, no. No, sir... Mayor... We're okay," NT stammered.

"We are so sorry, Mr. Mayor. We didn't see the car coming around the corner. Sorry!" Daisy repeated.

"If we hurt your car, we'll pay for it!" NT blurted out.

"No, no, son. The car is fine. Y'all just be more careful riding your bikes, ya hear?" the mayor responded.

"Yes, sir," NT and Daisy said in unison.

The mayor waved goodbye as the limo pulled off and headed for a parking spot near the entrance to the clubhouse.

"We just crashed into the mayor's limo!" NT exclaimed. "And the guy who yelled at us is the guy from Foley's!"

"Okay, calm down. Let's just act cool and go to your house." From across the lot, they saw Lenny come out to greet the mayor and his group as if they were old friends— with hugs and handshakes all around. NT and Daisy pretended to be checking their bikes for damage. On the sly, they watched as Lenny handed the mayor what appeared to be a thick wad of cash.

"Did you see that?" Daisy said.

"It looked to me like a ton of money," NT answered.

"It did, didn't it? Kind of like all that money in the golf bags."

"Right. Why would Lenny have all that cash?" Then NT answered his own question. "I think they're betting on sports."

"You do? Is that legal?"

"I have no idea. Let's get out of here."

* * *

"Heads, we play HORSE. Tails, checkers," said NT. He grabbed a quarter from BB's change jar, flipped it, and said, "Heads." Basketball won out over the quiet board game.

Daisy was ready for some competitive sport against NT. "Let's go! I'll whip your butt."

NT was not feeling his usual driven self—this day was different, and he was having a tough time focusing on beating Daisy. "Doesn't it seem like all these weird things have been happening since I first heard about my uncle Clay? I mean, what are the odds I would keep seeing that guy from Foley's? We found money stuffed in golf bags, old scorecards with dates circled, and money and notes in the programs from the attic."

"Yeah, it's creepy for sure—just like *Tony*. And the one thing we really want—the blue notebook—is nowhere to be found," she said.

NT shot and missed. He handed the basketball to Daisy who sank it effortlessly for the win. "Game over!"

"Until next time, when I thump you."

"Yeah, right. Dream on. Listen, I'm gonna go. My father should be home by five."

"Okay. I'll see you tomorrow at the club. What time are we meeting?"

"I don't know. I'll text you in the morning," Daisy said.

"Okay. Talk to you later."

Daisy rode off and NT wandered into the kitchen where Mimi was slicing peppers and tomatoes for salad.

"Hello there, young man," she said. "How's your day been going?"

"Hi, Mimi. Good," he answered, and stuffed two chocolate chip cookies into his mouth.

"Careful. It's close to dinner. Don't spoil it."

"I won't. I'm starving. What're we having?"

"Grilled chicken, corn, and marinated veggie salad. Would you please set the table? But wash your hands first."

NT washed up then reached into a drawer to pull out three yellow and blue plaid placemats.

"How far are you in *The Old Man and the Sea*?" Mimi asked.

"Close to finishing," he answered.

"Well, dinner is in an hour. Why don't you read a bit before we eat?"

28

Daisy rode home from Shady Acres and knew she'd find her father in his favorite spot—out on the patio. She walked around the side of the house, admiring the pink and fuchsia Impatiens that lined the walkway. As expected, Sheriff Taylor was relaxing in the lounge chair with a new novel about Abraham Lincoln. He had changed into shorts and his legs were stretched out in front of him. A frosty beer sat untouched on a side table.

Daisy plopped down on the chair next to her father. She knew he worked hard and that his job was not easy. Seeing him so relaxed made her feel bad about what she was about to drop on him, but she had to.

"Hi, Dad. How was your day?"

Sheriff Taylor looked at his daughter for a minute without speaking. He saw her as smart, kind, and beautiful. He had been convinced that baby number four in their family was going to be another boy—whom he would have loved and cared for just as much as he did the first three—but he was over-the-moon thrilled when he met his little girl. "Hi, sweetheart. It was a good day, for the most part." He thought back to his conversation with Hoot. "How about you? You and NT get into any trouble?"

"Nah, but I did beat him in HORSE."

"That's my Daisy."

Daisy cleared her throat to prepare for what she was about to tell her father. "Remember yesterday morning when I told you me and him saw something weird on Friday night?"

"*He and I*," her father corrected. "I sure do, and I'm sorry I let time get away from me without getting back to you. But I'm all ears now. What's up?"

"Well, on Friday night, NT and I were eating our dessert along the wall near the club parking lot and we heard two guys talking near the bag drop. They didn't know we were there. But they were saying something about money and a pickup, and they were pointing to three golf bags that were lined up on the bag drop. NT swears one of the men sounds like the guy from Foley's."

"And?"

"Well, when the men left, we snuck over to the bags and looked inside them. There was tons of money in them. I mean, *tons.*" She took a breath. "And then we—"

"Hold up." Daisy's father put up his hand to stop her. "What were y'all thinking, looking in someone else's golf bag? Daisy, honey, they're someone else's property. Lots of people keep their wallet in their bags. And other personal belongings."

Daisy pushed. "Yeah, but, Dad, there was tons of cash, mostly in ten-dollar bills. What does that mean?"

At the mention of ten-dollar bills, the sheriff straightened in his chair. "I'm not sure. More importantly, what made y'all look in those bags?"

Daisy shrugged. "We were curious, I guess. The second man said something like 'all of it was there' and we recognized that voice as Lenny," she answered.

"Lenny? The bartender?"

"Yeah."

Sheriff Taylor gave a long, slow exhale. He looked out toward the yard and up to the sky where the early evening sun displayed warm orange against a pale blue backdrop.

"Do you understand y'all had no business unzipping and looking in someone else's golf bag? You could've gotten into a mess of trouble—or worse."

"Yes, sir," was Daisy's sullen reply.

The sheriff's voice softened. "But I am glad you told me."

"There's more." Her facial expression was grave.

Sheriff Taylor took a much-needed swig of beer before listening to whatever else Daisy had to tell him. "Really? What?"

"They were talking about how someone was gonna pick up the bags, like, ten minutes later. So, we hid behind cars to see who it was."

"And?"

She took a deep breath and looked at her father. "It was Deputy Darman."

At first, Daisy's father said nothing. He then asked if she was absolutely sure.

"Yes."

And she was—he could tell by her tone. Their conversation ended. Nothing more needed to be said. Sheriff Taylor knew that what Daisy had seen and heard was accurate.

The patio door slid open and Daisy's mother's warm voice changed the atmosphere. "There you both are," she said, and kissed her husband on the head.

"Hi, Mom." Daisy stood to give her mother a hug. "What's for dinner?"

"I thought we'd grill chicken sausages tonight and have potato salad and corn to go along. Why don't you come help me shuck the corn and let your dad have some quiet time before your brothers get home."

Daisy followed her mother inside, leaving Sheriff Taylor to ponder what she had told him. Abe Lincoln would have to wait for another day. He needed the time now to figure out his next steps.

29

NT lay on his bed and daydreamed about the events in his book. Santiago had just hooked an enormous marlin and would now battle to bring the fish in. NT felt sorry for the old man, who was out on the ocean all alone. He wondered how Santiago would get the fish ashore by himself.

"Dinner's ready!" Mimi's voice floated up the steps.

"Okay. Be right down," NT answered. He bookmarked his place in the book and headed downstairs.

During dinner, BB, Mimi, and NT discussed NT's summer reading project, golf, and the upcoming end-of-summer party. NT mentioned how sad he was that summer was going so quickly. "I wish I could live with you guys all the time. It's so much easier than going back and forth between two houses."

Mimi glanced at BB and said, "I know, sweetheart. We wish we could help you understand why people do the things they do. But you know you're welcome to stay here with us every summer."

They were quiet for a while, each deep in their own thoughts, until BB finally broke the silence. "I was thinking that since it's such a nice night, we'd take Blackie into town and get some ice cream for dessert."

NT's demeanor changed. "Can't beat that plan," he said with a smile. He rose from the table, stacked the plates, and cleaned up the kitchen before heading outside.

In the driveway, BB was bouncing the basketball. NT usually put the ball away after playing with Daisy, but he'd been distracted earlier and forgot. BB bounced the ball to NT, who caught it and took it into the garage. NT opened the sports equipment closet and dropped the ball to the ground where it rolled up against Clay's old golf bag. That reminded NT that he'd been meaning to check out Clay's clubs all summer, but had forgotten to do so with everything else that had been going on.

The bag was black and made of genuine leather. The shafts of the clubs inside were made of heavy steel. The heads of the woods and driver maintained their shine. NT pulled out an iron and saw *Titleist* inscribed into the bottom of it. He squinted and read the letters *CHT* branded roughly into the toe of the club. The driver and other clubs were similarly inscribed. He looked again at the bag and then counted the clubs. *Huh. Thirteen? Did my uncle play with only thirteen clubs when everyone else carries the most allowed—fourteen?* NT moved other equipment around in the closet, but did not find the fourteenth club.

"Let's go, Nicholas!" BB called from the driveway.

Darn! I'll have to come back later to check the bag again. I need to find out which one is missing. "Coming!" NT ran out of the garage and hopped in Blackie's rumble seat. The evening air felt good on his face.

BB glided the LaSalle into a spot that had just opened up in front of Sweetwoods. They placed their ice cream orders inside then sat at one of the picnic tables outside to eat. Tubman Avenue was pleasantly busy on this lovely night.

NT was itching to bring up what he had found—or rather, *not* found—in the garage. He waited till he knew he'd have his grandparents' full attention. "I saw Clay's clubs in the garage. They're pretty cool."

"They don't make 'em like that anymore," said BB.

"Did you know he has only thirteen clubs?"

"Really? That's odd. I know he played with fourteen," said BB. "He would count them before each round and was meticulous about where he placed each one in his bag." He took a bite of his black raspberry-coffee cone.

Mimi nodded in agreement. "That's right, he was."

"I'll look again later to see what's missing," NT said.

"Good idea. Let me know what you find out," BB said.

They each finished their ice cream in thoughtful silence. When everyone was done, Mimi said, "Shall we?" and rose from the bench.

"Yup."

BB started Blackie's engine and the low, guttural rumbling caught the attention of those close by. He cranked the car into reverse, backed out of the spot, and headed toward home.

* * *

NT stayed behind in the garage after his grandfather had parked the car. On his way out, BB turned and asked NT, "You coming in?"

"In a sec. I want to check out Clay's golf bag."

"Sure thing. Then I'll say good night now."

"Good night, BB." NT opened the sports closet and dragged out Clay's golf bag. *How did Hoot carry this thing? It weighs a ton.* The clubs banged against each other, their sound reminding NT of bottles clanging together. He pulled out the driver and gave it a small swing. It was much longer than NT's driver. He felt wistful. *I'll bet Clay crushed the ball. I wish I could have played golf with him.* NT returned the driver to the bag and glanced at the rest of the clubs. It

A Letter for Hoot

looked like a full set, but he wanted to be certain. "One, two…"

Mimi called from inside the house. "NT, your father's on the phone!"

"Be right in!" NT finished his count. *Yup, only thirteen clubs. Looks like an iron is missing.* He pushed the bag back into the closet, shut the door, and ran inside the house.

30

The morning was muggy and soupy, thick with a blanket of gray clouds that trapped the humidity and stifled the air. Sheriff Taylor's mood matched the dull day as he drove through town on his way to the police station. He barely slept a wink the night before, as his mind had been on full throttle after what he had heard first from Hoot, then from Daisy. He checked his watch. *I have a few minutes before I need to be at the station. A cup of strong coffee from Wink's might help clear the fog from my brain.*

"Mornin', Sheriff. The regular?" Pete called from behind the counter.

"Mornin', Pete. Yes, please."

"Here you go. Fresh brewed." He handed Sheriff Taylor his cup.

"You've got the best coffee in town. Have a great day now."

"You too! Don't let the heat get to you," Pete replied with a smile.

The sheriff went out to his car to enjoy his coffee. The richness of the first sip jolted him. It slid down his throat and he instantly felt better. Tubman Avenue was starting to come to life. He was about to cruise past Al's Gas Station when he noticed a police car parked outside. He did a double take. *Why is there a patrol car here? One that looks just like Darman's?* He hadn't heard any calls over the police radio, so he decided to stop and see what was going on. He parked and walked through the spacious garage toward the office. He heard mumbling from inside—voices he recognized. He tried to listen, but they were speaking too softly. He poked his head into the office and said, "Mornin', fellas."

The conversation came to a grinding, awkward halt. Darman and Al glanced at each other.

"Uh, mornin' to you, Sheriff," Al responded quickly.

"Mornin', Sheriff. What are you doin' here?" Darman asked, his voice solid steel.

"I was on my way to the station when I saw your car out there. I was concerned. Is everything okay?" Sheriff Taylor asked.

"Why, sure. I stopped by here because my car was makin' a weird scraping sound," Darman replied smoothly. "And no one knows cars like Al here." The big man nodded at Al as he spoke.

Sheriff Taylor turned to Al. "I see. Did you find anything wrong, Al?"

"Well, I did just a cursory look, but saw nothin'. I recommended that Deputy Darman keep an ear out for that bangin' and bring it on back if he hears it again."

"Okay. Well, glad to hear there's no major concern with his car. I'd better be gettin' to the station. Got work to do. See you there soon?" He looked at Darman, who gave a curt nod in response.

"Good seein' ya, Sheriff!" Al called as the sheriff walked through the garage back to his car.

"You too, Al," he responded with a backhanded wave. He walked past Darman's car and glanced into the back seat. What he saw stopped him short. He stared briefly, knowing Al and Darman might be watching him. He forced himself to walk leisurely to his car where he got in and drove straight to the station.

Miss Brenda was already at work behind the front desk. "Good morning, Sheriff. You all right? You look a little—"

"Yeah, yeah. Just fine, Brenda. Got lots on my mind is all. But thanks for askin'."

"Oh, wait. You have a phone message." Brenda handed the sheriff a pink memo with a name and number written on it. "The caller said it was pretty urgent you call back as soon as you can."

Sheriff Taylor read the name and number. He thanked Brenda, walked into his office, and picked up the phone.

31

With two days remaining until the club championships, it was crunch time. NT and Daisy knew they could win, but it meant practice, practice, and more practice. They met on the range late that overcast morning. They hit balls and discussed the latest developments.

"Did you talk to your dad?"

"Yeah. I told him all about the money we saw in those golf bags. He was mad that we opened them."

"Really? Even though you told him about the money that was in them?"

"I told him everything—the voices we heard in the lot, the money pickup—everything."

NT swung his club and hit the ball clean. "Did he believe you?" Before Daisy could answer, NT admired his own shot. "Wow, I got that one."

"I guess." She shrugged. "He just sat there and stared out at nothing after I told him. Yeah, nice shot."

Daisy was clearly down, so NT tried to cheer her up. "I have another secret mission we need to go on."

"What?"

"Well, last night I was putting away the basketball and I saw Clay's golf bag."

"So?"

"I noticed there were only thirteen clubs in it."

"What does that mean? Just because you're *allowed* to play with fourteen clubs doesn't mean you *have* to, right?" Daisy said.

"That's true. But I checked to see which one was missing. It's his seven iron."

"Maybe he lost it, or it got lost?" Daisy said with a shrug.

"Remember the day at the clubhouse when we stopped in to order a sandwich? Lenny was in the back and I walked to the end of the bar to get some of their crunchy snacks? I saw a club behind the bar, and when I looked at it up close, it looked like there was a seven engraved in the toe of the club. It was also made by Titleist like all the other clubs in Clay's bag."

Daisy was focused on her swing and NT wasn't sure she was paying attention. But she was.

"And?"

"Come on. Do you think it's a coincidence that Clay's seven iron is missing and the club behind Lenny's bar is a seven iron that looks and feels exactly like the rest of the clubs in Clay's bag?"

Daisy slid her nine iron back in her bag and thought about what NT had just said. "Yeah. It is strange, actually. What did Lenny say about it before?"

"That he used to play golf, but now he likes to collect old clubs. He showed me some others too. He said he wants to hang them up in the bar to add to the décor. Whatever that means."

"Okay. When we're done here, let's go to the Grille Room and look. If we time it right, Lenny will be busy with lunch, so he won't even notice us."

"I'm in. But for now, my putting sucks. So guess where I'm going." NT wandered off to the putting green.

"Fine. We'll go soon." Daisy practiced her own putting alongside NT. When they finished, they walked toward the restaurant. Just as they passed by the pro shop, Hoot came out.

"Y'all been practicing?" he asked with a big smile.

"We did, for over an hour," said Daisy. "We're going to get some food." She set her golf bag down outside the shop and continued her way into the restaurant. "See you later."

"That's good, Daisy. Glad to know you're workin' hard." Hoot watched her go.

NT set his bag down next to Daisy's and said, "I put my putter to good use today, but I'm still—"

Hoot stopped him. "I got somethin' to tell you. Meet me in the shack at two. Don't tell anyone, including Daisy. There'll be time for that."

NT was scared by Hoot's tone. He was caught off guard. "Okay, but what's going on? Are you okay, Hoot?"

"Yes. Fine. I'll see you later. Don't be late."

"I won't."

Silverware clanked, people chattered, and ice clinked against glasses. Lunch was in full swing. NT took in the aroma of burgers and chicken sizzling on the grill. His mouth watered. He had skipped breakfast, and now his stomach was begging to be filled.

"Ooh, yum. It smells good in here," Daisy said.

"I'm going to get a burger, fries, and a chocolate shake. I need my energy before I crush you today in HORSE. I have to get my good name back after what you did to me yesterday."

"Yeah? Well, you can dream on," she answered. "Anyway, I can't play today. I have to babysit."

Lenny was hustling back and forth between the outside deck, the bar, and the kitchen.

"Look, there goes Lenny," said NT. "I don't think he saw us come in. We'll wait till he comes back, order our food, and when he goes back into the kitchen, I'll go around the bar and check that club."

"Okay, but, where is it?" Daisy scanned the area behind the bar. "I don't see it."

"No way. It has to be there somewhere." NT craned his neck to get a better look.

"Wait. Is that it? Over there?" Daisy pointed to a huge wooden cabinet filled with bottles of wine. A sole golf club stood leaning against the cabinet in the shadows.

NT could not resist. He ducked around the corner of the bar, picked up the club, and turned it upside down. He squinted to read the engraving. Sure enough, the letters *CHT* were carved into the toe of the club. He ran his finger over the initials. "It's his," he mouthed to Daisy.

"No way!" She ran over to see for herself. Just then, Lenny came in from the outside deck carrying a tray full of dirty plates and glasses. He stopped to empty the dishes into a plastic bin for the dishwasher to take back to the kitchen.

"Quick! There's Lenny. Put the club down!" NT put the club back in its place and he and Daisy walked nonchalantly around to the front of the bar.

"Hey, kids," Lenny said. "Your usual? Burgers, fries, and shakes?"

They nodded and Lenny dashed into the kitchen.

"That was close," NT said.

They wandered around the restaurant and out to the deck. Five minutes later Lenny appeared with their food. "Here you go. Enjoy."

Daisy watched Lenny walk away. "You were right. That club is definitely Clay's. Could he and Lenny have been friends and that's why he has it?"

"I have no clue," NT answered. He brainstormed the possibilities. "This is crazy. Why would Lenny have Clay's club? Do you think he knows it's his? Maybe he borrowed it. Maybe—"

Daisy stopped him. "I have no idea. None. Zip. If you think it would help, I can tell my dad." She wiped ketchup from her chin.

"That's probably a good idea. He might know why Lenny would have Clay's club," NT said.

"Okay. I'll tell him later today."

NT chomped on a fry. "Too bad we can't take the club and show it to him as proof."

Daisy tilted her head and responded matter-of-factly. "Why can't we? We'll just take it when Lenny isn't looking and then return it. He'll never miss it."

"Oh, yes he will. He really had his eye on it when I looked at it the other day," NT answered. "How about if I come over after dinner and tell him. Will you be done babysitting?"

"Yes. That's good. Come over after dinner and we can tell him together," she said.

They returned their empty plates to the Grille Room and Daisy saw the time. "Gotta go. Mom's picking me up at two to take me to the Davidson's. Those kids are bratty, but it's ice cream money. I'll see you later."

* * *

The sun had made its way high into the sky and now beat down relentlessly. Hoot was thankful he had looped the course earlier that morning and was done for the day. The other caddies were all out on the course, so he had the quiet and coolness of the shack to himself. NT would be arriving any minute. Hoot didn't have any grandkids of his own, so he enjoyed spending time with the boy, who had always shown himself to be kind, attentive, and loyal.

At precisely two o'clock, NT tapped on the door to the shack and entered. He joined Hoot at the rickety table where they made small talk.

"Sounds like you and Daisy had a good practice session?"

"Yeah, I guess," he sighed.

"What's that mean?" Hoot asked.

"My putting really sucks and it makes me not want to play."

"Now, hold on. You got a definite shot at winnin' the junior boys champs, but not with that attitude," Hoot admonished.

"I keep pushing the ball to the right, so it rolls completely off line."

"Just take a bit of a firmer grip with your left hand and make sure the back of it follows the line of your putt right to the hole. Got it?"

NT repeated the impromptu lesson. "Grip the putter more firmly with my left hand and follow the line to the hole. I'll try. Maybe you can watch me later. I hope we find out our tee times soon."

"Sure. You know I'll help. Did you ask Mr. Gates for your tee time?"

"I did, and he got really mad—he practically yelled at us."

"Maybe you just caught him on an off day."

"Maybe. But he's always in a bad mood." NT shrugged. "I think he just hates kids."

"Nah. I just think he's got a lot on his mind, is all." Hoot leaned back in his chair and eyed NT closely. "Do you have any idea why I asked you to come talk to me, Nicholas?"

"Not really. About golf? Or *Old Man and the Sea*?" NT ventured.

Hoot laughed. "No, son. None of that. I asked you here because I need your help with this." With that, he reached into his pocket and pulled out the letter Clay had written to him all those years ago.

He watched as NT's eyes followed the lines and grew wide with amazement. NT read the letter a second time and looked up at Hoot.

"Whoa. This is, like… I don't know… incredible." Then, in a hushed voice, he asked, "Where did you find it? Is it real?"

Hoot explained how he had found the letter stuck inside a book. "How it got there, I guess I'll never know."

NT was riveted. "I can't believe this. It's so cool you found it. He must have known something bad was going to happen to him one day."

"My thoughts exactly."

"But, I don't understand. What do you need my help for?"

"Well, actually, son, I need your and Miss Daisy's help. You two are gonna help get back Clay's blue notebook."

32

Sheriff Taylor sat at his desk and reflected on the phone conversation from earlier in the day. He decided to go for a run. Running helped him think, helped him focus on problems and often work through them. Yes, a run would be good, in spite of the heat.

He walked out of his office and went in the direction of the locker room to change. Along the way, he glanced in Darman's empty office. *Darman's out. After what Hoot told me, I have to find out what he could be hiding.* The sheriff backtracked and entered Darman's office. He yanked at the desk drawers, but had no luck—every drawer was locked. His eyes fell upon Darman's junk jar. He turned the jar upside down and assorted oddments fell out—paper clips, tacks, rubber bands, a chunk of blue glass, a few marbles— nothing helpful. He turned toward the file cabinet and noticed every drawer was partially open. *Why isn't the cabinet locked now, like it was the first time I checked?* He checked his watch. *Mid-afternoon. Darman's still on duty and could return at any time. I'd better be quick.* The top drawer was bulging with case files. The second drawer yielded the same. Sheriff Taylor wasn't sure if he should feel relief or anger at coming up empty-handed.

He gripped the cold metal handle of the third drawer and pulled. The drawer opened only an inch, then stopped. The sheriff yanked harder, but the drawer would not budge. He slid his fingers in and felt something like a piece of cardboard wedged inside. He grasped the cardboard with two fingers and yanked it out. He tossed the cardboard aside and pulled the drawer open. He thumbed through the files and again found nothing—that is, until he noticed a large envelope stuffed behind the folders. He picked it up and was surprised at how heavy it was. When he opened the envelope, he understood why. Inside he found ten-dollar bills—thousands of dollars' worth, he estimated—new and neatly stacked and bound with rubber bands. He also found a note pad, a piece of chipped red glass, and black and white photos. He flipped open the pad, scanned a few lines, then stuffed it in his pocket. He did the same with one of the pictures, a few ten dollar bills, and the piece of glass. He put everything else back in the envelope and returned the envelope to the drawer. *Take a breath. Get your sneakers and get the heck outside.*

Sheriff Taylor burst through the doors of the station into the summer day. He barely felt the sun scorch his head or the heat rise from the pavement and penetrate the bottoms of his sneakers. His stride was smooth, fast, and full of anger. He clutched the piece of broken glass in his right hand the entire time. He ran five miles nonstop. Exhausted and thirsty, he found himself on Twining Way, the road where NT's grandparents lived. *I could really use some water. I hope the Tysons are home.*

He slowed to a walk to cool his body down and saw Mimi working in her vegetable garden. He slipped the piece of glass into the pocket of his tee shirt and walked down the driveway to greet her. "Howdy, Mrs. Tyson. Mighty hot day to be pullin' weeds."

Mimi looked up and pushed her hair away from her face. "Well, hello, Sheriff." She looked him up and down and noticed his sweat-drenched tee shirt. "What brings you here?"

"I'm out for a run. I needed to clear my head, and runnin' does that for me," he answered.

"Running? On a day like this? Goodness, the sun will fry you like an egg! You sit down on the porch and I'll get you a drink to cool down."

Sheriff Taylor collapsed into a cushioned chair and enjoyed the cover from the sun.

Mimi appeared with a tray holding three drinks. "I brought you both water and lemonade. You look parched."

He reached for the water first and gulped the entire glass down. "Thanks, Marian. You were right. I was definitely parched. But I'll take my time and savor your homemade lemonade."

"Well, enjoy. I could use a break from the sun myself," said Mimi.

"Seems your Nicholas and my Daisy have been working hard on their golf game. I believe champs are coming up soon." He took a deep swallow of lemonade. "Now *that*'s good."

"Thank you. My secret recipe. You're right. They've been quite busy this entire summer," she said.

BB stepped onto the porch from inside. "I thought I heard a familiar voice. How are you, Sheriff? Everything okay?"

Sheriff Taylor stood and shook BB's hand. "Yes, sir. I was out for a run and before I knew it, I found myself on Twining Way. Lucky for me, Mrs. Tyson was out in the garden and offered me a drink."

"Well, it gave me an excuse to sit down," Mimi said with a chuckle. "We were saying how busy Nicholas and Daisy have been this summer."

"That's certainly the truth. Glad they're such good pals," BB replied. "I was just on my way to the garage. The LaSalle needs a good polishing."

Sheriff Taylor took advantage of the moment. "I know you take him out from time to time and you're in our annual Memorial Day parade, but I honestly don't believe I've ever seen the famous Blackie up close. Mind if I take a look?"

"Not at all. Follow me."

The coolness of the garage felt good.

BB pointed proudly at his car. "Here he is."

Sheriff Taylor walked slowly around the car and let out a low whistle. "Oh, boy. This is one spectacular car. How long have you had it?"

BB explained how his father had acquired the car in the late 1930s and eventually gave it to him and Mimi as a wedding present. "And I still have my brother Clay's Jag."

"I remember that Jag. Another beautiful car," the sheriff said.

"It is. I could never bring myself to sell it. It's one of the last things of his that I have."

"Can I see it?"

"Sure," BB said, and he led the way to the back of the garage. "I keep it protected under this tarp."

They lifted the tarp carefully and the sheriff stood back to take a better look. "Wow. It sure is a stunner," he said.

"Yup. Clay always treated this car like it was his child."

"It's as clean as when..." He let his words drift off so as not to upset BB.

"That's okay, Sheriff. Don't tell Nicholas, but my plan is to give it to him someday."

The two men stood admiring the car until Mimi's voice broke their reverie.

"Willy, George is on the phone!" Her voice carried through the garage.

"Be right there!" BB yelled. "I'll be right back. I've been expecting this call."

"No rush."

BB went into the house to take his phone call.

Sheriff Taylor removed the piece of red glass from his pocket and walked to the back of the Jaguar. He squatted down and gently inserted the glass where the taillight was broken. It was a puzzle-perfect fit.

33

NT looked at Hoot as if he had nine heads. "You want me and Daisy to get Clay's notebook? Seriously? Shouldn't *you*?"

Hoot was not about to tell NT what had happened to him in the locker room, as that would only frighten him. "No, I can't. But I have a plan."

"A plan?" NT could not believe Hoot had already thought things through.

"That's right. Now, listen. That fancy end-of-summer party is on Saturday. As you know, it's a big ole event. Everyone will be busy eating, drinking, and dancing. I'll be parking cars—which means I'll be right nearby to help you."

"Help us? Why can't you just do it yourself?"

"Hold on. I'll get to that. Now, when it starts to get dark, you and Daisy will steal away into the locker room and get the book. No one will miss you. You'll enter the side door by the second green, find Clay's locker with the secret drawer, and get the book."

NT was incredulous at the thought of him and Daisy skulking into a dark locker room, locating a locker that supposedly had a secret drawer, and finding Clay's notebook. "The kitchen windows overlook that green. Someone will see us," he countered.

"Son, no one will be lookin' out the windows on the busiest night of the year. Trust me. Plus, I'll be keeping an eye out from the parking lot." Hoot's deep voice resonated confidence.

"Okay. So, say we find the locker, the drawer, and the notebook. Then what?"

"Well, you take the book, hightail it out of the locker room, and meet me back here in the shack. Simple as that. And if I know your red-headed friend, she'll love every minute of it."

NT could not argue with that. "You're right about Daisy. She will." NT thought a moment longer. "I guess we could… I'm going over to her house later. Can I tell her?"

"You can, but make sure no one hears you. Got it?"

NT nodded. He stood to leave and gave Hoot a salute. "I do. But I think I'll play a few holes before going home. I need all the practice I can get."

"Out you go, then. Forget playin' any holes. Go right to that putting green." Hoot patted NT on the shoulder.

For the remainder of the afternoon and through dinner with his grandparents, NT was barely able to focus on anything other than Hoot's decision to put him and Daisy in charge of getting back Clay's notebook. The plan seemed easy enough. He couldn't wait to tell Daisy. And he still had to tell Sheriff Taylor about the missing golf club. As soon as he finished dinner, he raced out the door.

"Be back before dark," yelled Mimi after him.

"I will." NT hopped on his bike and sped off. A car parked down the street from NT's grandparent's house pulled slowly and quietly into the roadway and followed NT all the way to Daisy's house. In his excitement, NT never noticed the car. He swung into the driveway at the Taylor's house and the car continued down the road another tenth of a mile, then turned around, parked, and waited.

NT threw his bike down and raced up the stone steps to the front door. He rang the doorbell.

Daisy's brother Brett opened the door. In sing-song voice, he said loudly enough for the neighbors to hear, "Ooh, Daisy, your little boyfriend is here!"

"Shut up! God, you are so annoying!" Daisy pushed her brother out of the way and walked out the front door. NT smirked at Brett and followed her.

"Mom and Dad are out back."

"Hey, before we talk to your father," NT whispered, "I have to tell you what Hoot told me today."

"Something bad?"

"No. More like crazy, but really important."

"This sounds super serious."

"It is."

They walked to the top of the driveway and NT told Daisy all about Hoot's plan for them to retrieve the book.

"Geez. Are you serious? It sounds kinda scary." Daisy rubbed her hands together and looked at NT with a devilish grin. "And fun!"

"I knew you'd like this escapade. But we need to keep it secret. Got it?"

"I'm in!"

The friends rounded the corner to the patio. The sun had started to set and Daisy commented, "Look, a sky full of red raspberry, sweet lemon, and orange sherbet."

NT rolled his eyes at Daisy then greeted her parents. "Hi, Mr. and Mrs. Taylor."

"Good evenin' to you, Nicholas Tucker. How are you?"

"I'm good. How are you?"

"We're doing very well on this lovely evening," Mrs. Taylor responded. "But, I'm sorry to say, it's time for me to go inside and make a couple of phone calls." She sighed and rose from her seat. "Enjoy this gorgeous sunset for me."

"We will."

Without warning, Daisy came out with it. "Dad, NT has something to tell you."

NT gave Daisy a what-the-heck? look, but knew there was no going back.

Sheriff Taylor turned in his seat. "What's up, Nick?"

NT organized his thoughts and told the sheriff about finding Clay's golf bag and about the club—the seven iron—that was missing from it. He ended by saying, "I'm pretty sure the missing club is sitting behind the bar at the club restaurant."

Sheriff Taylor grew more serious with Nick's every word. His reaction was barely perceptible, but a small cloud appeared to have passed over his face. In a solemn tone, he said, "Thank you, Nick. I appreciate you telling me."

Daisy had never heard her father sound so somber.

"I hope I did the right thing."

"Oh, you did, son. You certainly did."

The driver of the car parked in the street watched as NT left Daisy's and rode in the direction of his grandparents' house. The man put the vehicle in drive and followed him.

34

The day of the Cascades Golf Club Junior Club Championship had finally arrived. Mr. Gates had called Shady Acres the night before to give NT his tee time. "You'll tee off at nine forty-five. Boys and girls will alternate teeing off ten minutes apart."

"What's Daisy's tee time?"

"She follows your group."

NT thanked Mr. Gates for calling. He was surprised the head pro didn't bark at him the way he usually did.

NT rose two hours before his tee time, got dressed, and wolfed down a hearty breakfast of eggs, scrapple, toast, and orange juice. He felt flutters in his stomach as he visualized how he would play each hole. Overall, he was confident about his game and knew he stood a strong chance of winning. *I just need to hit my tee shots into the fairways and not into the woods.* The other boys in his division were equally skilled, but staying calm, cool, and collected was key to success.

"I'm assuming Daisy will be ready when we pick her up in a few minutes?" Mimi asked as she entered the kitchen.

"She will be. I'll text her to tell her we're leaving."

Daisy was waiting in her driveway when Mimi pulled in. She got into the back seat beside NT, who noticed she was dressed in her power colors—black shorts, a red shirt, and a white baseball hat.

Daisy's belly was in knots. Her nervousness was apparent by her incessant chatter the whole way to Cascades.

"Hey, calm down," NT said. "You normally talk a lot, but, wow, you're going on and on," he said to her quietly.

"I just really want to win and I feel like I'm gonna puke," Daisy replied. The tense bouncing of her right knee further affirmed her anxiety.

"I know. I'm a little nervous, too. Just remember Hoot's tips, like keeping your head still, taking deep breaths, and letting the clubs do the work."

"I get it, but that's not always easy. Oh, my God, I'm so nervous." She sighed and looked out the window.

"I was watching the golf channel last night, and some guy said that when he was first learning to play, he used to pick a song to play in his head and that helped him keep the rhythm of his swing even."

"Really? I wonder if it also helps stop your heart from pounding."

"Try it. It can't hurt."

At the club, NT and Daisy carried their bags to the front of the pro shop while Mimi and BB parked the car. NT checked the clock outside the pro shop door and saw they had plenty of time to warm up. Mr. Gates required all players to be on the porch by nine twenty, at which time he would address rules, pace of play, and answer any questions the players might have.

BB and NT rode to the practice range in one cart while Mimi and Daisy drove in another. Hoot was already on the range waiting for them. Just seeing him calmed NT and Daisy's jingly nerves.

"Y'all ready?"

"Yup. A little on edge, but ready," Daisy said.

"Me too," NT agreed.

Hoot stared down at his two protégés. "Listen to me. You both have the swing, the mental toughness, and the patience to win this thing. I know you can do it," he said. "Remember, you're gonna hit some bad shots out there—that's the nature of this wonderful, crazy game. But don't go beatin' yourselves up over 'em. You have worked real hard for this, so just go out there and trust your swing." NT and Daisy looked at each other and felt bolstered by Hoot's vote of confidence. "One more thing," he added. "The most important of all? Have fun." Hoot gave each a wink and a pat on the back.

"Yes, sir. Thanks, Hoot," Daisy said. NT seconded Daisy's words with a nod.

On the porch, Gates ran down the rules and reiterated that all competitors had to be finished in the given time frame. "Since there are four foursomes playing, we expect you to finish your round in the time limit of four hours and thirty minutes." His words were more of a command than a statement. Gates also reminded the players that the maximum stroke count per hole was double par plus one. "For example," he said, "if you get into trouble on a par four, your maximum score will be a nine." He asked if anyone had any questions, which no one did. "Good luck, kids." The players all dispersed to the first tee.

NT watched Daisy as she colored her golf balls. "Feeling less nervous?"

"A little. Once I get out there, I'll be okay," she responded. "And look, my golf balls have red and pink hearts so they'll be easy to identify. I also have a song going through my head like you suggested, but I'm not gonna tell you what it is. So don't ask."

"You'll tell me later, I know." Daisy gave NT a wide grin. "Okay, I'm off. Good luck! Play well," he said.

"Same to you. Have fun! See you later for ice cream."

* * *

After eleven holes, NT was only four shots over par. He had parred the first five holes but then had a few bogeys. Regardless, he felt in total control of his game. His opponents were hitting their shots all over the map and reacted to their poor play with outbursts of profanity. NT did the smart thing and ignored their moaning and groaning, as they were not fully out of contention. He stayed in his own zone and focused on each shot. By the time they were down to the final four holes—NT's favorites—he had a healthy four-shot lead. He felt confident he could make par on these last few holes, maybe even bogey one, and still cruise to victory.

Trouble reared its ugly head on the fifteenth hole—a one-hundred-and-sixty-yard par three. NT usually parred this hole every time he played. He dropped his bag on the tee box and looked for his four iron, the club he always trusted to land his ball on the green. He looked again. No four iron. He checked his bag a third time. The club was missing. *Where the heck is my club?* He mentally retraced his steps and realized he had left it on an earlier hole. Panic took over his whole body. *Okay, take a deep breath. Hit your five iron and hope for bogey if you don't land on the green.* NT took a practice swing and teed up the ball. His heart was hammering. He breathed deeply then swung. He knew at impact that his back swing was off and his angle of attack entirely too sharp, which caused his club to hit the ground before it hit the ball. *Oh, my God. I totally chunked it! Idiot!* The ball sat in thick rough barely seventy yards off the tee box.

NT's opponents each hit their shots. Only one landed on the green. NT walked to his ball, pulled out his sand wedge and figured out his next shot. The flag was on the front downslope of the green. He would hit his ball to the right of the flag and let it run left toward the hole. *This time, choke down on the club and make sure it hits the ball first.* With the ball in the back of his stance, he swung. His club swooshed through the grass. The denseness of the rough caused the club to turn left and pull the ball smack into the side of an enormous sand bunker the regular golfers referred to as Jaws.

The face of the bunker stood at least nine feet high. *Oh, great.* From where he stood, NT figured he'd splash his ball out to be on the green in three and then putt for bogey or even double bogey. Upon closer inspection, he realized his ball was stuck in the face of Jaws like a fried egg, just six inches off the green. *So much for that idea.* But now, the face of the bunker reared up at him like the shark after which it was named. His double bogey was quickly turning into double par plus one—a seven. He stared in bewilderment at his ball. All he could think of was having to tell his grandparents, Hoot, and Daisy that he had lost the championship—not because he was outplayed, but because he was careless and had left his four iron on the course somewhere behind him.

"NT, come on! You've gotta hit," called one opponent from above the gaping face of the bunker.

"I know, dude. Calm down. This shot sucks," he responded. If he approached his ball from above, the ball might dislodge and roll down to the bottom of the trap, costing NT a one-stroke penalty. His only choice was to hike up the face of the trap from the bottom. With his right foot firmly dug into the sand behind the ball, and his left foot three feet above on the edge of the green, he leaned his weight into his left side in an awkward side-lunge position. Sweat rolled down his face and stung his eyes. He blinked hard to alleviate the burning. He choked way down on the club, took a deep breath, and chopped at the ball with all his might. Sand blew into his eyes and mouth as he struggled to maintain his balance. He watched in horror as the ball popped straight up, arced behind him, and landed at his feet in the bottom of Jaws. *This can't be happening. No way.* But it was. *Come on, NT. Get this ball out and close to the pin.* Fear of losing smothered him. *Stay calm. Remember, one shot at a time.* Luckily, he had a flat lie in the bunker which would allow him to hit a clean shot. He dug his feet into the soft sand, swung, and hit the ball over the massive face of Jaws. Bam!

"Whoa, dude!" said one of the boys waiting on the green, "You hit the flag stick!"

NT almost cried in relief when he heard that.

"Bad luck, man," said another of his opponents with a laugh. "It rolled against the rough. What took you so long?"

Seriously? Are they really asking me that? "Because if I moved the ball while trying to get a stance, I'd have to take a one-stroke penalty." *Moron.*

At that, the first boy pulled out his United States Golf Association rule book, thumbed through it to find the rule, and read, "According to USGA rule 18-2A, you're right."

"Yeah. No kidding. You guys should know the rules to this game too." NT felt as though he had been playing the same hole for three hours. His opponents naturally took the opportunity to laugh at his misfortune, which only fueled his fury. A routine chip shot landed his ball close to the pin, though that was no consolation. *Crap! I'm lying five. I have to make this putt. God, a triple bogey. There goes the championship.* He marked his ball while the two other boys on the green did the same.

The fourth player had also hit his tee shot into the thick rough. It was his turn to play. He lined up his chip and hit it. Click! His hit was clean and had enough loft for the ball to escape the gripping rough. The four boys watched the ball plop onto the green at the crest of the undulation. For what seemed like an eternity, the ball rolled languidly down the wide slope of the green, its dimples turning over perfectly. The ball's line was perfect. It clinked against the metal flag pole and found the bottom of the cup.

"No way! It went in! It went in! For a birdie!" The boy was ecstatic. "I guess that puts me even with you now, huh, NT?" He high-fived the other two boys first then went to NT with his hand raised.

NT returned the high-five, but inside, a tornado of sadness, anger, and despair raged. He tapped his own ball in the hole and wrote down a score of double par. Out of nowhere, Santiago's struggles with the marlin and the heinous sharks popped into his head. *Santiago fought back against sharks and survived. So can I.* "Yeah, you're even with me now, but don't get used to it."

* * *

Daisy played solid, steady golf through the first nine holes. She played with the same ball the entire time—the one she had colored with red hearts. She had been scoring well and did not want to jinx her game by changing to the ball with pink hearts. One of her three playing partners was also playing well, and Daisy figured they were either tied or very close in score. *Okay, Daisy, just keep steady and calm.*

She was on the fourteenth hole—one she loved—and saw NT's group up ahead, approaching the fifteenth green. She focused on her tee shot and crushed it down the fairway. On her next shot, the approach shot to the green, she fell short into the rough. Another girl's approach shot hit the green, while the other two girls' shots landed nowhere near the green. When it was Daisy's turn again, she chipped up to within three feet of the flag and marked her ball.

After they holed out, Daisy noted her par score and looked ahead to the fifteenth green. Her heart sank when she saw NT's awkward stance to get his ball out of Jaws. *Oh no, that's not good.* She saw him hack into the side of the Jaws and shoot the ball into the air and backwards. *Oh, God. Poor NT.* She next watched as NT's ball ricocheted off the flag stick and into the rough. *Oh, man, he must be lying at least four shots. NT's lost his lead.* His shoulders were slumped and his head hung low as he plodded off the green toward the sixteenth tee box. He glanced over his left shoulder at Jaws, which seemed to be licking its chops in triumph. He wiped his face with a towel and dabbed his eyes. *Is he crying? Oh, no. No, NT! Maybe he'll look back and I'll give him a thumb's up.* He didn't.

Daisy had to maintain her focus. If she could birdie two of the last four holes, she'd win. Especially since two of the other girls had just bogeyed the fourteenth hole. But she could not avoid sneaking a glance at NT when he teed off. She watched as he wound up like a top and striped the ball down the middle. He picked up his bag and marched down the fairway. *Phew!* Daisy got her mind back on her own game.

Two of the girls struggled on the fifteenth hole and it took the foursome close to fifteen minutes to play this one hole. Daisy bogeyed the hole, as did one other girl. Daisy was working hard to stay focused and not let their slow play take her out of her rhythm. *Okay, three holes to go. I'm certain I can get two birdies. Come on, Daisy, focus, focus, focus.*

The sixteenth hole was a long, uphill par four. Five large sand traps dotted the left side of the fairway like blobs of paint. To the right sat lovely, evenly spaced homes, one of which belonged to the Hardy sisters. White stakes in the ground at the back of each property indicated two things: the property line of the home and every golfer's nightmare—out-of-bounds territory. Daisy considered sixteen one of the easier holes to play because she possessed great length off the tee. All she needed was to hit her drive up the middle, get on the green in regulation, and make a birdie putt or, worse case, an easy two-putt par. Simple—or so it seemed. The three other girls all hit decent tee shots. It was now Daisy's turn.

She teed up her ball, picked a landing spot in the distance, and took her stance. On the downswing of her club, she felt it. A bug flew into her ear at impact and caused her to flip her driver over her head and onto the tee box behind her. She danced around and smacked at her ear like a crazy person. The intruder eventually buzzed off. Daisy turned to her playing partners who told her firmly that her ball had flown out of bounds along the right. The rules dictated she hit a second tee shot. She pulled the ball with pink hearts from her pocket and teed it up. She shook her head, steadied herself, then hit. This one also flew to the right. *Oh, no! No!* Daisy's opponents seemed convinced that this shot also landed out of bounds. Daisy turned on them and said, "Nope. No way. Totally disagree. I don't *need* to hit a third tee shot."

Her brain felt like scrambled eggs and her heart hammered in anger and frustration. She trudged down the fairway along the path her tee shots had taken. *What just happened? I totally screwed up! I totally just blew my first shot at winning the champs.* Tears stung her eyes, bile bubbled in her throat, and her head throbbed.

* * *

The Hardy sisters loved watching "Championship Saturday," as they called it, and reminiscing about the times they competed in different sporting events. Championship Saturday always started early for the sisters. They baked a batch of oatmeal cookies, stirred up sweet lemonade, and made peanut butter and jelly sandwiches—sans the crust— for the competitors, who would start to pass by at about one o'clock. They layered a large tray with the cookies, sandwiches, and lemonade, and placed it on a card table just inside the white property marker for their backyard. Cordie made a sign and wrote in large blue letters "Please Help Yourselves, Children. And Good Luck!" She even drew a golf bag on the sign as decoration.

When everything was ready, Cordie and Minnie plunked themselves down in lawn chairs in their pristine yard and watched the players come through. Succotash snored loudly at the sisters' feet and a huge pair of binoculars rested on the ground between their chairs. They were, of course, rooting for their favorites—NT and Daisy.

NT's drive from the sixteenth tee box landed in the fairway, near where the Hardy sisters were seated. Cordie and Minnie clapped as NT walked toward his ball. The noise woke Succotash, who snorted at being roused from his nap.

"Well, you sure hit that one, young man," Cordie noted. "If that shot is any indication of how you're playing, keep it going."

"Yeah, don't let that fool you. I need all the luck I can get because I just tripled fifteen. I suck," NT said, and shook his bag off his shoulder.

Minnie admonished NT for his negative attitude. "You banish that thought from your head and your heart, Nicholas Tucker. You are a Tyson, and Tysons never quit. Do you think your grandfather utters such nonsense if he botches one hole? And your great uncle? Do you think he carried on so? Certainly not. You can do this. Get your head straight and play your game. A negative attitude will get you nowhere fast, understand?"

"Yes, ma'am."

"That's better. Now, have a sandwich and a couple of cookies."

NT knew Minnie was right. He had had one bad hole and knew he could more than make up for it. "Thank you. I'll do my best, and thanks for the snack."

"Good luck and have fun!" they called out as NT continued down the fairway.

Minnie looked through her binoculars and saw Daisy on the tee box. When Daisy slapped at her head and jumped all around, she exclaimed, "My lord, what is that child doing?"

Cordie grabbed the binoculars from her sister. "What do you mean? I don't see—"

Thunk!

She was interrupted by the sound of a ball dropping nearby. The first ball was soon followed by a second one that landed about fifteen yards to the left of the first.

Cordie peered through the binoculars again and saw Daisy. "Oh, dear. Our little redhead does not look happy," she noted to her sister.

Minnie looked and saw Daisy lumber sadly down the fairway, eyes downcast. "Well, we're about to find out what's going on," she said.

Daisy approached and dumped her bag on the ground with a thud. She wiped her face and looked at her two fans. Her sad eyes tore at the Hardy sisters' heart strings.

"Daisy, honey, what's wrong? Not playing well?" Minnie asked.

Daisy practically wailed, "I was, until that bug flew in my ear just as I was hitting my tee shot and I know it went out of bounds and then I hit another one and *they* told me to hit *another* tee shot because they think the second one went out too!" She paused for a breath. "If they're right, I could be lying five on the easiest hole on the course! Now I'm totally out of contention for winning." She sniffled.

Minnie and Cordie frowned in confusion at each other and then at Daisy. Minnie said, "Daisy, dear, you're mistaken. Both of your tee shots are right over there." She pointed to the rough a short distance in front of their chairs.

"What? Really? Are you kidding? I could've sworn I sliced them out of bounds," Daisy responded.

"I saw you tee off, twice, and heard both thuds when your balls landed. I didn't understand why you hit two, but, then again, given your crazy dance up there, I figured something must've happened. Anyway, the tee shots we heard are yours because your opponents are in the sand trap and the rough on the other side. You're fine. Both balls are in bounds."

"Oh, my God. Really?" Daisy's face lit up with a smile. "Thank you!" she exclaimed.

The other girls came to see what was going on. The Hardy sisters explained what they had seen, then offered refreshments. The four competitors looked at the golf balls that had settled into the deep rough. The ball closest to where the Hardy sisters were seated had red hearts on it.

"Here's my first tee shot," Daisy said. The other girls saw a red heart through the blades of grass and had no choice but to concur. They each took a handful of cookies and a cup of lemonade, and walked back to their tee shots. Cordie and Minnie seized the opportunity to give their second pep talk of the day.

"All right, young lady, take advantage of the situation," Cordie said. "Keep focused and calm. We have no doubt you can win this. You're athletic, tough, and a real fighter. Now, you go and get yourself settled. We'll see you later at the party and watch you hoist that trophy!"

Daisy flashed a smile and expressed her thanks once again. She chose her club, walked to her ball, and let it go. The ball shot out like a rocket and spun to a dead stop about ten feet from the pin.

The Hardy sisters cheered. "Woohoo! That's our Daisy! You go, girl!"

* * *

With two pars down and only the daunting eighteenth hole to play, NT held onto a one-stroke lead. Without question, the eighteenth hole was the most difficult and demanding hole of the course. The fairway was narrow and loaded with traps, and Martin's creek serpentined through the base of the fairway. Junior boy and men golfers had to manage over four hundred yards from tee to green on this long, par four hole. Because of its length, the hole was a par five for junior girls and women. On the flip side, it was a spectacular and beautiful finishing hole.

NT knew that two or three solid shots would put him in position to hold the trophy. Everyone in his group hit the fairway with his drive. The hardest shot loomed next. Martin's creek babbled at the bottom of the sloping hill in front of the green. Like a witch's finger, it beckoned and dared NT and his opponents to try to hit their shots over her deep running waters. NT watched as his competitors each gave it a go. The first two came up short of the creek and avoided a certain disastrous, watery fate. The third player concerned NT the most. He trailed NT by only one shot. *If he makes it over the creek, I'll be forced to go for it too.*

NT watched his opponent choose a club, take a practice swing, and hit. The click of the ball off the club face told NT that his opponent had struck it perfectly. The ball sailed against the blue sky, poised for a soft landing on the other side of the creek. NT's hopes of a victory diminished as he watched. *Oh, man. That ball is gonna be perfect.* Then he heard a plopping sound. *What was that?*

"Aw, man!" his opponent moaned. The boy smacked his club on the ground. "I thought I hit that perfectly. Stupid wind must have kicked up."

NT stood on his tiptoes and looked down at the creek. He envisioned the ball splashing into the water and settling into the creek bed. Though he felt his opponent's pain, he now breathed a little easier. Time to visualize his next shot and find his line.

"You're not gonna lay up to the creek, are you? If you're gonna win, at least win with style!" the boy said to him.

NT ignored the comment. He knew better than be sucked into head games put forth by his opponents. This was the championship, and he wanted it so badly he could taste it. He was not about to do anything risky and had to calculate all his options. *The lay-up distance is tricky because I'm pretty close to the creek. The firmness of the fairway could make my ball roll into the creek if I don't hit it flush. My only smart play is to go for it.* He pulled out his beloved hybrid club and took a practice swing, then addressed the ball. Hoot's voice spoke to him loud and clear, "Remember, play smart and have fun out there. It's only a game."

NT let go a perfect, clean swing. The ball flew as if it had been shot from a cannon. It easily crossed the creek and took a single hop onto the green. The crowd of spectators gathered around the green erupted into loud applause.

"Wow! You killed that ball!" NT's opponents cried. "Totally awesome shot, dude!" With high fives all around, this time NT was happy to return their compliments. At that moment, he knew the championship was his.

The walk down the hill to the bridge and across the creek to the green was unforgettable. *This is the same fairway, bridge, and creek that Clay and BB crossed when they walked to their victories.* The hair on NT's arms and neck prickled at the thought. From the green, he saw Mimi and BB sitting at their regular table on the porch. He gave them a quick wave and they gave him a knowing nod in return.

The foursome putted out, shook hands, and went to the scoring table beside the green to turn in their cards to the head pro. After that, NT flashed his grandparents a million-watt smile, which they returned. He signed his card and handed it to Mr. Gates.

Gates quickly tallied NT's card and said, "You sure played with fire on that shot, didn't you."

NT was speechless at the compliment. He nodded then went to join his grandparents, where he plopped down in a chair at their table.

"Congratulations, my boy," BB said as he shook NT's hand. "That was quite a shot you hit across the creek."

"Not to mention a brave one," Mimi added.

"Thanks," was all NT could muster in response. He leaned back in his chair and shook his head.

"Are you all right?" Mimi asked.

He removed his hat and rubbed his face. "I don't know how you and Clay did this every year," NT said to BB. "The pressure and intensity was brutal. Every shot, every putt counted and just one bad decision could have cost me a ton." He let out a big sigh of exhaustion.

A waiter came and placed a large chocolate milkshake in front of NT. That got his attention. "Thanks!" He took a large slurp and actually enjoyed the brain freeze. "I wonder how Daisy is doing," NT said. "She was sooo nervous this morning."

"Any idea?" BB asked.

"She was three strokes up when we crossed paths on the twelfth hole," NT said. "I hope she kept that going."

"Speak of the devil," Mimi said. She pointed to the crest of the eighteenth hole where Daisy was marching along.

"Oh, no! She's marching. She only does that when she's really mad. This isn't good," NT remarked. Then, under his breath he begged, "Come on, Daisy, please be winning."

"Perhaps she's just very focused, dear," Mimi suggested.

"I hope so," he said.

Daisy played her second shot safely by laying up in front of the creek. She drew out a wedge and hit a gorgeous, arcing shot onto the green about thirty feet from the pin.

NT was oblivious to the pounding of his heart. He was truly nervous for her.

She nudged her putt to within a foot of the hole and knocked the ball in for par. The other girls putted out and the foursome shook each other's hands. Daisy could no longer contain her excitement. She pulled off her baseball hat, threw it in the air, and raised her arms in victory. The look on her face was one of pure elation and emotion. NT, BB, and Mimi smiled when they realized she had won for the girls. NT stood and gave her a standing ovation. He was the only one on the porch to do so, but he didn't care.

Near the scoring table, Daisy gave her mom and dad a big hug. Sheriff Taylor had snuck some time off from work to watch his daughter finish. Even two of her brothers were there, and NT laughed when they picked her up and swung her around. NT felt pride and a tug in his chest when he saw Daisy share a tender family moment. Deep inside, he wished his own mother and father had been there to watch him win, but when he looked at Mimi and BB, he knew they loved him just as much as his parents did. The events of the day made NT's summer complete, or so he thought.

After five minutes, Daisy appeared on the porch.

"Congratulations, Daisy!" Mimi said and gave her a hug. BB shook her hand and patted her on the back. And, in their own awkward way, the two friends gave each other a quick hug.

Daisy sat down next to NT. "Well?" she asked with wide eyes.

NT scrunched his brow. "Well what?"

"What happened to you?"

NT hung his head low. Daisy looked at Mimi and BB with troubled eyes and shook her head. "Oh, NT, I'm so sorry."

He raised his head and with a big smile said, "Ha ha! Kidding! I won too!"

"What? You had me thinking you lost!"

"Got you good, didn't I?"

Daisy socked NT in the arm and they high-fived. Magically, a second chocolate shake appeared and Daisy took a long, slurpy sip. She turned to NT and said, "Care to guess which song I was thinking of when I played?"

"Geez, knowing you, it could be anything," he answered.

"Ha ha. Seriously, take a guess. It's really famous," she said.

"Hmm, let me think." NT rubbed his chin. "The Rocky theme, 'Eye of the Tiger?'"

"Nope. Try again."

"I have no idea," he said.

"Here's a hint. It could be for both of us."

"'Don't Stop Believin' by Journey," NT ventured.

"Nope. Good guess though."

"I give up, Daisy. We could be here all day."

With that, Daisy stood and belted out the chorus from Queen's most famous song. "We are the champions. We are the champions. No time for losers, 'cause we are the champions... of the world!" NT laughed out loud. "Pretty cool huh, considering we both won. Right?"

"I totally agree," he said.

The two friends downed the last of their milkshakes and clinked their glasses in a happy toast.

35

The end-of-summer gala at Cascades Golf Club was *the* social event of the season. NT could hardly wait for the party. He'd be getting his golf trophy as well as his name engraved on the plaque that hung on the wall in the clubhouse. Yet, none of that compared to getting what he considered to be the *real* trophy—Clay's blue notebook.

NT and his grandparents cruised through town in the LaSalle, and NT felt like he was on top of the world. BB and Mimi were dressed up, as was NT in khaki pants and a blue dress shirt. The valet parking attendants practically drooled when they saw BB pull up in Blackie. But BB wasn't about to let anyone else park his car. He let Mimi and NT out at the front door then drove off to park the car himself.

Two massive white tents in front of the clubhouse reflected the late day sun. White, green, and blue balloons were tied to the tops of the tent support poles. The clubhouse porch was equally spirited, with each round table decorated in a white tablecloth with alternating blue and green napkins. Vases in the center of each table held bouquets of pink and white carnations, and grills located on and around the porch signaled the barbequed food to come.

BB caught up with Mimi and NT, and together they strolled to the party where lighthearted sounds of a Dixieland jazz band greeted them. Mimi bobbed her head to the rhythm of enthusiastic, uplifting notes being played on a trumpet and piano. The porch was filled with people decked out in their summer best, ready to enjoy the evening.

NT ordered his usual chocolate shake, then looked around for Daisy. He did not see her—not at first, anyway.

He then did a double take when he saw the girl who walked onto the porch wearing a white lace dress. Her tan arms were highlighted, and her normally wild hair cascaded over her shoulders in softly tamed waves that were crowned by a ring of daisies. A lightning bolt sizzled and crackled right through NT. Was this really Daisy? His summer friend, looking like that? He could not take his eyes off her.

"Here's your shake, kid." The waiter's voice shook NT out of his trance. "She your girl?" the waiter asked with a wink.

"Oh. Uh, no," NT stumbled. He was still staring at Daisy. "She's just a friend."

Daisy approached NT and said, "What are you staring at?"

"Uh, nothing. You look, um, nice... different." NT tried not to sound too surprised.

Daisy scrunched her brow and said, "Thanks... I think."

Before dinner, head pro Gates took the microphone to congratulate the junior club championship winners and award everyone their trophies. NT and Daisy accepted their trophies with pride and big smiles. "Again," said Gates, "congratulations to our junior winners, and may they never lose their love for the game. I'm being told now that dinner is served. Please help yourselves whenever you're ready."

On their way to the buffet line Daisy and NT ran into the Hardy sisters. Minnie Hardy gushed over them. "There are those adorable little champions! Congratulations to you both for winning the champs. It's always wonderful to see the next generation of golfers grow up."

"Thanks, Miss Hardy," NT responded.

"Are you going to be dancing up a storm tonight? I hear they have a young, hip band playing later. It's some crazy name, Big R and the Cat Paws? Of course, we old farts will be in bed long before they start," she said with a laugh. "Plus, little Succotash needs his nightly walk."

Daisy stifled a laugh and said, "Um, we might."

"You children have fun!" The sisters floated away into the crowd. The scent of their perfume lingered well behind and caused NT to sneeze.

The two friends joined a buffet line that wound its way around the porch. Immediately in front of them was an older man accompanied by two little girls. Daisy knew the man was a retired Latin teacher. He was tall and skinny, and always wore a bow tie.

NT whispered to Daisy, "Who's that? He looks like a know-it-all."

"That's Mr. Morehouse. He used to teach Latin and he thinks he's brilliant."

As if he sensed the conversation going on behind him, Mr. Morehouse turned and spoke to NT and Daisy. "Good evening to you, Daisy Taylor and Nicholas Tucker, junior club champions," he said. He looked down at them through horn-rimmed glasses. "I'd like you to meet my twin granddaughters, Ashley and Rachel. They are both future golfers and I thought it would be nice for them to play with you sometime."

NT and Daisy said hello in response, but the conversation was awkward because they didn't know exactly what to say in response to a comment about playing golf with six-year-olds. To make matters worse, one of the girls had a finger up her nose.

"Rachel! How unladylike! Stop that this instant!" Mr. Morehouse reprimanded his granddaughter, and was clearly embarrassed, as if the little girl had sullied his academic reputation.

Daisy and NT did not dare look at each other for fear they would burst out laughing. After a few more minutes of awkward conversation, Mr. Morehouse and the twins reached the food. The girls said no to every food item on the table, but Mr. Morehouse filled his plate with enough food for all three and then walked off with the twins trailing behind.

"Ribs, burger, or chicken?" the server asked.

"Chicken, please."

"Same for me."

With plates piled high with food, NT and Daisy walked to their favorite seats on the wall that bordered the main driveway. The sunset was brilliant. Shades of lavender, magenta, and yellow painted the entire sky, and the light cast the first fairway in a deep, emerald green.

It was almost time to set Hoot's plan in motion. They had rehashed it a hundred times—sneak into the locker room, find locker number eighty-six, open it, grab the book, and run to the caddie shack. Simple.

"It's almost dark, but we need to wait a little more. Let's get some ice cream. By then it'll be dark enough." On the porch, the party was in full swing with people dancing and eating and having a grand time. The Tyson and Taylor families were completely entrenched in the festivities. Daisy and NT got their cones and wandered around as they ate them. They thought it prudent that people see them among the crowd. They popped the last bites of ice cream cone into their mouths at the same time.

"Ready?" NT asked.

"Yep."

They walked casually around the driveway wall and confirmed no one was in sight. From there, they ran across the second green toward the Men's locker room. One last glance around told them they were alone—at least they thought so. A figure stepped out from behind a tree and followed them.

NT lugged open the wooden door to the locker room and they stepped inside.

Daisy wrinkled her nose. "It's dark in here and it smells like my brothers' rooms."

"I brought a small flashlight in case we need it. Let's just find what we're here for and get out," NT responded. He felt nervous.

"A flashlight. I'm impressed, Sherlock," Daisy teased.

They walked through the cavernous locker room and passed row upon row of tall lockers. Daisy's sandals click-clacked on the floor, so she yanked them off to be as quiet as possible. NT kept the flashlight in his pocket because the light from the exit sign overhead helped them read the locker numbers. Within minutes, they were standing in front of locker number eighty-six—Clay's locker.

Daisy rubbed her arms and said, "God, this place is creepy."

NT held his breath and pulled firmly on the door. Aside from a layer of dust and a small spider, the locker was empty. The flashlight would now come in handy. He clicked it on and examined the base of the locker. "There's a small space underneath." He reached in, felt the drawer, and pulled it out. They had struck gold. Clay's blue notebook lay face up in the drawer. He blew the dust off the cover and stared at it.

"It's actually here!" Daisy squealed.

"Shh! Contain yourself!" said NT, and he slipped the notebook into the back pocket of his pants.

Just then, they heard a loud click. Their blood turned to ice and they looked at each other.

"Did you hear that?"

NT nodded, wide-eyed, and his skin prickled with goosebumps. Fear squeezed at their hearts. Footsteps echoed from a few rows over.

"Someone's in here!" Daisy cried.

A figure at the end of the row pivoted toward them and charged in their direction.

"Run!" NT yelled.

Fear propelled them through the locker room and out across the second green toward the parking lot. The asphalt hurt Daisy's feet, but there was no time for her to put her sandals back on, so she threw them aside. They sprinted across the parking lot and deep into the woods. Blindly, they ran through branches and bushes that clawed at them. Lungs on fire, chests heaving, they longed to stop. Amid oddly shaped shadows, the moon emitted enough light for them to follow the small path to the shallow part of Martin's Creek. NT plunged in, grabbed Daisy's hand, and pulled her along through and up the muddy bank.

"Come on!"

"I'm trying, but my feet are cut and they hurt!"

Whoever was after them was gaining ground, so stopping to catch their breath was out of the question. The man's own loud, labored breathing echoed as he lunged through the water. His feet sank deeper and deeper into the thick mud. The route slowed him down, but only a little. Daisy turned to see the man crawling like a roach up the bank toward them. He was not to be stopped. He kept up his pace toward them when suddenly another figure stepped from behind one of the enormous Sycamore trees. The darkness obscured his face, but not the club he was holding in his hand.

"Oh my God! There are two of them! Keep running!" Daisy turned, and when she did, her right foot landed squarely in a hole. Down she went.

"He's going to kill us, NT!" she screamed, holding her foot.

Their pursuer saw his prey was down, but he kept up his pace. NT yanked Daisy off the ground before the man got any closer. They gained a bit of distance and turned around to see where he was. Instead, they saw the person with the club lift it high above the head of the man pursuing them. The stomach-turning thwack of the club, the man's roar of pain, and his drop to the ground made Daisy and NT run even faster. Next, the person with the club started toward them.

NT had an iron grip on Daisy's hand. They moved as fast as they could. The horror they had witnessed clouded their thinking. Rather than heading to Shady Acres, which was closer, they took the same path back toward the club. They glimpsed over their shoulders and saw no one. The other man had disappeared into the night. The woods were once again still and quiet.

NT and Daisy slowed their pace as they crossed back through the creek in the direction of the club. NT remembered Hoot's directions. *Get the book. Come to the shack.*

"We have to get to the shack," he said.

"I know, but I can barely walk." Daisy was close to tears. NT placed her arm over his shoulder and supported her as best he could until the shack came into view. The red door was a sign of safety and relief. They knocked. When Hoot opened the door, his jaw hit the floor.

"What in the devil is goin' on? Y'all look like you been rollin' around in slop! Get in here, quick!"

NT and Daisy hobbled into the shack. Hoot realized his initial reaction had been wrong. When he saw Daisy's bloody feet and the extent of their scratches and scrapes, he wrapped NT and Daisy tightly in his arms. The fear and horror of the previous thirty minutes drained out along with their uncontrollable tears.

"Now, now," Hoot said softly. "It's gonna be okay." His comforting and reassuring words helped.

NT and Daisy relayed how they followed his directions, but were not aware someone had seen them go into the locker room. Their tears started anew when they told Hoot what they had witnessed in the darkness of the woods. Guilt made the acid in Hoot's stomach churn like a tornado. He apologized for their horrific ordeal.

Then NT remembered. "We have the notebook." His face brightened at the recollection and he reached into his back pocket to pull it out. But the book was not there. Gone. "No!" he wailed. "It can't be gone!" New tears filled his eyes. "No!"

"Oh, son, it's okay. Maybe it's in the woods or somewhere outside near the shack. In the morning, when it's daylight, I'll take a look in the area to see what I can find. I promise." In actuality, Hoot knew better—the odds of finding the book now were slim. "If Santiago can hook a thousand-pound marlin, I can find that book." Hoot gave NT a wink, trying to reassure him—and himself.

"What are we going to do?" NT was saddened beyond belief.

"Well, for starters, y'all are gonna get cleaned up and head back to that party before anyone knows you're gone." Hoot handed them some towels. "Now, wipe that mud off your legs and faces." They did as told. "Y'all will need to use the bathrooms at the back of the clubhouse to clean up a bit more. Follow the path all the way to the back and you'll find two bathrooms there, by the kitchen door. I know you're both terrified and confused, but for now, let's keep this between the three of us. Lots has gone on tonight that y'all don't understand. I promise I will check those woods myself in the morning and see what I can find, okay?" NT and Daisy nodded. Hoot said he'd see them the next day and gave each a hug.

The doors to the bathrooms behind the clubhouse were locked. "Now what?" Daisy asked. "I can't go back looking like this."

The party on the deck was still in full swing so they snuck into the clubhouse and slipped into a bathroom by the main door on the opposite side of the porch. They locked the door and slid down to the floor. NT sat with his elbows propped on his knees and rubbed his hair. "What just happened? What if Hoot doesn't find Clay's book?" he moaned.

Daisy sat across from him, her legs outstretched and shoulders pressed against the wall. Her shoeless feet bore evidence of their run across asphalt and through woods. They said nothing for a full minute, until Daisy started to giggle.

"What?" NT asked.

"Look at your hair! It's standing straight on end!" Her giggles turned to laughter. NT rolled his eyes, but her joking was infectious. The strain and stress from the events they had just experienced were melting away.

"Well, you aren't exactly Miss America with mud smeared all over your torn-up dress. And talk about hair— you should see yours!" He pointed at Daisy and joined in her laughter.

She stood and looked in the mirror. "Oh no! How am I going to explain this to my parents? Mom spent, like, a *ton* of money on this dress!" Her tears returned. She dampened a hand towel and wiped the mud off her dress as best she could, although muddy streaks remained. She then dabbed at the cuts on her feet.

NT splashed water on his face and patted down his hair.

After a few more minutes of attempted clean up, they looked at each other and just shook their heads.

"Ready?" he asked.

Daisy took a deep breath and tried to regain her composure. "I guess. But I know I'll probably cry, and then we'll have to tell everyone what happened and…" She was practically hyperventilating.

NT took her by the shoulders and said, "You're the strongest person I know. You can do this."

"Yeah, but, what are we going to tell everyone when they ask how we got so gross and scratched up?"

He exhaled and looked up at the ceiling. "Good question." A minute later, his eyes got big with an idea. "I've got it! You know how Succotash is always escaping? We'll just say we saw him running down the fairway and we went to catch him and fell in the creek!"

The sad cloud lifted and Daisy's face lit up. "That's awesome! You're brilliant!"

After a final check in the mirror, NT and Daisy decided they looked good enough to rejoin the party. Daisy opened the bathroom door and almost tripped over something on her way out. She looked down and saw, just in front of the door, her sandals.

36

Hoot went straight home after learning what had happened to NT and Daisy. He needed rest and time to think about his next step. He walked into his tidy, comfortable home and found Janie in her favorite chair doing a crossword puzzle. She greeted him the same way she always did over their thirty years of marriage, "Well, hello, handsome."

Hoot loved Janie with all his might. He crossed through the small hallway and into the living room, planted a kiss on her cheek, and went to change his clothes. They sat together for a while, talking about the day and their plans for an upcoming family reunion. Janie planned the reunion every year and, despite her grumbling about all the work involved, loved it. At eleven, Hoot headed to bed and left Janie with her crossword puzzle. He needed sleep, but after hearing what NT and Daisy had witnessed in the woods earlier that night, shutting down his racing mind would be difficult. Sleep finally came an hour later.

He and Janie rose early the next day. Janie got ready for her regular sunrise church service and choir practice to follow. They enjoyed a light breakfast of coffee and fruit together before giving each other a goodbye kiss.

Hoot already had a plan mapped out in his head. He prepared an envelope with everything he needed to put his plan into action and was out the door by seven. Earlier, he had made two phone calls—one to leave word at the club that he would report to work by midmorning, and the other to arrange a meeting. In his car, he placed the envelope on the seat next to him and patted it with his large hand. *Quarry Lane, here I come.*

Hoot drove slowly to his destination. He finally stopped and parked along Quarry Lane where he looked out over the loveliness of Serenity Lake, so calm and peaceful at this early hour. He tilted his head back on the headrest and closed his eyes as he listened to the birds sing their morning songs. A few minutes later, he heard the crunching of car tires pulling up behind him. In his rearview mirror, he saw the person meeting him had arrived. Each man got out of his car and the two shook hands.

"Thank you for agreeing to meet me, Sheriff. I believe this belongs to you now." Hoot handed the sheriff the envelope. He then proceeded to tell him what he knew about the previous night's events, as told to him by Daisy and NT.

Sheriff Taylor was dumbfounded to hear what his daughter and NT had been through. "They explained things away by saying they'd chased the Hardy sisters' pig. I thought their story was a bit of a stretch, but the pig has escaped before, so I went along with it. I will be forever grateful, Hoot, that you are in Daisy's life."

Hoot's burden had been lifted. "You're welcome, Sheriff. Those two kids have been on the trail of this all summer. They just needed some protectin' from a distance."

Sheriff Taylor held up the envelope and added, "As far as what's going on with all this, this is just the beginning of the end for these guys. It'll take a while for me to digest what I've learned about people I thought I knew. Anyway, our plan is solid and I am grateful for you sticking your neck out. This whole thing will be wrapped up in a few days and a thirty-year-old mystery finally solved."

"I'm honored, sir. They've hurt too many people—or done worse," Hoot said. His reference to Sam Foley was not lost on the sheriff.

Sheriff Taylor gave Hoot a curt nod and pat on the back, then returned to his car and drove off.

Hoot drove toward the club, but pulled off the road just short of the main driveway. He had made a promise to NT and Daisy, and there was no way he was going to break it. *I've got to at least look for that notebook.* He found the path they had taken the night before and made his way to Martin's Creek. For thirty minutes, he scoured up and down the banks but found nothing—not even a sign of a struggle. He next removed his sneakers and socks, rolled up his pants, and forged the shallow part of the creek. The dead-earth smell of the mud that squished between his toes reminded him of the jungles in Vietnam. He saw footprints, but nothing else—no notebook, not even any broken branches. He scratched his head in disbelief. *Maybe the notebook fell out of NT's pocket on his way to the caddie shack.*

Hoot turned and was about to leave when something shiny caught his eye. The sun glinted off a small object that was sticking out of the mud. *What's that? A safety pin?* He picked the pin up and saw that it was glued to a two-by-three-inch piece of plastic. He wiped the mud off the front of the plastic and gasped. He looked twice, not wanting to believe what he saw. He sat on the edge of the creek, put his socks and shoes back on, and calmly decided his next step was to drive to the club.

37

NT slept in that Sunday morning. He, BB, and Mimi had returned home late, and his sleep was restless as thoughts of losing the notebook and being chased through the woods played over and over in his head. Mimi had not been happy about his filthy khakis and shirt but, thankfully, she did not question his story.

NT felt pulled in to the comfort of the bed, so he picked up his book and read. Just a few pages remained. Santiago had returned to shore with the marlin, but all that was left of the great creature was its spine and head. That saddened NT, but when he learned Santiago's helper continued to take care of the old fisherman, who now slept and once again dreamed of lions, he was glad. He closed the book and admitted to himself that he enjoyed it. *I wonder if Hoot finished it yet.*

He went downstairs and saw the time was close to noon. The house was quiet and still. On the counter was a note from BB saying that he and Mimi were out running errands and they would see him later. His stomach growled, so he slapped together two peanut butter and jelly sandwiches and poured himself a tall glass of chocolate milk. *Mmm. Best breakfast ever.* The phone rang and he hoped it would be Daisy.

"Hello?" he answered through a bite of sandwich.

"Hey. What are you doing?" she whispered.

"Nothing. Why are you whispering?"

"Because I don't want anyone to hear. Want to go back to the woods to see if we can find Clay's book?"

"Yeah. Definitely!"

"Okay. I'll meet you at the woods at twelve thirty."

"Cool." NT hung up, finished his sandwiches, and headed out the door. Ten minutes later, he and Daisy were entering the woods at the very spot they had entered the night before. They walked slowly, keeping their eyes peeled for the notebook. Even in the light of day, they soon became frustrated. Everything looked the same—overgrown brush, leaves, branches, roots, dirt, rocks, and the occasional wildflower.

"Are we in the right spot? I mean, it's hard to believe we actually ran through all this—in the dark and you barefoot!" NT's question was answered when Daisy spotted the crown of daisies she had been wearing in her hair, only now it was half smashed into the mud.

"Look. My daisies. We're definitely in the right spot." She pulled the crown from the mud and added, "Now all we need is the notebook."

"I don't know. I have no clue where it fell out. I'll *never* get it back for BB," NT complained.

"Let's go to the shack. It could be somewhere near there," Daisy said.

"I hope it didn't fall into the water."

"Oh, me too," she replied.

Their disappointment grew as they walked to the shack and still found nothing.

Inside the shack, Hoot sat thinking about his conversation with the sheriff and what he knew would unfold over the next few days. Bits and pieces of a conversation floated in through the open window.

"... he might know..."

"... could be in the shack?"

Hoot rose from his chair and saw NT and Daisy walking slowly in his direction. They looked dejected, as though they had failed. It hurt Hoot to know they felt that way. "Hey, y'all. Thirsty?"

They looked up and smiled. "Hey, Hoot."

Hoot thought his heart would melt. He loved them like his own and would miss them when the school year started and they'd no longer be able to come around. "What are you two up to?"

"Can we come in?" NT asked.

"Sure. Larry and James are here too."

All five sat at the rickety table enjoying a soda and the coolness of the shack.

Hoot repeated his earlier question. "And what, exactly, were y'all doin' out there?"

NT and Daisy looked at each other with mutual understanding. NT spoke first. "Since I'm the one who lost the notebook, I should be the one to look for it—not you."

Daisy said, "That's what we were doing."

"I'm really sorry, Hoot," continued NT. "It's totally my fault. I screwed up big."

"Now, now, son. Get that thought outta your head. You did no such thing. You did as you were told, and it could've ended up a whole heck of a lot worse. Heck, I felt so bad about puttin' y'all in danger, I almost lost my cookies. I mean that."

"Me too," said Daisy. "I'd never been so scared in my whole life."

"Same here. Everything happened so fast. It was like a movie," NT said.

"And who was chasing us?" Daisy asked. "We have no idea but, whoever it was, we really hope he doesn't have Clay's notebook."

"It sounded like he got smashed pretty bad. We had to take off because the man who clubbed him started to come after us. I guess we'll never know who either man was." NT sighed.

"Maybe not," Hoot said quietly. "But, then again, maybe so."

Hoot's tease got everyone's attention.

"What do you mean?" asked NT in a hushed voice. "You know who those guys were?"

"Only one of 'em," Hoot responded. And with that, he went to his locker and pulled out the piece of plastic he had found in the mud. "I went lookin' for that book too—earlier this morning. Y'all have to understand, the book is probably gone, but this here will tell you who was chasing you." Hoot opened his large palm and all eyes fell on what he was holding. It was a name tag. Engraved on it was the name Lenny.

"Lenny? As in bartender Lenny?" James asked.

"Yep," Hoot responded.

"Why would he... Wait! Lenny! He had to be the one who saw us in the locker room and chased us, right?" said NT.

"That would appear to be the case," Hoot answered.

"Hey, I have an idea, NT," said Daisy. "Let's go to the Grille Room and order something to eat. Then we can see if Lenny's wearing his name tag."

"Good thinking," NT said.

"Now, don't be too obvious, young lady," Hoot said to Daisy with a wink.

"I won't. I promise."

NT and Daisy walked casually into the Grille Room. The mayor and another man had Lenny cornered at the end of the bar. Lenny looked terrified. NT immediately recognized the other man as Tony—the rat-faced man who yelled at them when they smashed into the mayor's limo, the man with the squeaky voice, the man he had seen and heard in Foley's Hardware store. He nudged Daisy and jerked his chin in the direction of the men.

Daisy looked and gave a quick nod to indicate her understanding. She coughed to announce their presence.

Mayor Hall and his sidekick immediately backed away and walked out. Lenny had sweat on his brow along with a large bandage on the side of his head. He did not look well.

"Hi, Lenny," NT said.

"Hi, kids. Uh, get you something?" His voice was shaky.

"Sure. Two chocolate shakes, please."

"Give me two minutes," Lenny said, and he disappeared into the kitchen.

"I'd like to ask him what happened to his head," Daisy whispered.

"Go ahead," NT replied.

Lenny reappeared, his face dry of sweat, his smile pasted back on, milkshakes in hand.

Daisy squinted and leaned her head sideways, pretending to be concerned over the bandage on the side of Lenny's head. "Are you okay? What happened to your head?" she asked.

"Oh, this?" He patted the bandage and chuckled. "Yeah, dumb me. I tripped over Bogey at home and took a header down the steps. Smashed my head."

"Bogey?" asked Daisy.

"My cat. He's always underfoot. Loves attention, that one," he replied smoothly, then quickly changed subjects. "Y'all have fun at the party?"

"We sure did," Daisy replied. "You were pretty busy, huh?"

"That I was. I didn't budge from the bar all night. Had too many thirsty adults to attend to." He turned to leave, then stopped and looked back at NT and Daisy.

NT said, "Something else?"

Lenny shook his head. "Enjoy. I've got to keep a move on."

"Thanks. See you later," Daisy said.

NT thought Daisy deserved an Academy Award for her performance. "You were perfect. I don't think he suspected a thing."

Daisy ignored NT's comment and asked, "Did you notice?"

"The bandage? How could I miss it?"

"Seriously? Not just that—his name tag! That's why we came here in the first place, remember?"

"Oh, yeah. His name tag. Duh. I totally forgot to look."

"Lucky for you *I* remembered."

"And?"

"No name tag."

38

The day started out sunny and pleasant in quiet Cab Station. Unbeknown to its inhabitants, the calm serenity would soon be shattered, as their beloved, quaint town would be on display on every TV news show in the country.

NT was still in bed. His summer in Cab Station was winding down and he was unhappy at the thought of returning home. He glanced at the mini mountain of clothes on the floor, ready to be packed. That would come later. He dressed and joined his grandparents at the breakfast table.

"Easy on the syrup! Your teeth will rot out with all that sugar." BB laughed as NT poured a waterfall of syrup onto his blueberry pancakes.

"I can't believe I have to leave in two days," NT said.

They enjoyed the pancakes and made chit chat about the classes NT was going to take in high school and his return to Cab Station the following summer.

BB wiped his mouth and checked his watch. "Time to shove off. Does Daisy know our tee time?"

"Yeah. She's going to meet us on the range at ten," NT replied.

* * *

After finishing the front nine holes, the foursome stopped at the halfway house to get a snack. NT and Daisy each got a candy bar and stood munching as the group behind them came up to the ninth green.

"That's the mayor and his group," said NT. "They finally picked up their pace of play and caught up to us."

"Yeah, look at his ugly yellow-green golf pants," said Daisy. "They must be new. We would remember if we'd seen them before."

"That color is called chartreuse," said Mimi.

"Right. And what about his stinky cigar?" said Daisy.

Mimi smiled at her question. "I'm sorry, dear, but I don't know what that's called, other than *stinky cigar*."

They also saw the mayor's caddies—Hoot, Larry, and James.

Mayor Hall and the others in his group strolled back and forth around the green, lining up their putts from every angle and completely disregarding the advice given by their caddies. After ten minutes, they finally finished putting and walked off the green.

BB said, "The mayor spends a lot of time on the golf course—a *whole lot* of time." NT knew that was his grandfather's polite way of saying the mayor did not play as quickly as proper golf etiquette required.

* * *

Sheriff Taylor was in his office on the phone. He was standing next to a large road map of Cab Station that was pinned to the wall behind his desk. "Yes, Commander, I'll need backup in town on Tubman Avenue, plus extra cars on the surrounding roads... Yes, six or seven will do... I really appreciate you sending your best troopers to assist." When the call ended, he called Darman into his office. "I need you in here, Roy, to look over this map." The sheriff squinted and studied the map closely.

"What's up, Sheriff?" Darman asked as he entered the room.

"Listen, there's going to be police action and an arrest at Cascades Club today. I need you to stay here and run the operation. The target of the arrest is onsite. I was just tipped off as to his exact location and I am heading there now.

"Target? What're you talking about, Jackson? This sounds serious," Darman said.

"You'll find out the enormity of the situation soon enough. For now, I need you here, where you'll be most effective. The State Police are going to be assisting us, and they'll need someone who knows the streets and roads of this town to coordinate with them. As deputy, you will be in charge of ensuring officers are stationed on the major routes both to and from Cascades." The sheriff's words were forthright. He placed his hand on Darman's shoulder in a further display of confidence.

At the words *police action at Cascades*, the hair on the back of Darman's neck shot up. He got a clammy feeling and broke out in a cold sweat. He shook his head to clear his brain. "Are you sure I shouldn't go with you? If there's trouble, you'll need me by your side to help manage things," he replied.

"Not today. I need you here to organize backup in case there's trouble. But I don't think there'll be any. I know I can lean on you to organize more officers in case things don't go smoothly and we need to spread out our manpower there," Sheriff Taylor said. "The State Police are on our radio band, so you just need to make sure those officers are in place if needed. Obviously, you'll use our central radio for all communications. I'll update you via the radio as we advance on the target. You, my friend, are running command central," he finished with a smile.

Darman reluctantly agreed with the sheriff that he was the best person to run the action from the station. *This is not good. He knows something.* He couldn't shake the feeling and his mind raced as Sheriff Taylor imparted orders. Every possible scenario sped through his head as to what was going down at Cascades. *Are they on to me, or Lenny, or...? I need to warn them. Jesus, what if he's after Hall too? Lenny would sing like a canary and screw us all. And Hall... He'd throw us all under the bus.*

After the sheriff left, Darman contacted the State Police on the radio and had them set up roadblocks on the main roads around Cab Station, with one exception. He neglected to mention Quarry Lane. He then retreated to his office and called the club on his phone, hoping Lenny would pick up. After twelve rings with no answer, he hung up. He dialed another number and was met with, "You've reached Robert Hall. I am unavailable at the moment. If you care to—" Darman hung up. *I gotta find out what's going on.*

In Sheriff Taylor's office, Darman rummaged through the notes on his desk. He found nothing, but noticed the computer was on. He glanced down the hall to make sure the coast was clear. A tap of the space bar brought up a screen saver photo of Sheriff Taylor's family and at least twenty folders on the computer's desktop. He clicked on several and saw nothing relevant to what Sheriff Taylor had mentioned about problems at Cascades. Then his eyes fell on a post-it note stuck to the underside of the phone. *What's this?* He read aloud. "MH, eight eleven, thirteen hundred. *MH* must mean Mayor Hall, and eight eleven is today's date."

Darman checked his watch. "And it's almost one o'clock now. Oh, God!"

By now, Sheriff Taylor would be at Cascades, so Darman assumed the worst. He leaned back in his chair and stared at the radio. He was trapped at the station. The silence from the other end was agony. He felt his heart would throb right out of his chest. Ten minutes later, the silence was broken with the sheriff's voice. "The target is on the eighteenth hole, walking down the fairway. I'm going to wait until he's finished, then take him into custody. You ten-four that, Darman?"

"Yes, sir," Darman replied. He played along. "Backup needed, Sheriff?"

"Negative. Remain at the station to await further instruction."

"Ten-four." He called the club again. This time Lenny answered. "Hey, it's me. You see Taylor there anywhere?"

"Not in here. Let me check outside. Hold on." Lenny set the phone down then returned a minute later and said, "Yeah, he's out there. What's he doin' here? I don't like the looks of this."

"Okay, okay. Relax. Don't freak. You need to listen to me and trust me."

"What's goin' on, Royce?" Lenny squeaked.

"Get out. Now! Sneak out the back and cut into the woods up to Quarry Lane. I'll pick you up there. You'll see troopers, but I told them I've got that road covered. Got it?"

"Yeah, but hurry up, man. I can't take much more of this."

Lenny's nerves were already melting.

* * *

NT and Daisy were famished after their round. Lunch with BB and Mimi on the porch was a perfect way to finish a fun morning. The restaurant was packed with people who were enjoying one of the last summer weekends to play golf. NT's empty belly squirmed and poked at him.

BB patted Daisy on the shoulder as they sat down at the table where they could watch players finish up on the eighteenth hole. He said to her, "You hit the ball as well today, young lady, as you did in the junior championships."

"Thanks for taking me out. It was great," Daisy said. She took a sip of her water.

"You just keep playing, Daisy, and you'll have a fine future as a golfer. You never know where this game may take you," BB said.

Mimi looked around the porch. Every table was full. "My goodness, there are a lot of people here today," she said.

"I guess they're all here for the same reason we are— the awesome burgers, fries, and chocolate shakes," NT answered.

"I think you're right," Daisy responded.

Mimi and BB ordered their regular lunches—a Niçoise salad for her and a turkey club for him.

They sat back in their chairs to enjoy the beauty of the eighteenth hole. The mayor and his group eventually appeared on the crest at the top of the hill. The mayor's chartreuse golf pants were visible a mile away. Hoot, James, and Larry were all standing off to the side, waiting for their respective golfers to hit.

"He'd sure better hit the green with all of us watching, especially considering he's out here all the time and should know this course like the back of his hand," Mimi remarked.

"I once heard my father say he's lazy and lies about stuff," Daisy said.

"I'm sure he is, and does," BB said.

They watched the mayor swing and heard the thud of the ball as it landed solidly on the green. It rolled to within six feet of the pin.

In the distance, they saw the mayor follow up his shot with an awkward dance that reminded NT of the scene in the movie *Caddyshack* where Rodney Dangerfield dances on the fairway. Here, however, the mayor looked stupid.

The group hiked down the steep fairway and over the stone footbridge that led to the eighteenth green. NT saw Ratface was among them. He watched as Mayor Hall stepped onto the green to putt. The mayor rolled his ball in for a birdie.

"Ha! Just like Arnie Palmer! Good read, Hoot," Mayor Hall said, and gave Hoot a pat on the back. The others shook hands and tallied their scores. The mayor then reached into his pocket and pulled out a wad of cash. He peeled off several bills and handed them to Hoot.

Just then, a loud crash and the sound of shattering glass interrupted the normally serene atmosphere. The noise had come from the far end of the clubhouse porch. The lunchtime crowd dropped their forks at the commotion.

Lenny had dropped a large tray that had been loaded with glasses and bottles. His face sheet-white. With no warning, he leaped over the wrought iron gate onto the driveway and sprinted furiously around the side of the clubhouse toward the woods. He didn't get far. Another man came flying around the same side from the opposite direction and smashed full force into Lenny.

"What in the world—" Mimi started.

NT and Daisy jumped up from their chairs and weaved their way through the tables to see what was going on. They looked at the side lawn and gasped.

"Whoa! Mr. Gates has Lenny pinned to the ground!" NT yelled.

"Get off me!" Lenny yelled. "What are you doing?"

Simultaneously, three men and two women rose from their tables on the porch, hooked a badge onto their shirt pockets, and strode toward the eighteenth green. The crowd was mesmerized.

"Who are these guys?" Daisy asked.

"Who knows?" NT replied. "But look." NT pointed to the eighteenth green. Sheriff Taylor had just stepped onto the green and was standing with a grim expression on his face and his arms folded across his chest. "It's your dad. He looks cool with his aviator sunglasses—kinda like Arnold in *The Terminator*."

As much as Daisy wanted to call out to her father to ask what was happening, she knew better than to interrupt his official police business.

The mayor and his friends exchanged tense glances and moved slowly to walk off the green.

Sheriff Taylor had other plans. "Gentlemen, you need to stay right where you are. Do not move."

Mayor Hall was the first to break the tension. In a smooth voice he asked, "Afternoon, Sheriff. What's going on?" He threw his soggy cigar butt on the ground at Sheriff Taylor's feet.

The sheriff answered, "What's going on, Mr. Mayor, is that you will pick up that stub you just tossed and then you will place your hands behind your back."

The mayor kicked the cigar butt aside. "Place my hands behind my back? What's going on here? What's this about, Sheriff? I demand an explanation for this humiliation!"

"You want an explanation? My pleasure," answered the sheriff. He pulled out the envelope Hoot had given him several days earlier. "In this envelope is the indisputable proof that you've been using our fine club as the headquarters for your vile and destructive counterfeiting operation. For years. Those counterfeit bills you and your lowlife henchmen have been making in the basement of the club have been circulated not only throughout our fine town, ruining people such as Sam Foley and others, but in businesses up and down the coast." Sheriff Taylor lowered his sunglasses as he spoke and looked directly at the mayor to nail home his point.

The jaws of the diners on the porch fell open and the only sounds heard were birds chirping and cars driving by.

"Sir, I asked you to place your hands behind your back. Either do it yourself or I will do it for you." No one could miss the ice in Sheriff Taylor's tone.

* * *

Darman grabbed a bag he had packed with clothes, money, and other essentials. He glanced at his phone. 2:07.

He calculated that it would take him eight minutes to get to Quarry Lane to pick up Lenny and get the heck out of town.

Years of easy living were about to end unless he could get away and start a new life. His contacts up and down the east coast would help him and Lenny disappear. Forever. He turned up the volume on his police car radio and heard what was happening at Cascades. He knew this day would eventually come and he was ready.

As he drove, he reflected on his life. With the shattering of his dreams of playing college and pro football, he had enrolled in the police academy and planned to move up the ranks, eventually to Sheriff. But a penchant for money caught up with him, as did Mayor Hall's bookies, whom he owed big. His job as the drop man had paid off well, and he mastered the art of living two lives—those of dedicated police officer and cold, calculating criminal.

Darman turned his cruiser down Quarry Lane one last time. Lenny was nowhere to be seen. *He'll show up soon enough.* Darman's thoughts flashed back to the day when he and Lenny killed Clay Tyson on this very road. He remembered it clearly and smiled. They had followed orders perfectly—find a reason to stop him, get him out of the car, kill him, and dump his body in Serenity Lake. Lenny was so dumb he'd do anything the big man said. Darman truly thought he had gotten away with the perfect murder.

His line of sight was soon filled with four State Police cars that had arrived to block Quarry Lane. Eight armed officers were now standing in the road, their feet spread and weapons raised high. Darman had a split second to decide what to do. He threw his car in reverse, but he was too late. He looked in the rearview mirror and knew his fate was sealed. Sheriff Taylor's car had appeared. Darman waited, trapped like the rodent he was. He tasted blood inside his mouth, unaware he had chewed a hole in his cheek. He watched the sheriff exit his car and walk slowly toward him with gun drawn.

"Throw your gun out the window, Roy. Now," Sheriff Taylor said from the road.

Darman sighed, looked at the sheriff in the rearview mirror and knew he was beat. His gun clanked as it hit the ground.

The sheriff kept his eyes on Darman as he nudged the gun off the road. "Now, get out of the car, hands on your head."

Darman obeyed and said, "I'll make this easy for you, Jackson." He turned and leaned against the car with his back to the sheriff.

Cold metal encircled his wrists as the sheriff cuffed him and asked, "How could you?" He spun Darman back around and leveled him with a stare.

Darman gave it right back. He cocked his large head and spat on the ground before erupting. "How could I? Is that what you want to know? How could I kill the man who was gonna ruin my whole life?"

Sheriff Taylor stared at Darman. "You've been lying to me for thirty years. Thirty years." His voice was barely above a whisper. "Not just to me, but to this whole town."

Darman shrugged. "Plain and simple, Sheriff. He knew too much. Plus, the money was good and I wasn't about to let anyone ruin that for me."

Darman's response was so matter of fact that Sheriff Taylor didn't know what horrified him more—the response itself or the smirk on Darman's face. In a voice dripping with disgust, he said, "Well, Royce, it looks like you did a pretty good job of ruining your own life." He took Darman by the arm and shoved him into the waiting police cruiser.

39

NT and his grandparents were enjoying the porch at Shady Acres, recalling the amazing events of the summer. They, and the whole town, were still abuzz with the arrest of Mayor Hall and his henchmen.

NT heard a car approach and looked up to see Sheriff Taylor pulling into the driveway. The sheriff got out of the car, along with Mr. Gates and Hoot. "What's going on? Why are they here?" he asked. Next to arrive was Daisy. With red curls flying out behind her, she pedaled up the driveway and came to a sharp stop in front of the porch.

They all took a seat on the porch and Mimi brought out a large pitcher of lemonade and seven glasses. She served everyone, then Sheriff Taylor stood and addressed the little group. "As y'all know, Clay Tyson was senselessly murdered years ago. The case was cold, until a few months ago—June, to be precise—and may never have been solved had it not been for these three." He pointed to Hoot, Daisy, and NT. "You probably have a ton of questions, but I believe we now have the information to answer them all." NT and Daisy nodded. "I'll also bet you're wondering why Mr. Gates is here. Well, he's better suited to shed light on what's been goin' on, so I'll let him explain."

Mr. Gates stood and read from a piece of paper he was holding.

Dear Ben,
I know we have never met, yet I am writing to ask for your help. You are my last hope in helping to solve the mystery of who murdered my brother-in-law, Clay

Tyson. My husband William and I have recently discovered that you and Clay were very good friends. I would like to know if you have any information that would help.

The police here investigated, but the case went cold long ago due to a lack of evidence. The Medical Examiner, Dr. Nettleton, concluded that blunt force trauma is what caused Clay's death, not drowning.

I understand if you choose not to respond. You are our last resort and prospect for receiving answers and help.

I sincerely hope to hear from you.

Thank you,
Marian Tyson

Mr. Gates looked up from the letter and continued. "This letter is dated October 26, 1981. The *Ben* in question was my father. He was an FBI agent. I found this letter when I cleaned out my parents' house after my mother's death. I was in my final year at the police academy. I had always wanted to follow in my father's footsteps in law enforcement, and when I found the letter, I knew exactly what I wanted to do. As a boy, I used to hear him talk on the phone in a hushed voice. I never heard the whole conversation, but words like *Rouble Counterfeit Press, fraud*, and *paper currency*—all unfamiliar to me—stuck in my head. At the time, I had no real idea what my father did for work other than something with the law. In time, I learned what those words meant and it became clear to me that he was trying to break up an enormous, hugely successful and powerful counterfeiting ring. So, like my dad, I eventually became an undercover FBI agent. I'm actually Special Agent Michael Gates." He let his words sink in.

Daisy and NT looked at each other. Daisy was first to speak up. "Wait, but, you run the pro shop at the club and give golf lessons." She scowled, trying to put everything together.

"True. It's pure coincidence but, luckily for me, there was a golf course near the academy where I played. I even became a certified teaching pro. I've always loved the game," Agent Gates responded.

"So, you have two jobs?"

"Yes, Daisy, I do. I've decided, after spending all this time trying to break up this ring and solve Clay's murder, to take a less stressful position within the FBI."

Now it was NT's turn. "Okay, hold on a sec. That means you've been undercover this whole summer?"

"Yes. And that let me keep my eye on you and Daisy. After I saw you leaving the caddie shack several times and when you told me you talked to Hoot about Clay, I told him my real identity and everything that was going on. I needed his help. Good thing I did, especially after the night in the woods," he said.

"What? The night we were chased? You were there?" Daisy exclaimed.

He nodded, "Yup. That night and other times. Like when you two met at Sweetwoods and discussed Clay, and when you went to Mrs. Walker's. Anyway, I knew you were in trouble that night when I saw Lenny follow you into the locker room and then into the woods. I took a shortcut and leveled him."

"That explains the gash on his head. He said he fell over his cat! What a stupid liar," Daisy said, shaking her head.

NT absorbed what Agent Gates had just revealed about Clay. "Mimi said that Clay worked for the SCE or something like that? I'm so confused!"

"SEC, honey," Mimi chuckled.

Agent Gates continued, "Yes, NT, you're right. Clay was working in New York for the SEC, examining accounts for large brokerage houses. One in particular, Golden and Riley, also known as G and R, was receiving large sums of cash deposited into their accounts twice a month, but the depositor's identity was unknown. This bothered Clay. As he dug deeper into those large deposits, he realized something was wrong, but didn't have the authority to pursue it further."

NT asked, "If he was an agent, how come he couldn't dig deeper?"

Gates responded, "He was an examiner, not an agent. But he did a bit of investigative work on the sly into where the deposits were coming from. He realized he needed help, and he knew to call the FBI for assistance. My father, Ben, answered Clay's call and a relationship was born. Clay explained that he believed something was amiss and potentially illegal going on at G and R and—"

"What was it?" Daisy interjected.

"I'll get to that. Anyway, my father listened to what Clay had to say about these enormous amounts of cash being deposited into this account and where it was coming from. Clay said he connected the dots and figured that the influx of cash was coming from Virginia. After several discussions with my father, they decided Clay would go undercover and head here to Virginia. It made sense because Clay was a native Virginian and he knew the area where he had pinpointed the money trail. The area, of course, being his beloved Cab Station. He was crushed to learn that his own town could be involved in an illegal action."

"But, what was it? What was the illegal thing that was going on?" NT asked.

Gates looked first at NT then at Daisy and answered, "Your father said it the day of the arrest. Counterfeiting."

NT asked BB, "Did you know he was undercover?"

BB shook his head. "I knew he worked for the SEC, but I had no idea about the undercover part."

Gates went on, "My father and Clay kept in touch through notes and when they met at golf tournaments." He looked at BB and added, "He never told anyone about being undercover because he didn't want to put you in danger."

NT beaded his eyebrows together. "So, in theory, my great uncle Clay *kind* of worked as an undercover FBI agent? And no one knew it?" he said. "How's that possible?"

Agent Gates said, "Because he did his job well."

NT thought it through. He and Daisy had spoken to a lot of people. Everything they said made sense. Mrs. Walker the housekeeper, Mrs. Cavanaugh the librarian, the Hardy sisters—they all said Clay loved to travel and that he traveled a lot for work, but no one knew what he did. "BB, even you—Clay's own brother—didn't know what he did?"

"That's right, Nicholas," BB responded. "As an undercover FBI agent, Clay was sworn to secrecy. He couldn't tell anyone about his job."

"Mr., uh, *Agent* Gates, if you're leaving, then who's going to take your job?" NT asked.

"Well, I'm pleased to say that I have recommended Hoot to take over all golf operations, including the caddie program. I can't think of a person better suited than Hoot." Agent Gates smiled broadly at Hoot, who nodded his thanks.

Sheriff Taylor looked at Daisy and NT, then at Hoot, "When y'all told me everything that was going on, and when Hoot gave me all the stuff you found in the attic—the scorecards with the handwritten notes, the ten-dollar bills—I met with Agent Gates a couple of times to piece everything together. Everything you found was solid evidence that Clay had tried to communicate what was going on. When he was killed all those years ago, I made it my mission to find out who was responsible, no matter how long it would take. After Sam Foley was murdered, I had even more suspicions and did some detective work on my own. As you may have guessed, the people responsible for his death are these same people. Sam Foley was on the brink of breaking out of the ring, but Tony stopped that."

"Ratface?" NT asked.

"He's the man you saw at Foley's Hardware, the man with—" Sheriff started.

"He killed Mr. Foley?"

"Yes, and he's been the mayor's right-hand man for years, handling any and all dirty work that needed to get done. Directly or indirectly, he was always behind it."

"But, how is he connected to Clay's murder? And, why *did* they kill Clay?" NT asked.

"Tony's the one who ordered Clay's death. The *why* Clay was killed is all right here." And with that, Sheriff Taylor pulled Clay's blue notebook from his back pocket.

NT was stunned. "Clay's notebook! Where was it?"

Agent Gates answered, "It was near Martin's Creek, right where you dropped it last Saturday night. I found it after I dealt with Lenny. You two had safely escaped and I saw it lying on the ground. I grabbed it and hightailed it out of there before Lenny came to. I couldn't let him wake up and see it was me who'd hit him over the head."

"Can we read the book? Please?" Daisy begged.

"Sure. I don't see why not," Sheriff Taylor said. "It's all over now. Mayor Hall, his underlings, Lenny, Darman, and others are headed for a trial and prison and will remain there for a long time." The sheriff handed the notebook to NT, who held it in his hands like the long-lost treasure it was.

NT opened the book carefully and scanned the first few pages. He then stopped, closed the book, and handed it to his grandfather. "Here, BB. You're the one who should be reading this."

"Why, thank you, Nicholas." BB lifted his reading glasses from the table and proceeded to read aloud.

June 17, 1981, 9 pm -
Just back from the Open at Merion where Ben confirmed that the bills are all counterfeit. I taped one to the inside cover of a program. We have established that the counterfeit cash is being made every other Thursday in the basement of the Cascades Golf Club clubhouse, giving easy access to the mayor's

drop man (Royce Lee Darman, police officer) to pick up the bags and have the counterfeit cash distributed up and down the eastern seaboard, with enormous sums being deposited at G&R. Based on observations, we know that Lenny, the Cascades Grille Restaurant bartender, and Darman are in charge of production at this site.

NT interrupted, "Wait! The program? That's the one we found in the attic, signed by Ben! We thought it was Ben Hogan, but it wasn't! It was your father, right?"

Gates smiled and nodded. BB continued reading.

July 7, 1981, 11 pm -
After playing golf, I observed Darman and Lenny stuffing golf bags full of cash. They loaded them into their cars and drove off. I followed, and they stopped at several places of business in town to make their deliveries. Al's Gas Station and Foley's Hardware Store being two locations in town. Their last stop was at a restaurant outside town where Robert Hall, mayor of Cab Station, paid them.

July 21, 1981, 6 am –
It's time. In the next few days we are going to take down the mayor, Darman, Lenny, and everyone else involved. We have photographic evidence that proves the existence of a counterfeit ring.

BB closed the book after reading that final entry. Clay had been killed two days later. Everyone on the porch sat silent for a minute. BB gathered himself and thanked everyone for stopping by and sharing their information. "And, thank you, Agent Gates, for watching out for NT and Daisy. Apparently, they were in more than one precarious situation. Knowing there were eyes looking out for them gives us peace of mind." Lastly, BB asked Hoot to repeat the story of how he had found the letter from Clay that directed him to where Clay kept his notebook.

Hoot repeated the story of his accidental discovery of the letter in a book on a shelf in the caddie shack. "I don't know how he knew I'd find it, but he did."

NT's curiosity had not been quite satisfied, even with all the explanations he had just heard. He had to know exactly how Lenny and Darman executed what they thought was the perfect murder.

Sheriff Taylor explained what he had found in Darman's office file cabinet, including the piece of red glass from the taillight of Clay's Jaguar. "Lenny purposely broke the taillight while Clay was playing golf, probably the day before the murder. His easy access to the parking lot at Cascades meant he could break it when no one else was around, and the broken taillight gave Darman a reason to stop Clay on the road. Darman kept the broken piece in his cabinet for safe keeping which, of course, backfired." NT was stunned. He and Daisy stared with mouths hung open. Sheriff Taylor continued, "Hoot and I figured out that the dates on the scorecards were all Thursdays, which coincided with the day the counterfeiting was being done."

NT was still curious about the broken taillight. "Why would Deputy Darman keep a piece of glass from a broken taillight all these years?"

"Good question. I asked him the same thing. His reply froze me to the core," Sheriff Taylor responded.

"What did he say?" NT asked.

"That he wanted to keep it as a trophy of the perfect crime. He also said that if he kept the glass in his possession, no one else would find it. Well, you, Daisy, and Hoot turned that theory around."

NT's mind was working overtime. "That's creepy. So it *was* a kind of trophy. What about the murder weapon? Mimi told me his death was caused by *blunt force trauma*?"

Sheriff Taylor had saved the most interesting part for last. "Remember, Nicholas, when you told me about that club, a seven iron, behind the—"

NT jumped up from his seat. "*No way*! That's the murder weapon? Clay's own seven iron? I knew something was weird when I didn't see it in his golf bag!"

"Yup. I took a close look at the club and went back to the details Darman had written on a notepad and kept in his desk. It's all incriminating evidence that lays out the plan, and it was pretty dumb of him to write it out."

NT looked at his grandfather and said, "Now if only we could find Clay's good luck charm, that piece of blue sea glass."

"Blue sea glass?" Sheriff Taylor asked.

"That's right. Clay carried it with him whenever he played, but we've never been able to find it," BB said.

"I think I can help," said the sheriff.

"What? How?" asked NT.

"It's in the junk jar on Darman's desk. I'll make sure to get it to you later today."

NT was speechless, but BB spoke up for him. "Sheriff, that would be great. We sure do appreciate all you've done to help us get closure."

"Just doing my job, Willy. Well, this lemonade sure was good, Miss Marian, but I'm afraid it's time to go. Even though it's Sunday, I need to write up official reports on all this."

"Can I stay, Dad?" Daisy asked her father. "I need to beat NT one more time at HORSE." She snickered at NT.

"Sure. I'll see you later. Ready, Hoot? Mike?"

Everyone stood. Hoot stretched out his long arms and pulled NT and Daisy in close. "Y'all study real hard in school and get good grades, you hear?"

NT and Daisy buried their heads in Hoot's sides and gave him a long hug back. NT looked at the kind, weathered face and said, "Well, Hoot, like Santiago, we got the big fish."

"You got that right, son. You got that right."

40

NT was up early the next day. He stood at his bedroom window and looked out over the Shady Acres property one last time. His thoughts took him back to the beginning of the summer and his discovery of a great uncle who had carried a mystery with him to his watery grave. And now, at the end of summer, to find out that Clay's job at the SEC had led him to working undercover for the FBI, and that his work, all these years later, helped destroy a counterfeiting ring in Cab Station of all places was something out of Hollywood.

Mimi called up the steps, "Are you coming down for breakfast?"

NT smelled bacon, eggs, and fresh-baked biscuits. "Right now!" He was down the stairs and seated at the table in less than a minute. "This looks awesome."

"Since it's your last breakfast here 'til next year, I wanted it to be special." Mimi ruffled her grandson's hair.

BB joined them at the table. "We leave for the train station in half an hour."

NT finished off a plate heaped with food and washed everything down with a tall glass of orange juice.

Mimi watched him intently as he ate.

"What?" NT asked.

"I am so proud of you."

"What did I do?"

"For one, you won the club champs for your age group. For another, you helped solve the mystery of who took Clay away from us. You'll never know what that means to your grandfather."

"You're the one who got the case going, Mimi. Daisy and I were just running around looking for Clay's notebook. If you had never written that letter to Agent Gates's father, the case might never have been solved. Plus, it was fun, believe it or not, and it got my mind off Mom and Dad's divorce."

"Yes, you've had a few rough things to deal with this year."

NT retrieved his suitcase. In the living room, he asked BB, "Since it's so nice out, can we take the Jag?"

"Step outside," said BB.

From the front porch, NT saw the Jag and heard the quiet purr of its engine. He put his bag in the trunk and saw that the taillight had been fixed. "It was finally time to have it repaired," BB said.

NT asked if they could take Quarry Lane instead of Tubman Avenue.

"Sure," BB said as they drove off.

Quarry Lane was quiet and peaceful. The trees cast shadows on the gravel road while the sky above was bright and endless and the sun warm.

"Stop! Stop here," NT called out.

BB pulled to the side of the road and cut the engine.

"Mimi, I need to get out for a second, please."

Mimi let NT slide out of the back seat and watched as he wandered down to the lake. At the edge, NT reached into his pocket and pulled out the blue sea glass that had been Clay's good luck charm and that Darman had stolen. He looked at it and rubbed both sides between his fingers. Then he took a step back and, with all his might, threw the glass into the placid lake. The glass spun perfectly, carving its way through the air until it plopped into the water where it zigzagged through the depths and took a final resting spot in the soft bottom. NT turned to his grandparents and said, "I felt it belonged there."

The three stood silently with their arms around each other and gazed upon the still water. A strong, but brief, gust of wind blew out of nowhere and created ripples on the surface of the lake. To NT, the ripples resembled smiles, as if the lake were thanking them for bringing peace to the town at last.

"I guess Clay's letter for Hoot gave everyone justice in the end," NT whispered.

"Yes, especially for Clay."

Made in the
USA
Columbia, SC